NIGHT MAN

ALSO BY BRETT BATTLES

THE JONATHAN QUINN THRILLERS

Novels

Becoming Quinn

The Cleaner

The Deceived

Shadow of Betrayal (U.S.)/The Unwanted (U.K.)

The Silenced

The Destroyed

The Collected

The Enraged

The Discarded

The Buried

The Unleashed

The Aggrieved

The Fractured

Novellas

Night Work

Short Stories

"Just Another Job"—A Jonathan Quinn Story

"Off the Clock"—A Jonathan Quinn Story

"The Assignment"—An Orlando Story

"Lesson Plan"—A Jonathan Quinn Story

Takedown

STANDALONES

Novels

The Pull of Gravity

No Return

Mine

Night Man

Novellas

Mine: The Arrival

Short Stories

"Perfect Gentleman"

For Younger Readers

THE TROUBLE FAMILY CHRONICLES

Here Comes Mr. Trouble

NIGHT MAN

BRETT BATTLES

Brett Battles

Night Man Copyright © 2019 by Brett Battles

Cover art copyright © 2019 by Robert Browne

All rights reserved.

For more information about the author, please visit www.brettbattles.com.

CHAPTER ONE

Here they come.

They're in a gray Honda Accord. It's not the same car they used last time, but it's the kind of vehicle they favor. Ubiquitous, bland, and very blend-into-the-scenery-esque. I'm watching it on the feed from the camera I've set up to cover the street.

I've been waiting for over two hours, in case they showed up early. They haven't. Like clockwork, they're right on time.

I click the button on my laptop that shrinks the feed into one of four squares. In the other three squares are views from my other cameras—one inside the store, one outside covering the storefront, and one focused on the back alley. On the inside view, I can see the owner, Mr. Park, sitting on his stool and ringing up a customer while keeping one eye on his TV. I'm not familiar with Korean TV shows so I don't know what he's watching. Appears to be some kind of period drama.

There are two other customers, a pair of teenage girls hunting for drinks in the coolers at the back. I will them to hurry up. Not that I'm expecting problems, but the fewer people around, the better.

As expected, the Accord turns into the alley.

It's taken me nearly two weeks to figure out their pattern. I thought I'd had it worked out twice before, but both times they failed to show up. After going back over everything I knew, I realized where I'd made my mistakes. Their arrival today is the validation of that correction.

As the vehicle slows, my gaze moves to the feed showing the front of the store. The camera is across the street, giving me a wide shot that spans several units on either side of Park's Mini-Mart. Entering the frame on the right is the guy I've come to call Waste of Life No. 1. He's Caucasian, skinny, about five foot seven, with close-cropped brown hair and ears that lie flat against his head. Today, he's dressed in slacks, a dress shirt, and a jacket. No tie, but he doesn't need it. The outfit is enough to make him appear disarming.

WOL1 walks down the sidewalk, talking on his phone. I don't need a camera inside the Accord to know he's speaking with someone in the vehicle. His expression is jovial, as if he's talking to a friend about plans for the evening.

He pauses before he reaches the mini-mart, like the conversation needs his full attention. On the alley cam, the Accord stops behind Mr. Park's place. Three WOL passengers get out. Only the driver remains inside. Today they're wearing clown masks, which seems fitting.

If everything were to play out like the gang's previous jobs, WOL1 would enter the mini-mart, sneak into the back to unlock the rear door, then return to the front and nonchalantly shove a rubber doorstop under the front door to keep it from opening. At about the same time as this last bit, his buddies would slip in through the back entrance. After that, he and his asshole friends would take all the money from Mr. Park's cash register and make him open the safe.

Though they don't know it, things are going to play out a little differently today.

I check inside the store. The two girls are still trying to decide what they want, which means they won't be leaving in time and I will need to be extra careful.

I close my computer and open the door.

I've been hiding inside an empty store two units away from the mini-mart. It's a considerably more pleasant stakeout location than the Dumpster I used on one of my failed attempts.

When I step into the alley, I'm about a car's length behind the Accord, right in the sight line of the trio moving toward Mr. Park's door.

"Afternoon," I say, as I move my hands behind my back. "Nice masks."

I'm wearing one, too, only mine's a black ski mask with holes for my eyes and mouth.

This confuses them. One of them starts to say something, but before he can get a whole word out, I whip my hands in front of me and pull the triggers of the two Taser guns I'm holding. Sets of wires fly, hitting two of the three men and dropping them to the ground, where they writhe like frying bacon.

These Tasers of mine aren't your off-the-shelf, everyday kind of electroshock weapons. They're specially made and have detachable cartridges connected to the wires that keep the charge flowing. I drop one of the guns, pop the cartridge out of the other one, and replace it with a new wire set.

By the time I'm through, the third guy has realized things are going sideways and is running away from me, but he hasn't gone far enough. The needle-like pins hit him in the back and he crashes to the asphalt.

From my first shot to my last, fewer than five seconds have passed. Just enough time for the driver to panic. Before he can put the car into drive, I yank open the rear passenger door and toss in a smoke bomb. As I shut the door, he punches the gas and makes it maybe fifty feet before the bomb goes off. The device is designed to fill a good-sized room with smoke. In the Accord, the smoke is thick and opaque.

The driver is smart enough to slam on the brakes before he hits anything, but now he's faced with one of those damned-if-you-do, damned-if-you-don't situations. He can stay in the car and hope he doesn't choke to death, or he can get out where he'll have to deal with me.

He chooses option two, probably the smarter decision. But I'm sure that's not what he's thinking when I hit him with the Taser darts the second he steps out.

I return to the other three clowns. The battery charges on the wires connected to the first two guys have run out, and both men are starting to stir. Taking them in order of growing coherence, I apply a sleeper hold to each, cutting off oxygen long enough to make them unconscious. I then do the same to the third man and the driver.

After zip-tying each man's wrists and ankles, I head over to the back door to Park's Mini-Mart. It's unlocked, WOL1 having done his job. Before I enter, I check that my ski mask is still covering my face. In addition to the camera I sneaked inside his store, Mr. Park has his own surveillance system and I'd rather keep my face off the evening news.

I load a new cartridge into my Taser and ease open the door.

The entrance leads past the storeroom and down the side of one of the refrigerated cases. I can see only a small slice of the store, mainly the shelves along one wall and a little bit of the floor, but no one is standing there.

In the security tapes of the other robberies, WOL1 usually stays by the front door, where he acts like a victim when his friends come storming in demanding the cash. He even forks over his wallet.

I'm guessing right now, he's wondering where the hell his friends are and growing nervous. Which means he's bound to be looking at the end of the refrigerated cabinets, waiting for them to appear.

I walk fast and confidently into the store. WOL1 is right where I thought he would be. His brow furrows when he sees me, probably wondering why one of his crew is wearing a ski mask instead of the clown ones.

Mr. Park, on the other hand, jumps off his stool and reaches under his desk for what I'm sure is a weapon.

I raise my gun and aim it at WOL1, which has the added benefit of freezing Mr. Park.

WOL1 apparently decides that though my mask is wrong, the plan is proceeding. He raises his hands and says, "Don't shoot! Don't shoot! You-you can have my wallet."

Ugh. That kind of performance is never going to get him an Academy Award nomination. There's only one thing it deserves.

I shoot.

If he was perplexed before, the twin wires flying at him seem beyond his ability to compute. He stares at them as they sail across the room into his chest.

Screams come from my right, where the two teenage girls are standing, arms wrapped around each other.

I pop the cartridge off so that it will continue to deliver its charge, and point my now empty gun at Mr. Park.

"Please put your hands on the counter," I say.

He does as I request.

"If you want money, take it and get out of here," he tells me.

"I don't want your money." I wave the gun toward WOL1. "*He* wanted your money. Him and his friends out back."

The confusion bug claims another victim in Mr. Park.

"Come around the counter," I tell him.

He does.

"Go stand with the girls."

Mr. Park remains where he is, while the girls whimper in fear.

"Look, I'm not going to hurt anyone. I promise."

Once Mr. Park complies, I give WOL1 the sleep treatment and tie him up.

I retrieve the spent cartridge and wires, and detach the micro camera I hid on a wall support near the front door—can't go leaving any evidence around, after all. I walk over to where I can see the store owner and his two unfortunate customers, this time with my gun at my side.

"Call the police," I say. "Tell them you've caught those men who have been robbing convenience stores."

Mr. Park blinks in surprise. "You-you mean, the Masked Raiders?"

It's a terrible name given to the Waste of Life Gang by a local TV news reporter. A kind of play on masqueraders, I guess. I'm sure it sounded good in the reporter's head. The Raiders have been hitting up convenience stores on a regular basis. They didn't catch my attention, though, until they pistol-whipped a kid manning his mother's store three weeks ago. Technically it wasn't my attention they caught, but that's not important.

I nod. "The other four are in the alley."

The man is silent as he lets this sink in, then asks, "What about you? What do I tell them?"

"I'd prefer if you don't say anything." I nod up at his camera. "But I'm sure they're going to want to see your tape."

From the look on Mr. Park's face, I know he now believes I'm not a threat. "I...could tell them it doesn't work."

I'm not often surprised, but his offer is worth a raised

eyebrow. While it's very kind, it's unnecessary. The police won't be able to identify me from the footage.

"Don't put yourself in potential trouble for me," I say.

I look at the two girls and see from the cans of soda shaking in their hands that they finally picked their drinks. I pull a few dollars out of my pocket, set them on a nearby shelf, and glance back at Mr. Park. "For their Cokes."

I head out the back, where I quickly collect the other spent cartridges. I grab my computer and backpack from the store I was hiding in, and pull out a manila envelope. As I pass the Masked Raiders' Accord, I dump the envelope on the passenger seat. (I really hate that name—the gang name, I mean. I have no opinion on the car name.) Inside the envelope are photos of their other robberies, lifted from police reports, and a multi-page summary of all the information I've gathered on the members of the gang and how they pulled off their jobs.

After that, I head home.

CHAPTER TWO

J ust to set the record straight, taking out assholes like these isn't the way I make my living. I guess you could call it more of a hobby.

CHAPTER THREE

Actually, I don't know if you could even call it a hobby. I'm pretty sure a hobby is something one chooses to do. Like stamp collecting or plane spotting.

I'm not doing this because I particularly want to. I have more than enough opportunities to get into serious trouble with my day job. I'm doing this because...well, I have to.

CHAPTER FOUR

I live in Los Angeles. Until recently, I was house-sitting my business partner's home in the Hollywood Hills. He'd been spending more and more time over the last few years with his girlfriend at her place in San Francisco. After the birth of their daughter last year, he stopped coming back to L.A.

His place is a pretty plush setup. A great house. An *awesome* view. And zero rent. Why would I ever want to leave, right?

Let's just say something happened, and I felt it was time to find my own place.

I know, that's a little vague. Suffice it to say, things became strained between me and my partner after the death of someone we both cared about. I'll admit our problems are probably more my fault than his. The good thing is, while I'm skeptical that things between us will ever be completely back to the way they were, we've begun mending the wound and are working toward being okay. I guess that's all I can hope for. At least we've kind of figured out how to work together again.

The bottom line is, earlier this year, when things turned

sour, I moved into a rental a block from the ocean in Redondo Beach.

I like it down here.

If I stand at the very edge of my deck and lean as far as possible over the side railing, I can see a sliver of water between the two monstrosities that pass for homes across the street from me. I've fantasized about buying the one directly in front of my place and razing it to the ground, but while I have a nice nest egg, the price for beachside property in L.A. is ridiculous and I still wouldn't have enough. So I live with my little lean-to-the-side sliver of the Pacific, while enjoying the full effects of the coastal breeze and ocean atmosphere.

My favorite part of my townhouse is probably that deck. It stretches over my garage and is accessed through French doors off my living room.

And that's where I am, drinking a beer and getting a little late afternoon sun, when my phone buzzes with a news alert.

ARRESTS MADE IN
MINI-MARKET ROBBERY SPREE
Tap for Details

Well, that didn't take long.

I've been home for only about an hour, barely enough time to take a shower, set an alert for anything connected to the robberies, and crack open this beer.

Reluctantly, I go back inside and grab my laptop. On one of the local TV stations' website, I find a link to a live news feed. I click on it, and after several seconds of the Spinning Circle of Purgatory, the video kicks in, displaying a reporter standing in front of the entrance to Park's Mini-Mart.

"...sure, but we don't have confirmation yet," she's saying.

The shot shrank to only half the screen, revealing on the left a smartly dressed African American female anchor behind a news desk. The anchor said, "Thank you, Ashley. Right now, we're going to switch to Mark Francis at LAPD headquarters."

The image changes to a full-screen shot of a man with a I-may-be-good-looking-but-I'm-a-serious-reporter expression.

"Mark, I understand you have some new information."

"That's right, Sylvia. I just came from a briefing where an LAPD spokesperson confirmed that the five people who were taken to the hospital this afternoon have been arrested on charges of attempted robbery at Park's Mini-Mart earlier today. When pressed on whether police believe the five are connected to the so-called Masked Raiders robberies, the spokesperson would only say the investigation is ongoing. An announcement concerning the robberies, and the aggravated assault of Eddie Mauer, the son of an owner of one of the markets, will occur at a press conference with Chief of Police Mendoza scheduled for tomorrow at ten a.m."

The disembodied voice returns. "Is there any more information on this unknown person who helped subdue the suspects?"

Uh-oh.

I mean, not really uh-oh. I expected as much, but even the mention of me on TV in the abstract makes my stomach clench. In both my day job and this new hobby-that's-not-a-hobby, anonymity is key. I expect them to run a clip from Mr. Park's video surveillance system next, showing me taking out WOL No. 1.

"Nothing more than we already know," Mark says. "Just that there was a male customer in the market when the incident began who was able to disable one of the robbers."

I click off the website, and use the same backdoor pathway into the LAPD's computer network that I previously used to access their files on the gang. (Another perk of the day job.) It isn't long before I'm looking at the notes compiled so far on the

Park's Mini-Mart case. It's been only a couple of hours since things went south for the Masked Raiders, so there isn't much. There are, however, notes from a preliminary interview with Mr. Park.

I find the part I've been both looking for and dreading.

When asked for access to the store's video security footage, Mr. Park indicated that the camera hasn't worked for several months.

How about that. Mr. Park actually followed through on his offer.

As I close my computer, I make a mental note to send him a pair of tickets to a Lakers game. Anonymously, of course.

I told you, Nate. Nothing to worry about, Liz says.

I snort. There's always something to worry about. But she's right. It looks like I can file this one away as successfully completed and forget about it.

Thank you.

I shake my head. There's nothing she needs to thank me for. Not now. Not ever.

But she doesn't seem to share the same opinion, and says thank you again.

I go outside, grab my beer, down what's left, then head into the kitchen to snag another bottle.

CHAPTER FIVE

L iz. Dammit.

CHAPTER SIX

The next day is Sunday. And on Sundays, when I'm not working, I like to go on a long bike ride.

Though fall is only a week away, this is L.A., which means it's hot and likely only getting hotter until at least November. Even so, while I wear one of those slick biking shirts, below the waist I have on a pair of full-length workout pants. Yeah, maybe it looks a little odd with everyone else in shorts, but if I dress like they do, I get stares and questions. That doesn't fit well with my quiet lifestyle.

I take the bike path south to Palos Verdes, and go up and around the peninsula before turning back and heading for home. As I descend Palos Verdes Drive on the way to the beach, my phone vibrates in the zipped pocket of my shirt. I've assigned specific vibrations to the people who are important to me, so I know from the pattern it's Jar. I've been expecting her call.

I ride on until I reach the beach bike path, where I stop at an empty bench and call her back.

"A long ride today," she says.

No *hello*, no *how are you doing?* That's Jar. Just the facts. But she's right. I'm usually back at my townhouse by now.

"Went to the other side of the peninsula," I tell her.

"Which means you are not back home yet. If it is easier, I can call you when you get there."

"No, this is fine."

She's silent, then asks me the question I'm sure she's been sitting on since yesterday. "How did it go?"

"Just like I planned."

Jar knows about my hobby. She helps me when necessary and listens to me when I need to vent. Though I've never told her about the real reason I do what I do, there's no way she doesn't suspect, at least the essence of why. She's smart. I mean *super* smart. She's also eight thousand miles away, so that helps.

"The man and the girls at the market saw you," she says.

Of course she already knows this. I wouldn't doubt it if she paid a visit to the LAPD files before I did.

"All they saw was a masked man."

"You are lucky his camera did not work."

"Well, actually it does."

This pause is long. "He has you on video?"

"He's not going to show it to anyone."

"You cannot know that." She takes an exasperated breath. "I will erase it."

I almost tell her not to bother. I'm confident Mr. Park won't tell anyone, but I'm not sure about the two girls. They heard my conversation with Mr. Park, and they might not be as good at keeping a secret. "That's probably not a bad idea."

"You need to be more careful. How many times must I tell you this?"

I chuckle. "I will be, Mom."

"I am not your mother." She says this in complete seriousness because she means it.

"You're right. You're not. I'm sorry."

"Good."

"Can I get back to my ride now? Or is there something else?"

"I just wanted to make sure you are okay."

"And to tell me to be more careful."

"And that."

"I'm okay."

"Then you can get back to your ride."

She hangs up without saying goodbye. That's her way, too.

What can I say about Jar?

She's a tiny, scrappy, twenty-year-old Thai woman who is likely somewhere on the autism spectrum. She can take care of herself, no problem; she just has difficulty understanding and interacting with others. The fact that she calls me after each of my hobby-missions to make sure I'm all right is a big leap from where she was when I first met her. The truth is, she cares deeply about the people important to her and has feelings like the rest of us, but expressing them is where she sometimes falters.

What else?

She started working with my partner and me on the day job earlier this year and has quickly become a vital part of our team. She's also become one of my best friends over the last nine months.

Oh, and one more thing. She was there when my girlfriend died.

When I get back to Redondo Beach, I make my normal stop at Hey You, a juice bar a few blocks from my place. As I walk in, Nora, one of the girls behind the counter, starts making my usual.

The only other customers are a tourist family of four, sitting at a table by the window. How do I know they're tourists? Their matching shirts and sunburns.

The two kids, who look about six and eight, are trying to hurry their parents with a barrage of, "come on, come on," "we've been here *forever*," and "you promised we could go to the beach." Mom is doing all the deflecting, while Dad—clearly Father of the Year material—reads a newspaper and ignores everyone.

When the sound of the blender stops, I turn back to the counter and watch Nora pour my watermelon smoothie into a cup.

"Anything else today?" she asks as she hands me the drink.

"Not today," I say. I never get anything else.

As I pay, the kids finally win their battle and the family heads for the exit. I carry my drink to the table next to the one they used.

The dad has left his newspaper behind.

Take a look, Liz says.

I don't want to. It's too soon.

Take a look.

Against my better judgment, I grab the paper. While I savor my smoothie, I flip through the pages. Near the back, in a section that covers statewide news, I read a short item.

JENSON, CA—Seventeen-year-old Roosevelt High School student Marissa Garza is in a coma after being struck by a hit-and-run driver. The accident occurred Thursday night at approximately 9:20 p.m. Several people living in the area reported hearing a bang followed by a squeal of tires.

"I thought someone hit one of the cars parked on the street," said local resident Harvey Dawson. He went on to explain that he exited his house after the noise, and found Garza lying unconscious on his neighbor's lawn. According to the local police, an investigation is underway, but at this time there are no suspects.

I check the date on the paper. It's today's.

Nate.

I turn the page and scan the headlines.

Nate.

I try to concentrate on the words, but they start blending into one another.

Nate, go back.

I resist as long as I can, but we both know I'm not going to win. With a sigh, I return to the previous page.

Seventeen-year-old Roosevelt High School student Marissa Garza is in a coma…

This one, Liz says.

Dammit.

I guess I can't avoid talking about Liz anymore, can I?

Liz was my girlfriend, the person I mentioned before who, you know, died.

That happened nine months ago. Nine horrible, awful, painful, debilitating months ago. I don't think I'm any better now than I was right after she was killed. I've just learned to live with it.

In case you're wondering, my colleagues and I have dealt with those responsible. Not exactly the way I wanted to deal with them, but the more I think about it, the more I'm starting to come around to the idea that locking the perpetrators away for the rest of their lives is a much harsher penalty than the quick death I was advocating. Loads of time for them to just sit there and ponder what could have been.

Several months ago, Liz came back. It's just that I'm the only one who hears her.

Before you go thinking I'm a lunatic, I know it's my subconscious and not really her. At least, I think I know.

It sure as hell seems like her.

The voice is hers, not just the tone but also the way she says things. And the compassion. She had more of that than anyone I've ever met.

If you still think that makes me crazy, I'm not going to argue with you. Maybe I am.

This one, Liz says again.

She's the reason for my hobby. She is who drives me.

I read the article four more times as I finish my drink. When I leave the shop, the paper comes with me.

CHAPTER SEVEN

B ack at the townhouse, I grab my laptop, go out onto the deck, and plop down on an umbrella-shaded chair.

Liz has remained silent since the juice shop, but I can feel her hovering behind me, as if ready to nudge me again if she senses I'm not following through on her suggestion.

I know better than that.

I crack open my computer and search for information about the hit-and-run.

The first thing I learn is that Jenson is in Northern California, about forty-five miles north of Sacramento. According to Wikipedia, many families with at least one person who has a job in the state capital have moved there in the last ten years. The town is a good six-hours-plus drive from Los Angeles without traffic, or an hour and a half by plane with a much shorter forty-minute drive after.

The distance is a good thing. The takedown of the mini-market robbers was an aberration. I don't like partaking in my hobby so close to home. But Liz had insisted, and when she gets her mind set, it's not like I have much of a choice.

I find a post on a news site covering the Sacramento area.

Though most of what it contains is the same as what's in the paper, there are three tidbits of new information.

The first is a picture of Marissa Garza. It's a head and shoulders shot that was likely taken for school. She has long dark hair that falls in waves, bright brown eyes, and a smile that seems surprisingly genuine for a school photo.

The other two new items are contained in the final paragraphs of the article, under the heading UPDATE.

Connie Garza told reporters this morning that her sister Marissa remains in intensive care. When asked about her sister's prognosis, she said, "All I know is she's not out of the woods yet."

A Jenson PD spokesman indicated there have been no new developments in the search for the hit-and-run driver. Anyone who has information is urged to contact the department.

Liz leans in close, over my shoulder. I feel if I turn, I might actually see her, but I keep my eyes forward.

This one, she says.

"I heard you the first time."

Old Liz would have punched me in the shoulder for a comment like that. In-my-head Liz just looms over me, silently urging me to keep going.

I find a few more articles about the accident but they're all rehashes, so I turn my search to learning more about the girl.

Marissa does not have a Facebook page, but she does have accounts with Instagram and Hulla-Chat. Both accounts are private, meaning only those she approves can see her posts, so the only thing I can view is the picture she uses for her profiles. It's the same shot from the article. And why not? It's a good photo.

I open one of my legally questionable programs and set it to work hacking into Marissa's accounts. (Okay, maybe more than just questionable.) While it runs, I go back inside.

When Liz forced me to reread the article at the juice bar, I pretty much knew what was going to happen. Now that I've confirmed there's no new information about the hit-and-run, I'm positive.

In my bedroom, I remove two bags from my closet. Both are prepacked, one with clothes and toiletries, and the other with some of the milder tools of my trade. I check the bags, add a few things that might come in handy, and zip them back up. Hopefully, I won't need much from the gear bag, but I'd rather bring things I won't use than wish I had things I left behind.

In the kitchen, I open the large cabinet that acts as my pantry. It's about the same size as a basic American refrigerator and holds all the things you'd expect—canned goods, cereal, pasta, flour, that kind of stuff. I keep the items on the bottom shelf inside a lidless plastic bin, ostensibly so that they're easier to get to. The real reason has nothing to do with access to the food.

I remove the bin and set it on the floor. I then push down on the wooden shelf near the back, causing it to pop up along the left side. I raise the shelf like a hatch, and prop it up with the metal rod attached to the underside.

In the space below is one of those home safes people use for important documents. This one contains those kinds of papers, too. But the documents are fakes, meant to trick any enterprising thief who makes it that far. I even keep a thousand dollars cash inside, just to make the burglar feel good after getting the safe open. Of course, if someone ever *does* break into my place, I'd find him before he gets the chance to spend the money.

What I'm interested in this morning is the padded envelope I keep behind another board off to the side. I pull it out and carefully dump the two dozen smaller envelopes it contains onto the floor. Written on the outside of each are a name and a country. This is my stash of ready-to-go, never-used false identities.

I shuffle through them, looking for one that will work for my trip north. There are IDs from over a dozen different nations, but there's no need to waste one of my international personas for this trip.

I choose Daniel Bryce, United States citizen, and put everything else back the way it was. The Bryce envelope I carry into the living room and tuck into my gear bag. A check of my computer tells me that both of Marissa's social media accounts have been cracked. I'm tempted to scroll through what she's posted but that'll turn into a time suck. I'll have plenty of opportunities to go through things en route.

After I book a seat on a flight leaving in a couple of hours for Sacramento, I feel Liz finally relax.

Thank you, she says.

"I miss you."

Lips almost but not quite brush the back of my neck.

I swear this isn't a ghost story.

I swear.

CHAPTER EIGHT

How long have I been partaking in my hobby? That's kind of a tricky question.

Liz had a kind heart and would cry at stories about people being taken advantage of and those who needed help but were in no position to get any.

There were times when we'd be walking somewhere, enjoying each other's company, when she'd suddenly say something like, "You and my brother are wasting your talents. There's so much more you could do for people."

Did I mention that Liz was my partner's sister?

Yeah, there's that.

I know I mentioned my anger at how those responsible for Liz's death were dealt with. That's the reason my partner and I had our falling out. But, like I said, that's water under the bridge. Gelatinous, slow-moving water that might take the rest of our lives to fully pass.

Despite what Liz would say, she knew my job was important, and never pushed beyond those occasional nudges for me to do something different. Well, not until she started talking to me again a few months ago.

And hence the birth of my hobby.

In some ways, I've been doing things like this on and off for years in the day job. (Which, by the way, is not limited to daytime. On most assignments, it's a 24/7 kind of thing.) And what is this day job I keep talking about without really divulging anything? Sorry, it's one of those tell you/kill you situations.

I'm not kidding.

What I can say, in broad strokes, is that the team I'm part of operates in a world most people never come in contact with, other than in movies and TV shows.

Have I ever been shot at? Yep.

Have I ever been hurt? Ha. Yes. Yes, I have.

Have I ever shot back? Well, I certainly don't just stand around and act like a target.

Whether my colleagues and I are criminals or not would depend on who's talking. If you ask me, I would say no. To badly (and I mean *really* badly) paraphrase *Star Trek*, we few do what's necessary for the good of the many.

All of this is a way of saying my job has taught me very useful skills and exposed me to resources only a handful of people in the entire world have access to—skills and resources I can also use in my new hobby.

CHAPTER NINE

When I reach Sacramento, I rent a car using one of my Daniel Bryce credit cards. (Don't worry, I'm not scamming anyone. I pay my bills, no matter what name's on it.) I request a base model and am given a dark green Nissan Versa that looks like it's close to being retired. The rental agent probably thought I'd reject it, because he's visibly surprised when I say, "Perfect."

Standing out is my enemy. My goal is to leave few, if any, memories of me after I leave a place so that nothing can be tied back to me. A nondescript vehicle helps.

I make one stop in Sacramento before heading north. Though I have never been to the Sacramento Central Y before, I've been given detailed instructions so I know exactly where to go. When the attendant asks to see my YMCA ID, I flash him one with the name Daniel Bryce on it. YMCAs are convenient if you're working in the US and Canada. They're great places to wash up, exercise, hide out. A membership card for the Y is just one of several IDs that make up each of my false identity kits.

I find my way to the locker room and locate the correct

locker number. Using the combination I've been given, I open the lock and remove the bag from inside.

There are certain items best left at home when you fly if you'd rather not spend some serious time with the TSA. This is where the contacts from my day job come in handy. In almost any city in the world, I either know someone or can be networked to someone who can fulfill my particular needs. In this case, the contact is known to me, and the bag she has left me is full of goodies.

I return to my car and put the bag in the back. Before closing the hatch, I make sure everything I asked for is there. Two Glock 9mms, several spare magazines, two sound suppressors, three boxes of ammo, a selection of knives, a set of brass knuckles, and a baker's dozen of various incendiary devices. Like with my other gear bag, my hope is I won't have to open this one again.

By the time I arrive in Jenson, the sun is setting. An earlier internet search provided me with a list of potential places to stay. I could have booked something ahead of time, but I wanted to see the locations in person first. I work my way through the candidates until I find a suitably drab motel on the edge of town, near the interstate, called the Great 7. It's basically a Motel 6 knockoff. If there's a chain of them, I've never heard of it.

Room 218 is on the second floor, its door accessed from a breezeway overlooking the parking lot behind the motel. The room is pretty much what you'd expect—white walls, a serviceable bathroom, an uninspiring bed, a dinged-up dresser, and a dated TV.

A cardboard sign on the dresser informs me that for an extra five bucks a day, I can have unlimited Wi-Fi. That's a pass for me. Even if it was free, I wouldn't use it. I carry around my own mobile hotspot, which is both a hell of a lot faster and better encrypted than any public Wi-Fi.

I set the duffel containing my clothes on the bed—it's the only bag I've brought to the room—and return to my Versa to head out on recon. Though I appreciate downtime, when I have things to do and no reason not to do them, I'm not going to just sit around. I learned that from my partner back in the days when he was my mentor and I was his apprentice. Before I met him, I wasn't quite so smart with my time. (Which, by the way, is a colossal understatement.)

I drive first to the part of town where the hit-and-run took place. It's a nice, middle-class neighborhood of tidy yards and well-maintained homes. Nothing too outlandish, just average-sized places, probably three bedrooms per home at most.

When I turn onto the street where the incident occurred, there's no need to hunt for the exact spot. On a lawn, four houses from the corner, sits a patch of flowers and signs and burning candles. You can't call it a memorial because Marissa isn't dead, but that's what it looks like.

A small group of teens stands nearby, gathered around a woman in her mid-twenties. The kids are wearing your basic jeans and T-shirts, while the woman is in a stylish yet practical blue dress. She's also dangling a microphone at her side, which means she must have arrived in the news van parked nearby. There's no camera operator around, though.

Even without the kids and the news crew and the non-memorial memorial, I would have been able to pick out the accident location without any trouble. Black rubber smudges mark the curb and sidewalk where the unknown vehicle veered off the road. First impression: the marks weren't caused by sudden braking, but by a tire slamming into the curb and spinning across the sidewalk.

I drive by, making sure to face away as I pass the group. When I reach the end of the block, I park and pull the gear bag from L.A. onto the front passenger seat. I'm about to break my hope of leaving it closed, but this is a minor infraction.

I hunt around inside and pull out a case about the size of an average paperback book—think early Harry Potter as opposed to later. Inside are several lenses—telephoto, macro, wide angle— all designed to fit over the camera lens on my phone. I select the telephoto and aim my camera at the group by the news van. I snap several shots, getting as many close-ups as I can. The only person not giving me at least a profile is the newswoman, which is fine. She's of no interest to me.

Once satisfied, I drive by Marissa's house, located a block and a half from where she was hit. There are two more news vans here but no one on the curb. I wonder for a moment if the reporters have been invited inside the house, but then I notice movement within both vans and guess they're just waiting for something to happen. They're lucky to have found parking spots so close. Unlike elsewhere in the neighborhood, the curbs are filled in front of the few houses on both sides of Marissa's place.

Lights blaze from inside the Garza residence, and though I can't see anyone through the windows, it's not a stretch to guess the place is full of people.

This makes me worry that maybe Marissa has died. I checked the news at the motel and there was no change at that time. But contrary to what most reporters would like, information like that isn't always released right away.

If she *is* dead, that will take this to a whole other level. Not that it would change what I need to do, but murder has a way of thrusting law enforcement agencies into high gear, making it harder for me to move around without crossing their paths.

Half a mile from Marissa's neighborhood, I find a shopping plaza with a parking lot that's sparsely occupied. I take a spot far from other cars and pull out my phone. The number I want is near the top of the list I created on the flight up.

"Jenson Community Hospital," a female voice says. "How may I direct your call?"

"This is Dr. Hamon from Stanford Medical," I say, acting suitably gruff. "I received a call requesting a consult."

The woman says, "If you'd tell me who called, I'd be happy to put you through."

"Didn't anyone tell you to expect to hear from me?"

"I'm sorry. I haven't heard anything."

"Hold on." I'm in full annoyed-doctor mode now, so I give it a few seconds before saying, "It says here Dr. Tyler? Taylor? Oh, hell, I can't tell. Something to do with a patient named Goza."

"You must mean Garza. That would be Dr. Taylor. I'll put you right through to his office."

"Thank you."

Taylor is the medical director, something I learned from the hospital's website. (What did people do before the internet?) There is no way to know if he's in charge of the girl's case or not, but given the press Marissa has been getting, I figure he'd be keeping a close eye on things at least.

The line rings again.

"Dr. Taylor's office," another woman answers.

"This is Dr. Hamon, returning Dr. Taylor's call."

A slight pause. "Dr. Hamon? Dr. Taylor didn't say anything about a call."

"Then maybe you should ask him."

"I'm sorry, Doctor, but Dr. Taylor's in a meeting at the moment."

Well, crap.

I allow myself no more than a nanosecond of frustration.

One of the keys to success in situations like this is the ability to improvise. "Then I guess he'll have to call me back."

"Of course. Can you tell me what this is regarding?"

"He called *me*, remember? He wanted to consult with me about a patient named Garza."

"Marissa Garza? Oh, then I'm sure he'll want to call you right back."

"Is her condition still critical?"

"I believe she was upgraded to stable this afternoon."

I grunt, hoping I sound like I'm acknowledging the good news without caring that much. "Tell him to try me when he gets a chance."

"Of course. Can I get your—"

I hang up.

So, it's not a gathering to grieve at the Garza house. That's a relief.

I restart the engine and head off to get something to eat.

CHAPTER TEN

Like many small towns, Jenson rolls up its sidewalks a few hours after sunset. By ten p.m., the only things open are the town's four 7-Elevens, a handful of bars, and a 24-hour Del Taco. From the few cars I see in these places' parking lots, none has much business tonight.

Fridays and Saturdays are probably a little livelier, but this is Sunday night, and in the morning the majority of people return to work or school.

I'm hungry but don't fancy anything from Del Taco. Yelp tells me there's a place called Coyote Hill Bar and Grill in the town of Brighton, a fifteen minutes' drive south of Jenson. I decide to try it out. Unfortunately the meal isn't much of a step up from fast food, but I can't complain too much as it quells my growling stomach.

I return to my motel, but I'm not ready to sleep. I open my laptop, hoping I can dig up more information.

My first stop is the Jenson school district's database. The security firewall is laughably inadequate and a breeze to breach. It doesn't take long for me to locate photos of the students at Theodore Roosevelt High School, where Marissa goes.

Searching through them takes a bit longer, but when I finish, I've matched six students to the kids who were talking to the newswoman.

I cross-check the kids with photos in Marissa's Instagram feed. Four are featured multiple times. Fara Nelson, Luke Reed, and Julia Torres are seniors like Marissa, and Andrew Gomez is a junior. The two not in her feed are Noah Webb and Kaitlyn Gomez, both sophomores. Given the resemblances and the shared last name, I'm pretty sure Kaitlyn and Andrew are siblings. There's also a picture of Andrew in a high school baseball uniform that's been tagged #cuzluv, which I'm going to go out on a limb and guess it means he's Marissa's cousin. I'll verify later. If he is related to her, then the same's true for Kaitlyn.

I pull up Marissa's private Hulla-Chats, and see she has running conversation threads with Fara, Julia, and Luke. I learn she and Luke are in a relationship, or perhaps were. The chats between them stopped abruptly several weeks ago.

I lean back.

If Marissa was hit on purpose, then the culprit is likely someone she knows. In which case, there's a decent chance one of these six people was behind the wheel, and an even higher probability it's the (ex?) boyfriend.

Before I allow myself to go too far down that rabbit hole, I need to determine whether the hit-and-run was an accident or not.

It's no shocker that the Jenson police department's system proves trickier to get into than the school's. I'm actually impressed by its level of security. The base software is off-the-shelf garbage, but someone has done a fair amount of customizing. So much so that I almost call Jar to help me out. Thankfully, I get in before I resort to that embarrassing option.

The Jenson PD is about the size you'd expect for the area's population. In addition to the administrative staff, it employs three full-time detectives, thirty-six full-time officers, and a handful of part-timers who pick up shifts here and there.

The hit-and-run investigation (Crime Ref. No. #18-327K-12104) has been assigned to a pair of detectives both named Michael. Michael Dye and Michael Cook. According to their notes, they've interviewed Marissa's parents and several of Marissa's friends, including Luke, Fara, Julia, and Andrew, as well as several people who live in the vicinity of the accident. There are also pictures of the accident scene, including close-ups of the tire marks on the curb and sidewalk, and of the crushed grass where Marissa lay until paramedics arrived.

I read a sparse description of the events and an equally thin account of the Michaels' investigation to this point. I hate to be a critic but neither detective is a particularly good writer.

Their report boils down to three things. They have no idea who did it, they don't know why, and they aren't any closer to finding either answer than when they were assigned the case.

At half past midnight, I drive back to Marissa's neighborhood.

As I hoped, the accident scene is now deserted. I continue past it, checking the surrounding houses for signs of life. Like most of Jenson, the homes are dark and quiet. I circle the block and park around the corner, then hoof it to the spot of the crime.

Kneeling at the curb, I examine the tire marks. I also check the road in case there are skid marks from the rear tires. But there are no signs the car attempted to stop. It's as if the driver took aim, jumped the curb, hit the target, and swung immediately back onto the road. Which means the vehicle likely hit Marissa with the front passenger-side corner.

I spend a few moments hunting for pieces that might have broken off the car. The police report didn't mention any being found, so if there is something here, it'd be small.

I need some light to do this, but I don't want to turn on my flashlight. Luckily for me, a source of illumination is nearby that shouldn't draw any attention. From the not-memorial, I grab one of the few jars that still has a burning candle inside and slowly move it over the ground.

In the tiny depression between the sidewalk and the grass, I find a small, chrome-colored triangle. Maybe it's from the accident, maybe not. I slip it in my pocket to examine later.

When I find nothing else, I switch my attention to the spot where Marissa fell. The impression she made is gone, but I approximate the position from a copy of the police photo I saved to my phone, and estimate that the car threw her a good fifteen feet. Even though she landed on grass, she's lucky the blow didn't kill her.

There are only two reasons this accident occurred. Either someone wasn't paying attention—drunk or texting on their phone or whatever—and veered onto the sidewalk, or someone hit her on purpose.

I know it would be a mistake to discard either option before I obtain more facts, but I'm having a harder and harder time believing the first one.

Here comes poor Marissa, walking home through her quiet neighborhood, a little after nine p.m., and the only driver on the street swerves onto the sidewalk at the exact spot where she is and hits her? If it was a distracted or impaired driver, why hop the curb there? Why not twenty feet before the car reached Marissa? Or a hundred after? Or literally *anywhere* else along the block other than the only point where someone was walking?

I suppose it could be chalked up to bad luck or a freak accident. But neither feels right to me.

As I return the candle to its place with the others, I wonder if the perpetrator has made a contribution to the not-memorial. There are dozens of vases filled with flowers, several stuffed animals, and eleven candles in glass jars, all but four having burned out. A few of the vases and animals have notes taped to them.

Get well, Marissa

And:

We are with you.

And:

Praying for you.

If the driver left something, it's not obvious. I take a video of the display in case I need to reference it later.

After that, I return to my motel for some much needed rest.

CHAPTER ELEVEN

I wake with the sun on Monday morning and go for a run, keeping my route far from Marissa's neighborhood and the parts of town where the hospital and police station are located. Like when I bike in L.A., I'm wearing my full-length warm-up pants.

The reason isn't because I like to sweat a lot. I'd much prefer to be in shorts. But, like I said, I'd be noticed. Maybe you're thinking I was drunk one night and got myself an elaborate leg tattoo.

I wish.

The reason is the prosthetic that makes up the lower half of my right leg. I'd rather keep my superhero appendage under wraps. It's a uniquely identifying feature that doesn't play well with staying anonymous.

You may be wondering if this hinders me at all. The answer is not much. I went through a period of self-pity right after I lost that part of my leg, but it wasn't long before I was determined to prove to my mentor it wouldn't hold me back. Now, unless I bring someone in on the secret, no one can tell I'm not whole.

I have ten different prosthetic legs. No, eleven. I always

forget to count the first one I received, because I can't use it anymore due to the bullet damage. Four of the prosthetics are utilitarian, while the rest are designed for special situations.

One of them is a blade. You know what I mean. Like the kind Paralympians use. And yeah, like that one guy who used a pair in the regular Olympics, before he shot his girlfriend and his life went off the rails. I usually don't like bringing him up, but I know once I mention the blade and Olympics, the connection is almost always made.

Anyway, if I'm using my blade, I can really fly. Not as fast as I would be able to go if both legs were gone and I had a blade on each, but I go at least as fast as I did before that damn car smashed into me. Using only one does give me a weird gait, however, a kind of regular-step/bounce-step, regular-step/bounce-step pattern, which is why I don't use it that much and haven't brought it with me.

The only prosthetic I have on this trip is a jack-of-all-trades. I can run with it, too, just not as fast as with the blade, but at least my strides look almost normal.

See, I like to run. It's transformative for me. One of my concerns when I lost my leg—albeit lower on the list at the time —was whether or not I would be able to run again. That was another motivation for not letting the injury stop me.

Running has been particularly helpful since Liz died. I can get into a rhythm, and for however long I'm on the road, the crippling thoughts that sometimes rule my mind fade.

I don't listen to anything when I run, but I do wear earbuds. It makes it easier to pretend I can't hear people if they try to talk to me. I'm positive I'm not the only one out there who does this.

As I run this morning, I let my mind wander, making sure not to focus on any one thing. What I'm hoping is that some insight will bubble to the surface that'll give me a clue as to who hit Marissa. But clearly I don't have enough data yet, because by the time I get back to my room, all I have for my efforts are a lot of sweat and the refrain from that old U2 song "Where the Streets Have No Name" playing through my head. (Just because I don't listen to music doesn't mean I don't hear it sometimes.)

After a shower, I head to my car for a look at Jenson in the daylight. I start downtown, at the south end of the city. It's a mixed bag of mom-and-pop places and chain stores, like Gap and Rite Aid and Starbucks. I have a feeling in the next year or two, most of the mom-and-pop ones will be gone.

Even with the new businesses, it's not hard to picture the quaint, sleepy little town Jenson once was. I can even imagine folks on horseback moseying down the road, looking to stock up on provisions.

As I move down Central Avenue, the town's main drag, I see signs sticking out from lampposts, trumpeting the upcoming Prospector Days Festival in October. There's also a banner stretched over the road asking people to be mindful of water consumption during the continuing drought.

Like I said—quaint.

I find the police station a few blocks off of Central, in a suitably civic-looking building. When I drive by, the place seems quiet. I imagine that's the status quo.

My tour of downtown complete, I branch out.

Jenson has four main residential areas. The northeast (where Marissa lives), the northwest, and the west are mostly populated with relatively new homes. The fourth area borders downtown and spreads to the southwest. It's filled with older homes, and I'm guessing it's the town's original neighborhood.

Sitting between the old area and the westside neighborhood is Theodore Roosevelt High School. The campus is decent sized, built in the California mostly-one-story-buildings style. At the north end are the football and baseball fields, both well maintained.

In the blocks surrounding the school are several fast-food places, a café called the Sunny Creek Diner, and one of the town's several 7-Elevens. Typical school-adjacent fare.

The hospital is on the east side of town, and, at four stories and a whole city block long, is the largest building in Jenson. It's way too big to be a holdover from the pre-population boom era. In fact, it even seems too large for the town's current size so it probably serves the whole region.

As the hospital's parking lot comes into view, I spot several news vans, all with antenna dishes extended above their roofs. Something must be going on.

I turn into the lot.

Sure enough, just off to the side of the hospital's main entrance, a podium is set up, and news crews and other people are gathered in front of it. An older man in a police uniform is speaking into a bouquet of microphones. A doctor about the same age stands to his side, and behind them are several other medical personnel and police officers.

Thinking it unlikely there's a local story other than the hit-and-run that the Sacramento news stations would be interested in, I park the car and walk over.

My hope is that the officer is announcing the arrest of a suspect. That would put a quick end to my trip, which is fine by me. I don't care whether or not I'm the one who finds the person responsible, just that the person *is* found.

As I reach the back of the crowd, I get a better look at the speaker and recognize him from the Jenson PD website as Chief of Police Norman Sparks.

"...at this time," he's saying. "I want to stress how important it is that if anyone knows anything about the incident, they should contact us immediately. That's all I have for now. Thank you for your time."

"Chief Sparks!" one of the television reporters shouts. "Have you at least identified any persons of interest?"

The chief walks away without saying anything. The doctor who was standing next to him—I'm pretty sure it's Dr. Taylor—and the other officers and hospital employees follow.

More questions are shouted, but none get a response.

One of the questions, however, hits me like a punch to the gut.

"Do you know when services will be held?" This from a female TV reporter, whom I think is the one I saw last night.

I step closer to a couple of women standing at the back of the gathering and ask, "Was this about Marissa Garza?"

One of them nods.

"Has there been a break in the case?"

The other woman glances at me, a grimace on her face. "She passed away an hour ago."

For a split second, I can feel Liz hovering, crying. Then she goes away again, wherever it is she goes.

I know I should let my conversation with the women end there, but I can't help but say, "I thought she was doing better."

"Some kind of setback this morning." The woman looks at me, longer than I'd like. "Are you a reporter?"

"Me? No. I'm just visiting a friend inside."

She turns away, no longer interested, and I slip away.

CHAPTER TWELVE

The hit-and-run has been upgraded to manslaughter or murder.

I have no proof yet, but I'm more convinced than ever that it's option number two.

You have to find the driver, Liz says. There's a quiver in her voice. Sadness, yes, but anger, too.

"I will," I promise.

If it was an accident, there's at least an even chance the driver will go to the police once he or she knows Marissa has died. Many people can't handle that much guilt.

I monitor the news for the rest of the day, not just on the radio and online, but also by taking periodic dips into the police department's files. As of ten p.m., no one has come forward.

It looks like instead of a quick solution and return to Los Angeles, I'm going to be here for a little while. Which creates a problem. Jenson is a small town, and I'm a stranger. The longer I'm here, the greater the chance I'll be noticed. I need a plausible reason for hanging around. Something that will allow me to blend into the background.

The Help Wanted sign, Liz whispers.

It takes me a few seconds to understand what she means. On my drive around town earlier, I saw a sign hanging in the window of that diner near the high school that read BUSBOY WANTED.

"Good call," I say.

Not only will a job legitimize my presence, this one in particular will place me close to the high school, putting me in indirect contact with students and teachers looking for something to eat. Perhaps I'll pick up a few clues as I clear off tables.

The next morning, after the breakfast rush, I walk into the café and am hired on the spot to be the weekday first-shift busboy. This means I'll be covering breakfast and lunch, and will have the rest of the afternoon and all night to hunt.

I need to do something about my lodging, though. The Great 7 is a budget motel, but it still costs more than a busboy can afford. I downgrade to a rent-by-the-week place called the Sleepy Daze Residential Inn.

It's a dump, with water-stained wallpaper, brown carpet that I don't think started out that color, and a worn mattress with a questionable history. It's all okay, though. The room's only for appearances.

I mess up the bed so that it looks slept in, and crumple and drop a towel on the bathroom floor. I then head to Brighton, where I take another room, this time at a Residence Inn along the freeway. I'll have to make daily stops at Sleepy Daze, but I'd rather do that than risk picking up some kind of disease from hanging around there.

I spend the first part of Wednesday cleaning tables at the diner and the rest on the internet, trying to build a clearer picture of who Marissa was, and creating a list of everyone she ever came into contact with.

Can I take a moment to sing the praises of social media? I don't use it myself, not in my line of work. I can't have some rando bad guy just look me up. That would be dumb.

Your average citizen, though? Most don't seem to care how much information they expose to the world. Even those who are cautious and try to keep a low social media profile have way more personal data than they realize floating out there. Give me a single picture and I can start building a profile of someone. Add a comment, and—God love them—maybe a hashtag, and it's like the person is handing me the keys to their front door.

Can I tell you my favorite thing?

It's when other people in a picture with my subject are tagged or post a comment. Because even if my subject is digitally discreet, at least one (if not all) of the person's friends won't be. And those friends? Oh, man. They often have a treasure trove of photos and comments about the very person I'm researching.

(Please understand, I use these powers only for good, but a lot of others out there are mining data for more nefarious purposes. Consider yourself warned.)

What I learn from snooping is that Marissa and Luke were together for just over seven months when they stopped talking. Given the number of pictures of him at Garza family dinners and other functions, he seemed to have ingratiated himself into her family,

So why the sudden rift? Had she cheated on him and sent him into a jealous rage that ended with him running her down in his car? I have to say, that's a pretty tidy solution. After all, most murders are committed by someone the victim knows and often loves.

I take another dip into the Jenson PD files, and find a transcript of the interview one of the Mikes did with Luke. It's surprisingly extensive, so a gold star for Detective Dye. The most important part can be boiled down to this short exchange:

DETECTIVE DYE: Can you tell us where you were at 9 p.m.?
LUKE REED: I...I was at work.
DETECTIVE DYE: Where do you work?
LUKE REED: McDonald's. The one on Cherry.
DETECTIVE DYE: What time did you start?
LUKE REED: Five. I was supposed to close.
DETECTIVE DYE: Supposed to? Are you saying you didn't?
LUKE REED: No, I didn't. Andrew...uh, Andrew Gomez, Marissa's cousin, he came in and told me what happened. I left right away and went straight to the hospital.
DETECTIVE DYE: What time was this?
LUKE REED: I don't know. Nine forty-five, maybe.

There's a note in the file indicating that Detective Dye confirmed with someone name Brad Sorenson at McDonald's that Luke had indeed been at work when Marissa was hit.

So, unless Luke hired someone to do it, he's not a suspect. I'm not yet going to dismiss the possibility that he did, but I think it's unlikely a seventeen-year-old kid would pay someone to run over his girlfriend.

While the Michaels have also cleared Fara, Julia, and Noah, they haven't talked to Andrew or Kaitlyn yet. No big deal. I've already looked into Marissa's cousins.

Ignoring the fact that Kaitlyn hasn't even learned how to drive yet, they were both in Sacramento with their parents that night, as evidenced by a photo Andrew posted—not ten minutes before Marissa's accident—from the Buffalo Wild Wings at the

Promenade Shopping Center in Sacramento. And no, I'm not taking the photo at face value. I asked Jar to check the mall's security footage, and she found more than enough to confirm Andrew and Kaitlyn were there.

Since I'm in the police files, I check to see if there have been any new developments. I find a report from a crime lab in Sacramento. The techs have been unable to determine the brand and size of the tire, though they put the likelihood of it being a Michelin at seventy percent. They are more confident the vehicle is a sedan as opposed to a truck or a van.

Which narrows things down to seventy-five percent of the personal vehicles on the road, give or take. Not the most helpful piece of information, but it's something, I guess.

The technicians calculated that the vehicle had been going about fifteen miles an hour when it hit Marissa. They also speculate that, given the damage her arm received, there's likely a dent in the car's hood, possibly also one on the front passenger-side fender. There's likely some grille damage, too. I think about the triangular piece I found next to the sidewalk and again wonder if it came from the car.

On Thursday, a customer in a nice-looking suit comes into the diner around eight a.m. and takes a booth by the front window, or, as I've learned to refer to it, table two. The problem is, I haven't had a chance to properly clean it yet.

"Hey," the man says, when he sees me. "Can you hurry it up?"

"Sorry, sir," I reply as I hustle over.

"Damn right, you're sorry."

I clamp down on my natural desire to put him in his place, and keep my expression calm. The thing is, table one, the next table over, is clean and ready for use.

Maybe table two is his favorite.

Fine. Whatever.

I wipe down the table. "There you are, sir."

He looks at the surface like he's the health inspector, gives me a grunt, and turns his attention to his phone.

Man, I do not know how service industry people can do this day in and day out. Working directly with the public sucks.

CHAPTER THIRTEEN

M arissa's funeral service takes place at ten a.m. on Saturday at St. Matthew's Catholic Church.

It's my day off from the diner, but not from the real reason I'm here. Since there's a strong probability her killer will be at the service, I head over to the church. I'm not sure I want to go inside, though, as people might wonder who I am and why I'm there. But at the very least, I can observe the mourners from my car as they go in and out.

When I see how many people have shown up, I change my mind about going in. I should be able to lose myself among the crowd.

I park in one of the last spaces available and walk inside. Many people have already made their way to the pews, but several are loitering in the vestibule, talking. I scan their faces, picking out a few I've seen on one of the several Instagram accounts I've gone through, and memorizing the ones that are new to me. I proceed into the nave.

St. Matthew's is bigger than I expected. There's enough room for several hundred parishioners if everyone squeezes together. Which is a good thing, because I think Marissa's service will be pushing the building's capacity.

I pause near the back and take a look around. My research has led me to conclude Marissa wasn't at the very top of the Roosevelt High popularity pyramid, but she was well liked. That's reflected in the amount of kids around her age in attendance. It appears as if half of her school's student body has turned out. There are plenty of adults, too, most talking in hushed voices to one another.

I take a seat in the third to last row, next to the outside aisle. Not having brought a suit with me, I picked up a jacket and pants the previous afternoon at a secondhand store in Brighton, the slightly worn outfit reflecting the economic status of my assumed identity.

Okay, time for a peek into my day job.

A big part of what I do is dealing with the dead. No, I'm not an assassin, though I guess I could play the part in a pinch. My associates and I are more in the disposal end of things, as in making inconvenient corpses disappear. I tell you this to point out that the sight of a dead body—or even lugging one over my shoulder—doesn't faze me.

Oddly, funerals do.

That's not to say I haven't been to my fair share. I have. (Not Liz's, but that wasn't from a lack of wanting to be there. It was because I was busy trying to find her killers.)

My problem with funerals goes back to the very first one I remember going to. In many ways, that one was much like Marissa's. It was for this kid I knew at school (middle school, not high school). He died of leukemia or a brain tumor or something like that. I don't remember exactly. Just some crazy disease I didn't understand.

My parents took me because I said I wanted to go.

I didn't know what to expect. We weren't big churchgoers. I just assumed there would be some talking and some praying and that would be it.

The church was packed then, too. I remember feeling like I was both in and hovering above my body. I'm sure the preacher talked, and that there was music, and that others got up and shared their remembrances. I know now that's how these things work, but I honestly don't remember any of that. What sticks in my mind is the open casket that sat at the front of the room. An open casket with a kid lying inside I used to play with.

I was old enough to know he wasn't sleeping, but from where I sat, that's exactly what he looked like he was doing. That sounds like a cliché, doesn't it? I can't help it. In my head, he was both sleeping and dead and it freaked me out. But I held that in and said nothing.

When the time came for people to approach the casket, my father said, "We don't have to go up if you don't want to."

Oh, I *didn't* want to.

I didn't want to go anywhere near that box.

What I wanted to do was go the other way, out the door, to our car, and back home, where I could play with my friends who were still alive. Maybe I was afraid if I got near my dead friend, I'd end up in a box, too. I don't remember what was specifically fueling my fear, just that it consumed me.

But he had been my friend. And if it had been me lying up there, I would have hoped he wouldn't be too scared to come up and say goodbye. So I shook my head, moved into the aisle, and joined the line.

Though it was the right thing to do, Older Me wishes I had taken my dad up on his unspoken offer. Up close, my friend didn't look like he was sleeping at all. He didn't even look like my friend. I mean, he did but he didn't. There was something off. How I held it together and didn't run down the aisle scream-ing, I'll never know.

Maybe I did run.

See, the last thing I remember is standing by his casket, staring down at him. I still wish I did a better job of honoring his memory. It's something that eats at me, now and then.

Marissa's casket is mercifully closed, saving her friends from that awful experience.

This being a Catholic funeral, there is a rhythm to the service steeped in centuries of tradition. Of course, there's an extra sadness in a ceremony for a person who died too young.

I can hear people around me sniffling and softly crying. Those closer to the front must be in even worse shape. I'm not immune to what's happening, either, and can honestly say my eyes are moist.

When the priest begins reciting the closing prayer, I slip out the back, and head for my car, not wanting to get caught in the crowd exiting the church. Plus, my work here isn't done yet.

In the footwell of the front passenger seat, under a black T-shirt, is my Canon EOS 5D camera, already mounted on a bendable tripod. I set it up on the seat so that the lens is just above the windowsill and point it at the church's door. I zoom in and program the camera to take pictures every three seconds. Then I let her rip.

There is a second tripod on the floor, this one with an attachment designed to hold a smartphone. I snap my cell into place and put the rig in the backseat, also aimed at the church. Instead of zooming in, I leave it wide and hit the VIDEO button.

After climbing out of the car so that my movements won't disturb the shots, I stand by the Versa as if I'm waiting for someone.

The first of the departing mourners appears a few seconds later, and soon the bulk of the crowd is pouring out. The mood is predictably somber, with everyone walking slowly and not a smile to be seen.

"Hey!"

I jerk my eyes toward the sound, thinking someone has noticed what I'm doing. But the bark came from a man who's just exited through a side door of the church and he isn't talking to me. The shout is intended for a young man who apparently came out the same exit ahead of the older guy.

I recognize the man who yelled. He's the asshole from the diner. The one I heard Donna the waitress call Mr. Linderhoff.

The kid he yelled at is lanky, at least as tall as Linderhoff, and has a mop of black hair that hangs over his forehead and is short on the sides. He can't be much more than twenty or twenty-one.

It takes another "Hey!" for the kid to stop and look back.

Linderhoff marches over to him until their faces are no more than half a foot apart, and begins reading the kid the riot act. Unfortunately, I can't hear what he's saying. Whatever it is, though, it's turning Linderhoff's cheeks red. My hot take is that the kid is his son. I expect the younger man to verbally fight back or walk away, but all he does is stand there and take it, even though he's clearly distressed.

I reach into the car and aim the Canon at them. I'm able to get a few shots before the kid nods and walks away. Linderhoff looks around, like he's wondering if anyone has seen them. He even looks in my direction, but I am leaning inside my car now, and he doesn't notice me.

After he completes his scan, he straightens his suit jacket and heads over to where the other mourners are gathered.

I look around for the kid and, for a moment, think I've lost him. But then I hear the roar of an engine and see a black Camaro (from one of the model's uglier years) pull out from a spot along the street. As it drives by, I spot the kid at the wheel.

I move the camera again and take a picture of the Camaro's license plate as it speeds away.

CHAPTER FOURTEEN

I t isn't until I'm going through the pictures back in my room that I realize this isn't the first time I've seen the guy in the Camaro. At least, I'm pretty sure that's true.

I think he's in a photo on one of Marissa's friends' Instagram accounts. I don't remember which one, so I begin flipping my way through them once more.

Turns out he isn't on one account, but two.

The first image is in Julia Torres's feed. A candid shot of Andrew and Noah sitting in what looks like a school cafeteria or maybe a food court, laughing. Sitting in the background is the mystery kid. It isn't clear from the shot if he's part of the group or an unintentional photobomber. The reason I didn't make the connection right away is his hair is shorter now. In the photo it almost touches his shoulders.

Hoping that Andrew or Noah posted photos taken around the same time, I check their feeds but find no joy.

I hit pay dirt, however, on Fara's account.

It's a picture that must have been taken seconds after Julia's, only from the other side of the table. Again, Andrew and Noah are the heroes of the shot. Mystery kid is there, too, but is on the very edge of the frame because of the angle. The surprise is that there's a fourth person in the photo.

Marissa. She's sitting directly across the table from Mystery Boy and smiling in his direction.

I compare the two pictures side by side. It sure looks like he has a bit of a smile, too. He doesn't in the other photo, so they must have been taken a few moments apart.

I'm well aware this is only a momentary slice of time and their expressions could have nothing to do with each other. But they just as easily could. Given how few leads I've found, the kid is a new avenue I can look into.

If he and Marissa were friends, it stands to reason they would have interacted on social media. In Marissa and her other friends' cases, their messaging app of choice seemed to be Hulla-Chat. When I went through the messages in Marissa's account earlier, there were a couple of conversations I couldn't link to a specific person. The messages seemed innocuous, so I had no reason to suspect anything then. I check both of these chats again.

In one it's clear Marissa was talking with someone she worked with. It contains messages about covering shifts for each other, one short exchange about a manager neither of them liked, and that's it. The last set of messages occurred nearly two months ago.

This is the only mention I've seen about Marissa working. When I discovered it the first time, I poked around and discovered she had a job at the same McDonald's where Luke worked but quit in the summer.

I pull up the second chat thread. It's only four lines long. What's interesting is that the conversation happened the day before the accident.

The exchange is with someone Marissa labeled APPLE.

MARISSA: Don't you have a bio test coming up next Friday?

APPLE: Not next Friday, the one after.

MARISSA: U start studying for it yet?

APPLE: What do you think?

MARISSA: Didn't think so. Don't worry. I'll make sure you pass.

APPLE: Can't wait.

What strikes me most is that this back-and-forth feels too familiar to be the only conversation these two have ever shared, but there's nothing else in their chat history. Of course that doesn't mean there's nothing else anywhere.

Using a pathway Jar created for me, I worm my way into Hulla-Chat's servers and hunt for any deleted messages between Marissa and Apple. And boy, do I find some. Their chat history is hundreds of interactions long. After saving them to my computer, I turn my attention to unearthing Apple's identity. According to Hulla-Chat's records, the account was created by someone named John Smith.

Right. That sounds legit.

I'm good at what I do because I've been taught to be thorough. So I check Roosevelt High's enrollment records, and—surprise, surprise—there's no John Smith registered. There are five current students with that last name, and nine with the first. The latter seems kind of low to me, but I guess John doesn't hold the same prestige it used to.

When I go through the deleted Hulla-Chat messages, it quickly becomes clear that both Marissa and Apple/John were concerned someone might see their conversations. Most of their exchanges were conducted using memes—you know, pictures with pre-written, usually smartass comments on them. Marissa and Apple/John seemed to have created a whole language out of them. Several images made multiple appearances, leading me to guess that each represents a specific word or phrase. Without more context, I have no idea what they mean.

Jar might, Liz whispers.

I frown.

While Jar is closer to Marissa's age than I am, her first language is Thai. She's barely spent any time in the States, which is why my immediate thought is that the messages will be as much a mystery to her as they are to me.

What do you lose for trying?

Liz does have a point.

I upload everything to a server Jar and I use and send her an email. I also ask if she can track down the location of the computer John Smith used when creating his Hulla-Chat account.

I bring up the pictures of Mystery Boy again.

"Are *you* Mr. Smith?" I ask.

Unfortunately, he doesn't answer.

Maybe he is, maybe he isn't. I'm going to leave figuring that out to Jar for the moment. What I can do is see if I can uncover Mystery Boy's real name.

I dive back into Roosevelt High's student records and search the pictures of the males in the senior class. I'm so confident of finding him there that when I come to the end without seeing his face, I figure I must have skipped his picture. But a second pass proves equally unsatisfying.

I try the juniors. He's not there, either.

I'm 99.9 percent sure he's too old to be a sophomore, but I check anyway. Kids are sometimes held back or have unusual growth spurts. But he's not a sophomore.

I must be looking in the wrong direction. After hunting around a bit, I find the files for former Roosevelt High students.

Instead of slogging through the photos, I try what I hope will be a short cut and look for anyone with the last name Linderhoff.

Two results come back, both boys, with parents listed as Raymond and Vera Linderhoff. The oldest son, Michael, graduated three years ago, and the youngest, John, that previous spring.

Bingo.

I click on John and stare perplexed at an image of a meaty boy with light brown hair. He is not Mystery Boy. I try Michael. Another big guy, not fat, more football linebacker than offensive tackle. Neither he nor his brother has anything in common with the guy I'm looking for, save for the fact they all have eyes, noses, and mouths.

Maybe the Linderhoffs are a blended family, and Mystery Boy is from a previous relationship the wife had. I google Raymond and Vera Linderhoff, and confirm right off the bat that the husband is indeed my grumpy friend from the diner. He's apparently a lawyer, with his own practice right here in Jenson. He also seems to have his hands in a lot of other businesses. He's a former president of the local Kiwanis Club, served as campaign chairman for the area's state assemblyman and state senator, served on an advisory committee to the district's US congressman, been grand marshal of the Jenson Christmas Parade on three separate occasions, and is a member of the local school board. There's more, but these appear to be the highlights.

Impressive. But it doesn't make him any less of a dick.

I'm less successful in trying to tease out Vera's maiden name. I check the county registrar's records for marriage licenses, but apparently the Linderhoffs got hitched somewhere else. I'm sure if I keep at it I'd eventually uncover it, but who knows how long that might take. Searching for the kid's photo in the former student database would likely go faster. If he's not there, then a) crap, and b) I go back to hunting for Vera's name.

Lucky for me, neither a nor b comes into play. After fourteen minutes of clicking through images, I find him.

Adam Nyland.

He's two years out of school. His record while attending Roosevelt High isn't exactly something to brag about. Adam graduated 297 out of a class of 322, maintained a solid C-minus average, made six disciplinary trips to the principal's office, and received one two-day suspension for "disrespectful behavior in the classroom." A real class act.

For the record, he is not part of the Linderhoff family. His mother's first name is Judy and she's married to a Scott Lester, who I'm guessing is the stepfather.

Unless Adam is attending college (and I have my doubts about that), there's no reason for him to worry about a bio test. In which case, he isn't John Smith.

I type the address from Adam's file into Google Maps, and the pointer plops down in front of a house in the old section of town.

719 Rhonda Way.

CHAPTER FIFTEEN

I t's late afternoon, and a cool wind that wasn't around earlier in the day blows through Jenson. I'm a lot farther north than my home in L.A., so I guess the heat of summer doesn't have quite the stranglehold on mid-September here as it does down south. At least not today.

I drive across town, hoping Adam is the kind of lost boy who has yet to move away from home. It won't be the end of the world if he isn't, but it'll sure make my search easier if he is.

The streets of Adam's (current or former) neighborhood are laid out in a grid that straddles Central Avenue. Rhonda Way is a short road on the south side, a two-block stretch of homes tucked away between Knutson Lane and Evert Street.

The houses are mostly clapboard boxes with small porches and yards hidden behind fences. A handful of the places have been renovated into two-story beasts with all the charm of stucco-sided dentist offices.

Seven-nineteen is in the middle of the second block. I'm pretty sure it was originally painted white, but years of weather and sunlight have turned it gray. The asphalt shingled roof is showing its age, too. A blue tarp lies over a section of the roof's apex, held down by rocks. The grass in the front yard has been left to brown and appears ready to morph directly into dirt.

Parked in the driveway are an old green Buick Riviera and a twenty-year-old Mercedes station wagon. No sign of the Camaro.

I drive by slowly, allowing my Canon, which I have set up in the backseat, to shoot a series of photos. When I reach Knutson Lane, I turn right and pull to the curb. There, I shuffle through the pictures. The place is even sadder in photos. I study the home's windows and see no signs of anyone inside.

Just because the Camaro isn't present doesn't mean Adam doesn't live there, though. If this neighborhood were in a big city, I could probably get away with parking down the street and watching the house from my car. But here in Jenson, doing something like that would end with someone calling 911. I could put a miniature remote camera in one of the trees lining the road. Only I can't do that until the wee hours of the morning, when everyone's asleep.

I'd rather not wait that long.

Jenson isn't that big, and when I was Adam's age, I would be out and about on a Saturday. Maybe I can drive around and spot his car. It's worth a try.

I cruise past the fast-food places near the high school first, then do a drive-by of the Sunny Creek Diner. When none of those work out, I head toward the interstate, where there's another group of burger places, including the McDonald's where Luke (and previously Marissa) works.

The food vendors there prove to be a bust, too. Before I leave the area, my stomach starts to growl. It's almost seven p.m. and the sun is balancing on the horizon, ready to cede the sky to the night. The last meal I had was a banana and a cup of coffee this morning, before the funeral. I really don't want fast food, but I don't have time to stop and sit down somewhere. I settle for Subway and grab a veggie sandwich on flatbread.

As I'm walking back to my car with my food, I hear the rumble of a familiar engine, and look out to the road to see the Camaro drive by.

I grin. Gotta love a small town.

I don't hurry back to the Versa because the Camaro is slowing and its left-turn blinker is flashing. As soon as traffic clears, it pulls into the McDonald's parking lot.

Interesting choice.

I hop into my car, drive over to the gas station next to McDonald's, and park near a Dumpster. The Camaro's in the drive-thru lane, waiting its turn. I grab the Canon and zoom in on the vehicle.

Yep. Adam Nyland is behind the wheel, all right, and he's got friends with him. There's a blond guy in sunglasses in the front passenger seat, wearing a white T-shirt that bulges from an impressive pair of biceps. Two other guys are in the back. Blondie's currently blocking my view of one of them. The one I can see is another white guy, only he has brown hair.

The car at the speaker finishes ordering and pulls away. As Adam rolls the Camaro forward to take its place, the back door of the restaurant flies open and Luke comes barreling out.

Whoa.

Plot twist.

What's he doing at work? If I were him and my girlfriend—or recently *ex*-girlfriend—had been buried today, I wouldn't have gone in.

You were working when they buried me, Liz says.

I wince.

Touché.

The guys in the Camaro don't see Luke until he rounds the menu board and sprints straight toward them. I raise the camera again, this time backing off on the zoom so the lens can take in the whole scene. I also spin the function dial to video and let the camera run.

When Luke reaches the Camaro's hood, the doors on both sides fly open and Adam and Blondie climb out.

Luke heads straight for Adam, yelling. I don't know what he's saying, but it is clear he's enraged. A group of customers walking through the lot stops to watch. Two McDonald's employees are sticking their heads out the back door.

Luke shoves Adam in the chest. Though they're about the same height, Luke has more muscle on him and Adam staggers back several steps.

Before Luke can push him again, Blondie grabs him from behind and shoves him toward the building. Luke whirls on him and, despite Blondie being bigger both in height and mass, balls his fists as if he's going to throw a punch. Blondie clenches his own fists and takes a step toward Luke.

What happens next is probably as much of a surprise to me as it is to Luke and Blondie.

Adam rushes forward and grabs Blondie's arm, stopping his friend from attacking. He says something to Blondie as he steps between him and Luke.

After a second, Blondie lowers his fist and takes a few steps back. Adam says something to Luke. If I'm reading his body language correctly, he's trying to defuse the situation. Which is fascinating since he seems to be the cause of Luke's fury.

Adam raises a hand in front of his chest, in a I-don't-want-to-fight-you gesture, but he's barely put it up when Luke rushes him and grabs him around the chest.

They fall to the ground, next to the car. It's hard for me to see exactly what's happening because Blondie is now between me and the action, but they seem to be rolling back and forth. I get glimpses of Luke hitting Adam, but don't see Adam returning any shots.

Blondie tries to get into the action, but once more he suddenly backs off. I'm guessing at Adam's orders.

Movement back at the restaurant's door. A big man dressed like management runs out. When he sees the two guys on the ground, he grabs Luke by the back of his uniform, lifts him into the air, and plops him on his feet.

Luke tries to get by him, but the manager is having none of it, and clamps on to both of Luke's arms. He yells at the kid, then turns him around and shoves him toward the back door. It's obvious Luke doesn't want to go, so the manager shouts at a couple of the employees who have come out to watch. They hurry over and escort Luke inside.

Once they're gone, the manager attempts to help Adam up, but Adam jerks away and gets up on his own. Though the manager tries to talk to him as he gets back into his car, Adam ignores the man.

As soon as Blondie gets in on the other side, Adam drops the Camaro into gear and shoots past the menu board, out of the drive-thru line. Apparently, his craving for McDonald's has waned.

I head back to the road and turn onto the street moments after the Camaro roars by. Adam is driving fast, and if I try to stay with him, there's no way he'd fail to notice me. So I go as fast as I dare, and keep an eye on the Camaro's taillights as the distance between us grows.

A couple of red traffic lights prevent Adam and his friends from getting completely away from me, and after a third light, it appears Adam's anger has subsided, as he's eased back on the gas pedal.

It's not long before I have a pretty good guess where he's headed. Sure enough, near the high school, he turns down the road where the fast-food places are and pulls into the parking lot of Carl's Jr. Instead of using the drive-thru this time, he parks, and he and Blondie and the two in back get out.

I pull into the lot as they go inside. Through the window I can see Adam's companions head to the service counter while Adam turns toward the back of the restaurant. I can't see exactly where he goes, but I assume he's heading to the restroom, to clean up after his roll on the asphalt with Luke.

I've worked in the world of secrets for years now, and from my earliest days it was hammered into me to never hesitate when presented with an opportunity to gain an advantage. As soon as I'm sure the Camaro gang won't come right back outside, I park on the far side of Adam's car, where I can't be seen by anyone inside the restaurant.

I climb out, and remove one of the many tracking disks from my gear bag in the back. The disk is small, about the size of a quarter, with a sticky side covered by a piece of protective film. After removing the film, I glance around to make sure no one else is in the area. I wait until a car goes by on its way to the drive-thru before I crouch and attach the disk to the underside of one of the Camaro's rear fenders.

Next, I move to the hood of my car, from where I can examine the front of Adam's. Looking for signs of damage, I pay particular attention to the grille and the right front corner, but I don't see any dents or places where my little triangle piece would fit. I also don't spot any signs of recent body work.

Back in the Versa, I check my tracking app to make sure the disk is working, and upon confirmation, I drive off.

At the Dairy Queen next to Carl's, I pick up a soda then sit in my car and wait.

Adam and his friends have apparently chosen to eat inside, as it's another twenty minutes before they return to the Camaro.

I let them get a few blocks away before I follow.

CHAPTER SIXTEEN

I follow the Camaro to a house on Conrad Street, on the western edge of the old part of town. As I drive by, the last of Adam's friends walks inside. Is this where Adam lives?

There's no place nearby to hang out where I won't be conspicuous, so I find a bar a few blocks away, with a large, half-empty parking lot. I have no intention of going in, but there's an isolated spot in back that should be a good place to wait.

Once I'm settled, I set an alarm on my tracking app that will alert me if the Camaro moves more than a foot. I then hack into the county tax assessor database. According to the records, the house on Conrad Street is owned by Timothy and Brenda Fletcher. Maybe Adam rents from them, or maybe Fletcher is the last name of one of his friends.

I check my email and see a response from Jar.

Am doing something for Christina. Will look at this as soon as I have a moment.

J.

It's not exactly what I hoped she'd say, but at least she's not telling me she can't figure out Marissa and John Smith's meme exchanges. (Just so you're not completely in the dark, Christina's the person Jar worked for before she started doing projects with my partner and me.)

I recline my chair as far as it can go and lie with my phone on my chest, thinking a little nap would be the perfect way to kill time.

What wakes me is not the alarm, but a persistent tapping on my window.

I open my eyelids and immediately snap them closed again as someone shines a light in my face. I shield my eyes with one hand, find the lever for my seat with the other, and return myself to an upright position.

"Please step out of the car," a male voice says.

The light is still aimed at me so I can't see who's out there, but from the nature of the request, I have a pretty good idea who it is.

Apparently, this wasn't as good a place to wait as I thought.

I fumble for the handle and push the door open. Finally the light moves away, and as I climb out, I see a cop waiting for me, and another next to a patrol car stopped nearby.

"Sir, what's going on here?" the cop with the flashlight asks.

"Nothing. I was just resting my eyes."

"How many drinks have you had tonight?"

"I haven't had any."

He snorts. "Is that right?"

"I haven't had a drink of alcohol in almost a week," I tell him. It's true.

"Can I see your driver's license?"

I pull out my fake ID.

A note on that. The license is not like the kind you get when you're a teenager so you can buy beer at the local convenience store. Mine is only fake in the sense that it's not in my real name. In all other aspects it's genuine, as is proven when the silent partner takes the license to their car to check it and doesn't immediately come running back to cuff me.

While he's off doing this, the talkative one—his nametag reads DRAKE—says, "You don't mind if we conduct a sobriety test, do you?"

"Not at all."

The alarm on my phone starts to ring. I tap the screen to turn it off and put the phone in my pocket.

"You need to get that?" he asks.

"It was just a timer to wake me up."

He gives me a yeah-sure half grin. "If you'll step over here, please."

We go through the battery of balancing and coordination tests that I'm sure everyone's seen on TV, and I pass with flying colors. Not that he tells me this. In fact, he seems quite annoyed.

"Would you consent to a breathalyzer test?"

"Of course," I say. Whatever will get these guys off my back and let me get on my way.

He looks toward the patrol car. "Hey, Rosen, bring the breathalyzer."

Rosen returns with my license and the device. In the exchange of glances between the two men, I infer Rosen is letting his partner know nothing negative popped up when he ran me through the system.

"Blow in here, please."

Again, I pass the test.

"Well, Mr. Bryce," Drake says, glancing at my license, "looks like you were telling the truth. You want to tell us why you chose here to take your nap?"

"Seemed quiet."

"Says here you live in Santa Barbara. Just passing through or are you staying someplace around here?"

"I'm staying someplace."

"Then I ask you again, why did you choose to nap here?"

"I'm meeting a friend and had a little time to kill. Did I do something wrong?"

The cop studies my license for a few more moments before holding it out to me. "You'll need to move your car. This is private property. Next time, I suggest you do your sleeping at home."

"Sure. Sorry if I caused any problems."

The cops return to their car. But instead of heading out, their vehicle remains stationary, engine running and headlight illuminating the back of my rental.

As I pull out of the parking lot, the police car follows me.

I've seen this game before. Not that it's happened to me, but to people I've been keeping an eye on. Cops employing the not-so-subtle intimidation tactic of following someone for a while. Don't get me wrong—I'm not bagging on cops. They have a tough job, and the vast majority is out there doing the right thing day in and day out. Some, though...

Playing the part of Mr. Law Abiding Citizen, I keep my speed just below the limit and drive across town to the Great 7 Motel. I'm not staying there anymore, but I think it would be better than leading them to the Sleepy Daze Residential Inn and reinforcing their already low opinion of me.

Sure enough, once I am parked and have turned off my lights, the cops speed off.

I lean forward and let my head rest on the steering wheel.

Dammit, dammit, dammit, dammit.

I've just violated one of my prime rules for remaining anonymous. Never ever draw the attention of local authorities. And all because I decided to take a nap. Yep, that's right. I was literally caught sleeping on the job. Feel free to laugh.

I need to be extra careful from now on. And I absolutely must avoid coming into contact with Drake and Rosen again.

Focus, Liz says.

"I am focused," I whisper.

She makes no reply, though I can feel her judging gaze.

I sit back up and check the tracker.

The Camaro is on the move. The interesting thing is that it's not in Jenson at all, but on the interstate heading south.

After checking the street to make sure the cops haven't secretly returned, I leave the Great 7 and soon am cruising down the freeway. The Camaro exits in Brighton, the town where my other hotel is, and stops in what I assume is a parking lot.

As I continue on, I keep expecting an alarm to go off, letting me know the Camaro is in motion again, but I reach the Brighton exit without a peep.

I haven't done much research about this town and am unfamiliar with the area. So I am mildly surprised when the route takes me into an industrialized zone of small warehouse-like buildings and professional business parks.

The Camaro has stopped at one of the latter, a place called the Larkin Professional Center. It consists of three parallel wings protruding at ninety-degree angles from a fourth structure—kind of like a squared-off W. Security lamps hang from the sides of the building every twenty feet or so, illuminating the area.

The glowing dot representing the Camaro is coming from the space between the middle fork and the one at the far end. No way I can drive by. The building complex is surrounded by asphalt and parking spaces and there are no other cars in sight, which means most, if not all, of the businesses that call this place home are closed. If I drive by, I run the very real possibility of Adam and his friends seeing me, and I've had enough of being seen for one night.

The building next to the business park has a sign on the side identifying it as Brighton Hill Machine Shop. Most of its parking area is closed off behind a chain-link fence, but there's a customer parking area in front that's accessible and empty.

I leave the Versa in the spot farthest from the road and make my way back to the business park on foot. As I set foot on Larkin Professional Center property, I hear occasional thumps and bangs coming from ahead.

I circle around behind the complex. Big rolling doors, large enough for small delivery trucks to use, line the backside at equidistant intervals. Beside each is a second, regular-sized door. Most of the two-door combos have etched metal signs next to them identifying the name of the tenant.

What I don't see are the Dumpsters I was hoping I'd find back here.

I jog down the entire side, peek around the other end, and grin. Ten feet away is an enclosure attached to the building that, given the smell, contains the garbage receptacles.

I pull on my leather gloves and use one of the Dumpsters to get onto the wall of the enclosure. From there, I'm able to reach the lip of the roof and pull myself up.

Staying low, I move onto the outside wing and to a spot overlooking the space where the Camaro should be parked.

There is only one door that isn't closed along the courtyard-like area—a business on the middle wing, its big roll-up door halfway up. Directly in front of the unit sits the Camaro. Light from inside the shop spills through the gap under the unit's door. There's noise coming from the unit, too, the crash of metal and plastic, followed by someone yelling, "Oh, yeah!"

The only camera I have with me is the one on my phone. I aim it at the opening and zoom in as much as I can. But because of the angle, I see only a small slice of the floor. It's concrete, and appears to have a puddle of dark, glistening liquid spreading across it. I can't tell what the substance is. Oil, maybe. Or muddy water.

At first, the banging sounds make me wonder if it's a garage and Adam and his buddies are working on a car. But I quickly dismiss the idea. The racket they're making is too chaotic.

I move along the roofline, looking for a better angle, but the best I can come up with gains me only a few more inches of the floor. Whatever they're doing continues for another ten minutes before I hear voices approaching the door.

The light inside the unit goes out, and the shadowy forms of the four men exit the building. Though there is little chance they'd see me, I pull back from the roof's edge and raise my camera high enough so that I can still see what's going on.

On the screen, one of the silhouettes pulls the roll-up door down. It hits the ground with a bang, and a whoop of satisfaction from the guy who did the shutting.

One of his friends steps up to the door and begins moving his arm around. As he does this, I hear the distinct sound of an aerosol spray can.

It's got to be spray paint, and from his arm movements, I surmise he's spelling out words as opposed to creating a piece of street art.

When he finishes, one of the others claps him on the back and they all pile into the Camaro.

After the car backs out of the parking area, I stand up again and track the headlights as the Camaro makes its way out of the business park and onto the street. Once it's out of sight, I open the tracker app and watch the Camaro's dot make a beeline for the interstate.

I wait until it's on the freeway before climbing off the roof and circling around to where the Camaro was parked.

The message on the roll-up door is painted in orange neon and is neither subtle nor elegant. Nor is it particularly original.

EAT
SHIT
ASSHOLE

The artist needs some education in comma use.

I grab the bottom of the door and give it a test lift. It's unlocked. Not terribly surprising given their disregard for this particular piece of property.

The last place I want to be is inside the unit if someone shows up, especially if it's the cops, but I need to see what Adam and his friends did. I pull the door up just far enough to duck under, then close it behind me.

Instead of turning on the lights, I use the flashlight on my phone. The puddle I saw from the roof is blue paint that's been dumped out of a five-gallon paint barrel. The lake of thick liquid has oozed to only a few feet from where I'm standing, but it looks like its forward progress has stopped.

The rest of the unit isn't in any better shape. It appears to be used as storage for a hardware store, or maybe the home base for a small construction company. Shelving units have been toppled, spilling nails and glue and metal brackets and the like all over the place. In a back corner is a stack of wall insulation that Adam or one of his buddies has poured some kind of liquid over. The same is true for a pile of two-by-fours and a stack of plywood panels.

There are more messages painted on the interior walls, most even cruder than the one on the door. The general theme is *you blew it and you're screwed now*, though not in quite so polite terms.

Near a desk that has been upended along one of the walls, I find a business card for a Chuck Owens, General Contractor. I shove it in my pocket then take a final glance around.

This wasn't a simple act of vandalism. The words on the

wall make that clear. This was a targeted hit meant to deliver a message.

Has this Chuck Owens guy done something to anger Adam or his friends? Or did the Camaro Crew wreck the place on someone else's orders?

There's no way to know which at the moment, but my gut is telling me it's number two, and my gut is seldom wrong.

What any of this has to do with Marissa, though, I don't know. Probably nothing.

I return to my car and check the tracker. The Camaro is almost back to Jenson. I shift the Versa into drive and return to the interstate.

CHAPTER SEVENTEEN

S eems the trashing of the contractor's facility isn't the only
message Adam and his companions are delivering tonight.

When I catch up to them, they're parked in front of a fancy
house in the northeast part of town. Again, my first theory is
that one of them lives here, but a few moment later, when they
escort a hair-challenged, middle-aged man out the front door, I
revise my thinking. While the man is walking under his own
power, it's pretty obvious he's less than thrilled to be in their
company.

Upon reaching the Camaro, he's put into the back, sand-
wiched between the two who have been in the rear all night.
They drive off.

If I didn't like what happened at the business park, I hate
what I'm witnessing now.

Once more, I can't see how this has anything to do with
Marissa, but that doesn't matter. Solving Marissa's murder has
temporarily been moved to the backburner.

With the tracker as my guide, I follow the Camaro east
across the city and onto a county road out of town. The country-
side is mostly open fields with a few scattered copses of trees.

The road is flat and straight, making it a lot easier for me to be seen.

I'm tempted to ease back. I have the tracker, after all. It's not like I need to keep them in sight. But I'm concerned about their unwilling passenger, so I maintain a two-hundred-yards buffer between us.

Five minutes farther on, the Camaro slows and turns left. I see no corresponding road on the map but something must be there, because the car continues moving away from the highway.

A few seconds later, I pass the spot and see the beginning of a dirt road. I keep going in case they're watching me. When the county road passes a group of trees that take me out of sight, I remove my foot from the accelerator and turn off my lights. When my momentum has slowed enough, I make a U-turn without using my brakes.

I drive back to the dirt road and roll to a stop. The Camaro is about a quarter mile in and still moving.

I grimace. What the hell am I doing?

Turning down the road will put me at risk. This isn't why I've come here. Whatever's going on is not my problem.

You need to turn, Liz says.

She's becoming *very* cavalier with my personal safety. But, like always, she's right. I can't just stand by and do nothing.

I make the turn.

Since I don't have my lights on, I drive more slowly than the Camaro. After two minutes, the other car stops. Needless to say, this ramps up my sense of urgency. I increase my speed a little and stare at the dark road ahead, hoping I don't hit anything.

When I'm about three hundred yards away from the others, I slow again so that the sound of my engine doesn't give me away. At the two hundred yards mark, I spot a copse of trees on the right. I kill the engine and let the Versa coast, then angle off the road right before I reach the trees. When the vehicle comes to a stop, I'm satisfied it's hidden well enough.

I shove a few items into my backpack, strap it over my shoulders, and run.

The Camaro is parked in front of a dilapidated old mobile home sitting in the middle of nowhere. Through the windows, I see flashlights are moving around.

I scan the area. There are no other cars. I also don't see Adam or any of the others standing around. I pull on my ski mask (the same one I used at Mr. Park's market), hunch down, and move quickly to the back of the Camaro. From this new position, I can hear a voice inside the trailer. It's loud and commanding.

"Well? Where is it?" the voice asks. There's a pause of several seconds, and then the voice speaks again. "Where the hell is it?"

This time, the demand is followed by the slap of flesh.

I move up to the trailer and circle around the end to make sure no one is standing on the sides I couldn't see from the trees. I'm alone.

"It was due at noon today," the voice says. "Did you think he would forget?"

"No, no," a new voice says. It's weaker and trembling, and I have no doubt it belongs to the balding man from the big house. "I'm sorry. It's just—"

Another slap.

"We're not here for an apology! We're here about the transfer."

"I-I-I'll check first thing Monday morning. I'm sure it will be here by then."

"Monday? No. Now."

"It's not in my control," the weaker voice says. "And I have no way of checking it here."

"Then we have a problem. The boss was very clear. You don't leave our sight until this is resolved."

Flesh hitting flesh again, but this time more a punch than a slap, followed by a groan of pain.

It's a shakedown. And based on what the interrogator said, Adam and his crew do indeed work for someone else.

Their hostage doesn't sound like he's a particularly stellar character himself. Does that mean he deserves to get the hell beaten out of him? In the grand scheme of things, I'm probably not the right person to judge that. In the here and now, though, the answer is clear.

As the interrogation continues, I move to the front door, stand at the hinged side, and knock twice.

The voices go silent. Someone then whispers something, and I hear the trailer creak as one of the guys approaches the door.

"Who's there?"

Nice try, buddy.

I remain silent.

Another step, bringing him right up to the exit. The handle rattles, then the door swings open.

"Who's there?" he repeats.

I remain out of sight, waiting for the moment when—

He puts a foot on the top of the metal stairs outside the entrance.

"I said who's—"

I shove hard against the door, slamming it in his face and bouncing him backward into the doorframe. He falls onto the threshold and slides partway down the steps, groaning.

I swing around the door, pull him all the way outside, and shove the door closed again. It's one of the guys who was in the Camaro's backseat. He tries to get to his feet, but the brass knuckles I introduce to his jaw ensures he'll stay down for a good long while.

As I finish the punch, I hear the door open again. The first guy to exit is the other one from the backseat, and behind him is Blondie. The guy in the lead pauses for a fraction of a second in the doorway, assessing the situation. This is all the time I need.

I grab his belt and yank him out, sending him tumbling to the ground.

Blondie has stopped just inside the trailer. He smiles now, his eyes narrowing. He's got a good three inches and fifty pounds on me, which I can see makes him think this is going to be a cakewalk.

As he starts to take a step outside, I shoot a glance at the guy I just dealt with. He has an arm under him now and is pushing himself up.

While I'm trained to deal with multiple attackers at once, I'd rather take them one at a time.

Since I'm closer to Blondie, he wins the who-goes-first lottery.

As he steps off the stairs, I feign throwing a punch. He leans sideways and brings up an arm to block the shot. Instead of taking my swing, I adjust my center of gravity and kick him hard on the side of his leg, right at the knee.

Knees are designed to bend front to back, not side to side. Something snaps and down he goes, screaming. Unfortunately for him, I think he has some serious surgery in his future.

The other guy is back on his feet, and he looks *pissed* (American definition, not British.) He's also not too smart. If I were him, I would take a few moments to assess the situation. Two of his friends are already down—within seconds, I might add—and neither laid a hand on me. This might be a good time to run away.

He, of course, rushes me head-on.

Right before he reaches me, I jerk sideways and wrap an arm around his neck. He's able to get one of his around my waist, but I bat it away with little effort, and twist around so that I'm behind him.

As you might have guessed, sleeper holds are a specialty of mine. Squeeze the neck in the right way so the brain doesn't get enough blood and boom, out go the lights. (It's a learned skill, kids, and an easy way to accidently kill someone, so please don't try this at home.)

While I put the guy to sleep, my eyes are on the trailer door, waiting for Adam to appear, but he doesn't. The guy in my arms goes limp and I lay him on the ground. Blondie, who's wincing in pain, reaches out and tries to grab my ankle.

"You son of a bitch!" he growls.

Son of a bitch is one of my partner's favorite phrases, and it's always weird hearing someone else use it—especially someone as morally questionable as Blondie.

That's not why I strike him with the brass knuckles, however. I do that to shut him up on general principle. I mention the SOB thing only as a point of interest.

The punch has the desired effect as Blondie joins his other two friends in dreamland. He should thank me. At least for a little while, his knee won't be bothering him.

I pause outside the trailer doorway. Based on the fact that none of the three on the ground brandished a weapon, I doubt Adam is armed, but I'm not stupid enough to barge in and hope for the best.

I am armed, however. I pull my Glock and attach the suppressor.

"Adam?" I say. "I suggest you come out with your hands on your head."

"He-he's not here," says the pleading voice from earlier, coming from deep in the trailer.

"I'm not playing games. If you come out, I won't hurt you."

I *really* don't want to shoot anyone.

"He's not here," the voice repeats. "He went out the window."

It could be a trick. I aim through the doorway at the wall across from me and pull the trigger. There's a satisfactory crunch as the bullet smashes through it.

"That was just in case you were wondering if I'm armed."

"He's not here. I swear!"

Staying low, I creep into the trailer. The only light is from the partial moon, but it's more than enough to see that the interior space has basically been stripped bare. The only thing present is a lumpy shadow down at the other end.

"Please, don't shoot me! He's gone!" the lump says.

I step farther inside, my gun held in front of me. Soon, the lump takes the form of a human sitting on a chair.

"He went out the window." The lump nods to his left, at a glassless window on the back wall.

As I move to it, I hear a car door opening. I whirl around and rush outside just in time to see Adam drop into the Camaro's driver's seat.

I run toward him, my gun raised. "Out of the car!"

Either he doesn't hear me or he figures it's worth taking a chance, because he fires up the engine and jams the pedal to the floor.

I don't normally bluff when it comes to threats, either stated or implied, but I did in this case. I hoped it would work. I really would have liked to question him, but it's not worth shooting up his vehicle to get him to stop.

I watch as he races down the dirt road, and I pay particular attention as he nears the spot where I've hidden the Versa. He blows right by it without slowing.

When he moves out of sight, I return to the trailer. Adam

will have to come back at some point to get his friends, but I have a feeling he'll need some time to calm down first.

The man in the chair is tied in place. He's sweaty, and what hair he has left is a mess. There's blood around his mouth.

"Who are you?" I ask.

"Please. Untie me."

I don't move. "I asked you a question."

He blinks twice. It's easy enough to read his mind. He thought he was being rescued but now is wondering if he's just exchanged one oppressor for another. "Collins," he finally says. "William Collins."

"Well, Bill, you seem to have gotten yourself into a little pickle here. Want to tell me what's going on?"

"It's...a mistake. That's all. They took the wrong guy. Now please, can you untie me? My wife is going to be worried."

"Didn't sound like they had the wrong guy when they were talking to you."

From his startled reaction, he obviously didn't consider that I might have been listening in. "It's not important."

"It sounded pretty important to me. In fact, it sounded like you've disappointed their boss."

"It's a misunderstanding, that's all. Can you please—"

"What's their boss's name?"

"What?"

"You heard me."

Collins shakes his head like he's scared to even make a sound.

"If you don't tell me, I guess I'll have no choice but to leave you here. When those guys outside wake up, they're probably going to start in on you again, and I have a feeling they won't be as nice as before."

Collins's eyes widen. "Guys outside? But they left. I heard the car."

I give him my best you-poor-delusional-bastard look. "The guy who went out the window left. His three buddies are still here."

"I-I don't believe you."

"What do you think happened when they went outside? Do you think they just stepped out of my way and let me walk in?"

"You...? You took out all three?"

"Now you're catching on. So, are you going to tell me who their boss is, or do I leave you here?"

I watch as he struggles with what to do. In the end, he realizes he has only one option. "Linderhoff."

Well, well, well.

The conversation I witnessed between Linderhoff and Adam must have been work related.

"Are you late paying some legal fees, Mr. Collins?"

"Some...thing like that."

He's lying. Whatever his business is with Linderhoff, it has nothing to do with the practice of law.

"Do you know a contractor by the name of Chuck Owens?"

His brow furrows. "Owens?"

"He's based out of Brighton."

Collins shakes his head. If he was a good actor, I might think he's trying to pull a fast one on me. But I've dealt with good actors before and he's not one, so I'm convinced he's telling the truth.

You don't have to be a genius to conclude that Adam and the other three work as Linderhoff's enforcers. And if the vandalism at Owens's shop and Collins's kidnapping are unrelated, that leads me to think whatever business Linderhoff is into is not only shady but fairly widespread. Which means—

I force myself to take a mental step back.

Marissa is my focus. She's the reason Liz has brought me north. Whatever all this is about, it's not my business.

But maybe it is, Liz says.

I close my eyes for a moment. "No, it's not."

"No, what's not?" Collins asks.

"I'm not talking to you."

That seems to confuse him enough to shut him up.

Liz, whatever Linderhoff's into could be a lot more trouble than I'm prepared to deal with. I'm here for Marissa, remember?

I never forget anything, she says. *You can at least figure out what he's doing.*

I think I mentioned before I never win these conversations, but this one's a little different from others we've had. I'm serious when I say this could be more than I can handle on my own.

Rule number one in doing these little projects for Liz is that I never physically bring in anyone else to help in any kind of dangerous situation. These are my problems to fix. I don't want to put anyone else at risk.

I convey this to her more in scattered thoughts than articulate sentences.

There's always a way.

I want to tell her she's not being reasonable, but the truth is, even without Liz in my head, I would eventually force myself to do something about this whole Linderhoff business. Once I know about a wrong, it is extremely difficult for me to turn my back on it.

Dammit.

"What?" Collins says.

I focus on him again. "What do you mean, what?"

"You said dammit."

I consider telling him to mind his own business, but instead I say, "How about I give you a lift home?"

"Oh, God. Yes. Yes, please. Thank you."

"There's just one little thing I need to do first."

CHAPTER EIGHTEEN

I leave Collins in a park on the east side of town.

He's unconscious, another recipient of my well-honed skills.

If you really thought I would drop him off at his front door and give him a chance to see what kind of car I'm driving, then you don't know me very well.

My tracker tells me Adam is still in Jenson, parked behind an apartment building on West Ash Street. I do a drive-by and discover the Camaro in a covered carport behind the building. I park around the corner and make my way back.

Lights are on in only one of the apartments, a second-floor unit at the opposite end from the driveway. There are no cameras outside the building—small towns, less need for that kind of thing—so I'm able to sneak into the carport without being seen.

The building might have lax security, but the Camaro has an alarm that's been turned on.

There's an app for that, though.

Heh.

(Working in espionage definitely has its privileges.)

I disarm the alarm and ease the driver's door open. Under the dash near the steering column, I stick another one of my handy little disks. This one isn't a tracker. It's a microphone with a built-in relay that will send anything it records to a server, as long as it can piggyback on a nearby device's signal. I figure anytime Adam uses the vehicle, he'd have his phone with him, so I should have no problems hearing any conversations that take place.

When I'm done, I walk back to the street and look at the apartment building again. The same apartment is still lit up. It's got to be where Adam lives, but I'm not about to go up and knock on the door to find out. I might, however, take a look inside when he's not around.

Which probably will be happening soon.

Before leaving the trailer with Collins, I left one of the Camaro gang's phones within easy reach of Blondie. As soon as he or one his buddies wakes up, I have a feeling Adam will be receiving a call.

I consider hanging around until that happens, but I'm beat. *And* I promised to cover the weekend busboy's Sunday morning shift. I head to the interstate and make the fifteen-minute drive to my room at the Residence Inn.

But my plan of crawling into bed and going straight to sleep is thwarted by an email from Jar. It's my own fault. If I didn't check my inbox, I would be snoring away by now.

The majority of Marissa and John Smith's Hulla-Chat conversations are meaningless without some idea of what was happening in their lives at the time, but there are some I believe I have figured out. More are unimportant, but a few stood out to me (see below). I have also attached a file with all the ones I have deciphered so far, if you feel the need to go through them. Please note in the transcripts, instead of referring to his chats by the screen name Apple, I refer to him as John or simply J.

Also, the majority of John Smith's messages were sent from an iPhone that was reported stolen six months ago. The few messages he sent from a computer were done on a machine at the High Sierra Coffee Shop in Jenson.

I hope this helps.
Jar

At the bottom of her message are the translations she thought I would be interested in.

JULY 10

Marissa: Where were you?

John: Had to work late.

M: I waited for you. (Note from Jar: *There is another image here that I believe denotes the amount of time she waited was long.*)

J: I'm sorry. I'll make it up to you.

M: You'd better.

J: Dinner tomorrow?

M: Can't. Already have plans with (Note from Jar: *She uses the following picture here to identify a person. I have no context to match it to.*)

Below this is an image of Luke Skywalker. I don't think Marissa is trying to be subtle here. It's got to mean her boyfriend Luke.

J: Trying to make me jealous?

M: Shut up. I told you not to joke like that.

J: Relax. I didn't mean anything by it.

M: I've got to go.

J: I'm sorry! I was just kidding!

J: Marissa?

The other messages Jar has highlighted are along the same lines.

It's hard not to get the impression Marissa really was cheating on Luke, but openly cheating on a boyfriend like that doesn't jibe with what I've learned about her.

Could my instincts be that far off?

I crawl into bed, exhausted. But my mind is whirling and does not let me sleep for some time.

CHAPTER NINETEEN

S unday morning at the Sunny Creek Diner.

I'm paying for my late night. I had maybe four hours of sleep, and that's only because I didn't get out of bed until thirty minutes before I had to be at work.

The first hour or so of my shift isn't bad, I guess. We have a handful of customers and none of them are in a rush. But let me tell you, come eight a.m., the pre-church crowd starts rolling in and they are a demanding bunch. Not all of them, of course. Maybe not even the majority of them. But there's a substantial subset of the suit-and-dress-wearing crowd that acts like they got up on the wrong side of the bed.

Donna, Bree, and Tally, the morning waitresses, deal with the brunt of the gruff behavior, but I'm brought in on several occasions to clean up spills or remove finished dishes and am subjected to plenty of people barking *watch what you're doing* and *careful, or you'll spill that on us*.

Just to reiterate: service-industry workers, you can't tip them high enough.

At around 8:25, as I'm trying to stifle a yawn, Raymond Linderhoff enters with a woman I recognize as his wife, Vera, from my earlier search. He stops just inside the door, looks toward table two, and frowns upon seeing it occupied.

Bree stops long enough to greet them and point toward an empty table in the back. Vera smiles and thanks her, but her husband is clearly annoyed. As soon as Bree walks off, he whispers something in Vera's ear, his face taut. Her smile slips a little, and she responds in a similarly snippy fashion. Whatever his beef, they walk over to the booth and get in.

I'm clearing the table next to the Linderhoffs when Tally comes to take their order.

"The usual," Linderhoff says, and hands Tally his menu before she has even opened her mouth.

"Good morning, Tally," Vera says.

"Good to see you, Mrs. Linderhoff. How are you today?"

"Fine, just fine, thank you."

"What can I get you?"

"Um, French toast today, I think."

"Sausage with that?"

"Bacon."

"Coffee?"

"Yes, please."

"Great. I'll be back in a minute with your—"

"Put a rush on it," Linderhoff says. "We're running a bit late."

I look over to see him shoot an accusing glance at his wife.

"Sure thing," Tally says and heads back behind the counter.

Busboys are members of the invisible world. Even though people see them, they don't really register them.

So even though I'm still within earshot, once the Linderhoffs are alone Vera says, "It's not my fault we're late."

He grunts, pulls a napkin from the dispenser on the table, and puts it on his lap.

I have no idea what the grunt was supposed to convey, but

Vera is obviously well versed in her husband's communication methods, as she says, "Well, it's *not*."

"Enough," he said.

There's no gruffness in his tone, no anger, no emotion at all. The word is spoken like one would say, "Pass me the salt," or "Gesundheit." But it has power nonetheless, as Vera shifts uncomfortably in her seat and says, "I-I'm sorry."

I can't see her face from where I am, but I have no doubt she looks contrite, maybe even a little scared.

I don't know what her husband's deal is (yet), but I do not like the man.

Not one bit.

His presence here, though, does present me with another opportunity. And you know how I don't pass up on those.

I carry the dishes into the kitchen and place them on the counter next to Ferdinand, the dishwasher, then I go out and find Bree. She's in charge of the dining room this morning.

"Can I take a bathroom break?" I ask.

She looks around, sees there are no tables that need my immediate attention, and says, "Make it quick."

There are restrooms off the dining area, but those are only for customers. Employees are supposed to use the one at the back of the building, behind the kitchen. When I reach it, I glance back into the kitchen to make sure no one is watching me, and then I sneak out the back door. My car is close by, in one of the rear parking spots. I grab another tracker from my gear bag and move to the side of the building that serves as our main customer parking area.

When Linderhoff was here during the week, I saw him drive off in a gray Lexus G SF sedan and noted its license number. It was an automatic response. I'm trained to notice everything, and to remember. In my job, it can be the difference between life and death. And now, the same thing can also be said about my hobby.

There are several gray cars in the lot, but only one is a top-of-the-line Lexus sedan. It's parked on the edge of where it can be seen through the dining room windows on this side of the building. Keeping out of view, I walk to where I can verify the license number.

Not that it was really a question, but it's Linderhoff's, all right.

I move toward the sedan until I can see the diners sitting at the booths on the other side of the window. To my pleasure, no one is looking in the direction of the car.

Pretending I've dropped something, I bend over right next to the Lexus's fender and, in a maneuver I've done a million times, I stick the tracker inside the car's wheel well.

By the time I'm back in the restaurant, no more than two minutes have passed.

Bree looks at me, surprised.

I shrug. "You told me to make it fast."

We're able to get the Linderhoffs fed and out the door by five minutes to nine, and for the next couple of hours, business slows. At around eleven a.m., the place is packed again, this time with the post-church crowd.

When I finish my shift at two p.m., all I really want to do is take a nap. But I'm still on the clock—Liz's, not the diner's—so before I can even contemplate heading back to the Residence Inn, I check my tracking app.

Linderhoff's Lexus is parked at a large property in the town's affluent northwest neighborhood, the same general area where William Collins lives. I check the address and confirm it's the one listed in the school district's database as the family's residence. I scroll backward through the tracking info and see that after leaving the Sunny Creek Diner, the Linderhoffs went to the Methodist church on Moreland Avenue before heading home.

I switch over to Adam Nyland's tracker.

He's been a busy boy since I last saw him. Around five a.m., he returned to the mobile home in the middle of nowhere. From there, he drove back into Jenson to...huh, a private doctor's office a few blocks from the hospital. I seriously doubt the office was open in the predawn hours of Sunday morning. Not officially, anyway.

My guess is that Adam and his buddies didn't want to go to the emergency room as that might draw unwanted attention, maybe even enough to provoke one of the medical staff to call the police. Someone at this doctor's office—there are three physicians listed—must have a prearranged agreement with Linderhoff or—and I like this idea more—he has something on a doctor and uses that to get his people off-the-books treatment. In Blondie's case, the doctor probably gave him something for the pain, but there's no way the man could have put the asshole's knee back together without a full surgical team.

I switch from the tracker app to my browser, and go to the server where the audio from the Camaro was sent. Only nothing is there.

That doesn't make any sense. There's no way I'm going to believe that Adam and his friends didn't have a conversation after he picked them up. Besides, even if everyone *was* silent, the noise of the engine alone should have triggered the record function. Something's got to be wrong with the bug. Either it doesn't work, or the upload signal isn't getting through.

While disappointing, I'm buoyed by the fact the bug contains a memory card with more than enough space to hold a couple days' worth of talk. If it *is* recording, I should still be able to hear everything. I just need to break into his car again.

Oh, joy.

I return to the tracking app.

After the stop at the doctor's office, where the Camaro gang stayed for nearly two and a half hours, Adam drove to three different locations. Again, it's not hard to puzzle this out. His buddies would need rides home.

"Thanks, Adam," I whisper as I note the addresses.

The next stop is even more interesting. At eight a.m., Adam visits Linderhoff's place.

Huh. I'm pretty sure that explains why the Linderhoffs were running late this morning.

The Camaro was there until 8:15, leaving Linderhoff and his wife just enough time to drive to the diner. While they did that, the Camaro returned to the same apartment building where I found it the previous evening.

Adam remained there until thirty minutes ago, at which point he drove to the Dairy Queen near the freeway. Twenty-five minutes later—at approximately the same time I was walking out of the diner—he left the fast-food place and drove onto the interstate, heading south.

That's where he is now.

The last time he headed in that direction, he was up to no good. Is he going on another one of his intimidation visits?

Do I go back to my hotel? Or do I follow him?

Follow him, Liz says.

CHAPTER TWENTY

By the time I get onto the interstate, the Camaro is almost to Brighton. I've been assuming that's where Adam's headed, so am surprised when he drives right past the last Brighton exit and continues south.

After that there are a few scattered small towns, but he avoids them all and soon nears Woodland, just west of Sacramento.

A thought hits me. Maybe Adam is heading to the Sacramento airport. It's just on the other side of Woodland. Perhaps my little stunt at the mobile home has scared him so much he's decided to leave town. Could be he went to Linderhoff's house to tell him he's quitting. It would certainly explain the lawyer's bad mood at breakfast.

No, scratch the airport. He's still basically a kid. He's not going to think about flying somewhere when he's got a Camaro. He'd just drive to wherever he's escaping to.

As much as I might believe that, I'm still nervous when his blip passes through the other side of Woodland and closes in on the airport. So, when he stays on the interstate and continues into Sacramento, I breathe a sigh of relief.

Up until now, I've been maintaining a gap of about ten minutes between us. Now that he's in the city, his speed slows enough that I make up ground fast.

When he passes downtown and remains on the freeway, I begin to think I was right about him running away. I decide if he does exit before passing all the way through the city, I'd call off the chase. I can't waste time that would be better spent tracking leads back in Jenson. Besides, if I really need to confront him, the tracker will tell me where he is.

But he doesn't continue south. Just past the junction with I-80, he exits onto Sutterville Road.

I'm not very familiar with Sacramento. Not counting when I flew into the airport a few days ago, I've been here only three times. Twice on jobs that kept me in very specific locations, and once in college, when a group of us drove up from UCLA on a ski trip to Tahoe and made a stop at the home of one of the people with us. None of these three places is anywhere near the part of town the Camaro has just entered.

I exit a few minutes later, and by the time I turn onto Sutterville, the Camaro has turned north onto Freeport Boulevard. A few minutes after that, it turns again on 12th Avenue and parks.

What I'd like to do is bring up a satellite image of the area but there's too much traffic, and I'm going to be there in less than four minutes anyway.

I turn onto Freeport and find a large, beautiful park on my left. It's the kind of place Liz and I might have gone to, with a basket of food and a bottle of wine, disguised as something nonalcoholic in case there were rules against that. On the right are several businesses, with a lot of room between them. If this was L.A., they'd be packed in, one against another.

After a stoplight, I pass a brick sign reading SACRA-MENTO CITY COLLEGE. A community college, I presume. It's a nice place for it. I'm surprised by the size of the campus as I continue along Freeport. It goes all the way to 12th Avenue, where the Camaro turned.

The hair on the back of my neck starts to tingle, not with a warning of danger, but with the flickering of intuition. For the moment, I just let it simmer.

The road is only about two blocks long, and the Camaro is parked down at the end of it. Not on the road itself, but in a parking structure that is part of the college.

The tingling becomes a full-on burn, and I know exactly what it's telling me. But I won't allow myself to go down that path just yet. I want to focus on what's in front of it, and if that parallels with my thoughts then fine.

I don't have a sticker that will allow me to park in the structure, so I find a spot on a nearby side street and walk back.

I'm in another one of those situations where it's easy to be seen. Next to the structure is a wide, mostly empty parking lot. Half a dozen people are walking through it, but I'm still young enough to look like I belong there. If Adam is around and sees me, hopefully he won't give me a second glance.

That is, if Adam is the one who drove here in the first place. I haven't actually seen him yet, so it's possible I've been following someone else entirely this whole time. But if I was his age and that was my car, I wouldn't want anyone else behind the wheel.

The tracker leads me to the third floor of the structure. The Camaro is parked along the side overlooking the all but empty lot. There doesn't appear to be anyone inside it so I walk over.

One of the first things I notice is a tag hanging on the rearview mirror. It's a plastic placard with a hook on top, like a hotel's Do Not Disturb sign, only instead of a message telling people to keep out, a square sticker is affixed to it, printed with the words SACRAMENTO CITY COLLEGE PARKING PERMIT • STUDENT LOT.

The burning intensifies.

I look out toward the main part of the campus. No sign of Adam anywhere.

If that sensation at the back of my neck is right, there's something I can do that might help me find him that doesn't involve me scouring the campus and peeking through doorways. Unfortunately, my laptop is back in my hotel room. I had every intention of heading back there after work. And though I'm no slouch when it comes to hacking, I'm not nearly as good at it on my phone as some of my friends are.

I leave the structure and cross the parking lot to the shade of one of the buildings, where I sit on a bench and call Jar.

She answers in her normal, no-pleasantries kind of way. "Is something wrong?"

It's the wee hours of the morning in Bangkok, but I've stopped worrying about waking her. If I hadn't seen her sleep myself, I'd almost think she never does it.

"Nothing's wrong," I say. "I just need your help. Do you have a few moments?"

"I can give you seven minutes, no more."

"Knowing you, you'll only need half that time."

I laugh. She doesn't. It's the way it goes sometimes.

I tell her what I'm looking for, and she puts me on hold.

Approximately four minutes later, she comes back on. "Your assumption is correct."

"So, Adam *is* enrolled here."

"That is what I just said, is it not?" She has little time for wasted words.

"How many classes is he taking?"

"Three. Intermediate Algebra, College Writing, and Introduction to Concepts of Human Anatomy and Physiology."

"Do you mean biology?"

"Yes. It is a Biology 101 class. Whatever that means."

It means the burning sensation I've been trying to ignore is very likely right. "What days does he have biology?"

"Mondays, Wednesdays, and Fridays. Eleven a.m. to noon. Do you want me to send you his schedule?"

"Yes, please."

A pause. "It should be in your inbox. I need to go now."

"Wait, one more question. He doesn't have any classes on Sunday, does he?"

"No."

"Then why the hell is he here?"

This question is more for myself than for Jar, but she answers anyway. "He is a student. I would think he is studying."

The thought has also occurred to me, thank you very much.

"I appreciate the help, Jar."

"Be careful," she says and hangs up.

Adam's class schedule is not proof he's John Smith, but it's damn close.

Marissa: Don't you have a bio test coming up next Friday?
Apple/John: Not next Friday, the one after.

Adam has biology on Fridays. If this exchange was indeed between them, then the test she is referring to would be this coming Friday.

So where does a student go when he or she studies on campus? The library, of course.

I find a map of the school online and make my way to the library, or as they call it here, the Learning Resource Center. To my surprise, the door is locked. The posted hours of operation state the center is closed on Sundays.

Well, that's not helpful.

So much for my powers of deduction.

Adam's here somewhere, but I'm not going to perform a building-to-building search.

I have a couple of choices. I could pack it in and head back to Jenson. Since he's not running away, he'll be heading that way eventually. Or I could wait and see if he makes any more stops before heading home.

While the first option pulls at my desire to take a nap, the second is the smarter move. Plus, it will provide me the opportunity to swap out the bug inside his car. I return to my Versa, grab a new bug, and head over to the parking structure.

Before I enter, I check to make sure Adam hasn't returned, and then I head up.

The bug in the car is right where I left it. The moment I pull it out, I see what the problem is. There's a tiny switch along the bottom of the device that turns the bug on. It's stuck between the ON and OFF positions. I try pushing it all the way to ON, but it seems to be jammed. When I put the bug in last night, I activated it by feel, and when the switch stopped moving, I assumed it was on.

That sucks. That means there won't be anything on the memory card.

I exchange the good bug for the bad one, this time visually confirming the device is on before attaching it under the dash. To be extra sure it's working, I speak a few words into the car and check the server to see if the audio has come through.

It has. Time to strike up the band.

I'm back in my car, parked where I can see the structure, when Adam finally shows up about forty-five minutes later. He's in the company of three other people around his age, two men and a woman. The three all have book bags slung over their shoulders, while Adam is carrying a large textbook and a note binder. They walk across the parking lot to the structure.

When they come out again, one of the boys and the girl are

together in a car, and the other boy is on a motorcycle. Adam comes down last, blasting a song from Kendrick Lamar's latest album. I know this because I'm listening to a live feed from inside his vehicle.

I follow him at a safe distance back to the interstate, and we head north. We're just past Woodland, a little over twenty minutes into our drive, when Adam's music is replaced by a ringing phone.

I hear him curse under his breath. A second later, the ringing stops and he says, "Hello?"

Over the speaker, a man says, "Did you get it?"

It's only three words, but I'm pretty sure it's Linderhoff's voice.

"I'm heading there now."

"What the hell's taking so long?"

Yep. Definitely Linderhoff.

"I had some other things I needed to do."

"What things?"

"For my mom, all right?"

"No. Not all right. What you do for me *always* takes priority. Am I clear?"

Adam mumbles something that I can barely hear.

Linderhoff is obviously having the same problem. "Am. I. Clear?"

"Yes, sir."

"Let me know as soon as you're done."

"All right."

There's a click, and the music comes back on. I can hear Adam mumbling to himself, but the volume of the song is way too high for me to understand anything. Jar might be able to filter out some of the music to make his words clear, but that's not something I want to waste her time on. Not at this point, anyway.

Adam exits the interstate in Brighton.

Interesting.

As I veer onto the off-ramp, it gets even better. He appears to be heading back to the business park.

I speed up until I'm only three cars behind him. I want to see what's going to happen.

Sure enough, he turns into the Larkin Professional Center and heads straight to the wing he parked in front of last night. Even though it's Sunday, some of the places are open and there are more cars around. I follow him in.

I don't turn down the gap between buildings where he goes, but I do drive by it slowly. He's stopped in front of the shop he and his friends vandalized. The neon orange on the roll-up door has been mostly covered up by new paint. A middle-aged guy holding a paint spray gun stands in front of it, looking over at the Camaro.

As much as I'd like to stop and watch, I keep rolling, and that's the last thing I see as I move out of sight.

On the audio feed, I hear Adam say, "Good afternoon, Mr. Owens."

From the nearness of his voice, I know Adam is still in his car.

I drive around the side of the complex where the Dumpsters are.

"What do you want?" I'm guessing it's the guy holding the paint sprayer. The one and only Chuck Owens, General Contractor. His voice is more distant, so I picture him leaning down at the passenger side window.

"What do you think?"

More silence, then, "Give me a minute."

"Take two if you need it."

I wouldn't be surprised if Adam has learned his tough-guy

talk from mob shows on TV. Seems to be working for him, though.

In the silence that follows, I turn along the back of the complex, drive out to the street, and park a block away.

The next sound I hear is not a voice, but the thud of something with substance landing on something else.

"There," Owens says.

I hear the crinkling of heavy paper before Adam says, "It's all here?"

"Yes."

"Plus the penalty?"

"Plus the penalty."

"Good. Just one more thing. Mr. Linderhoff wanted me to remind you that it would be best if everything went smoothly next time."

"It will."

"Then we'll see you in three weeks. Have a nice afternoon."

The Camaro's engine growls as Adam presses down on the gas.

I don't know how this Owens guy kept from spray painting the side of Adam's car. I bet the idea is at least going through his mind.

I tail the Camaro again. As soon as we reach the interstate, Adam calls Linderhoff.

"I got it."

"Everything?"

"He said it was."

"You didn't check?"

"Not yet. I'll—"

"You should have checked, goddammit!"

"You want me to do that now?"

"Just do it before you drop it off. If it's not all there, you're going back. Understand?"

"Yes, sir. But...I thought you wanted us to deal with Collins again this afternoon."

"He came by earlier. He's good now."

"Oh. Okay. Great."

Linderhoff hangs up before Adam finishes speaking.

The rest of the ride to Jenson is done without any further interruption to the music. When we get to town, I figure Adam will head to Linderhoff's house to give him the package. (It's money, right? It's got to be. It's certainly not tile samples.) But instead of heading in that direction, he goes toward the east side of town. Maybe Linderhoff doesn't like receiving the offerings at home, and he and Adam have an alternate place where they make their handoff.

Worried the exchange might last only a few seconds, I close the gap again.

We're on the road that will take us to the hospital, but before we get there, Adam pulls into an empty parking lot surrounding a single building sporting a sign that reads JENSON NATIONAL BANK.

No way I can pull into the lot without being seen, but there is a strip mall on the other side of the street. I pull into a perpendicular slot that gives me direct line of sight to the bank.

Adam has parked the Camaro in front and is getting out of the car. I grab my bag, pull out the Canon, and attach the telephoto lens. Before aiming it across the street, I flick the camera to video and press Record.

Adam is carrying what looks like a thick manila envelope. The side I can see has no writing on it. He walks up to the night deposit drawer, but as he starts to slip the envelope inside, he suddenly stops and pulls it back.

He looks around, checking to see if anyone else has driven into the lot. When he sees he's alone, he opens the envelope and sticks his hand in.

I snort as I shake my head. He's forgotten to count what's inside.

I zoom in on the top of the envelope. There are flashes of green and white. It's money, all right.

I zoom back out so that Adam is fully in the frame again.

When he finishes counting, he reseals the envelope. From his lack of agitation, I'm guessing the required cash is all there.

As Adam lifts the envelope to the night deposit slot, I get a look at the other side of the package. There's no writing there, either. It's just a blank envelope full of cash. Whoever's going to retrieve it inside the bank apparently is involved in Linderhoff's world, too.

As soon as Adam finishes his mission, he gets back into the Camaro, has a short conversation with Linderhoff confirming the cash is all there, and leaves.

I pick up the chase again, but it lasts only until Adam drives into the carport behind his apartment building. Once he exits his Camaro, I head back to the interstate and drive to the Residence Inn, more than ready for that nap.

CHAPTER TWENTY-ONE

The problem is, I can't sleep.

Adam confuses me.

He's into something pretty bad, there's no question about that, but I'm having a hard time equating his job as a thug with the fact he's going to college. I mean, yes, I understand. Being a thug doesn't necessarily mean a person is stupid or not interested in getting an education, but I've got to believe the percentage of people who fall into that category is low. I admit I may be prejudiced.

Okay, fine. For argument's sake, let's go with Adam being a thug who wants to get a degree. Given his previous academic record, going to a community college is a good choice. But a quick check online tells me there's a closer community college in Brighton. There's also a closer one in Woodland.

Maybe Sacramento City College is a better school. But Adam's current classes—all basic-requirement types—should be perfectly adequate at a more convenient campus.

I can't help but think he's going there because he doesn't want anyone—or, more likely, someone specific—to know. But why? Is he afraid that person will force him to quit?

Wait.

Perhaps I'm overthinking this.

Maybe the reason he's keeping it a secret is he's afraid he might not succeed and doesn't want anyone to know in case he ends up dropping out. That makes more sense.

But I still have questions.

What's his goal? Is he thinking that with an education, maybe he can become the boss thug? And if he's John Smith—which I'm now all but convinced he is—why was Marissa helping him?

After a half hour of these questions going around and around in my head, I finally drift off.

CHAPTER TWENTY-TWO

I'm in Jakarta again.

Around me are high-rise apartment buildings and a few large homes hidden behind towering walls. I'm standing in the middle of a wide road scattered with streetlamps, but there are no cars.

I'm walking. I thought I was standing still, but I'm actually walking.

I don't want to walk. I want to go back to where I was.

No.

I want to go as far away from here as possible, but I'm not in control.

Ahead, I see a gap between properties, a place where a wall would be if there was a home on the lot. I can see the silhouette of the top of a tree protruding above the property, but I can't see the bottom yet. It's blocked by the walls of the home next door.

A flash of light illuminates the branches. The source, which has gone dark now, is also hidden like the tree trunk. My feet move faster.

Stop, I try to yell, but I'm no more in control of my lips than I am of my legs. *Please, stop!*

I reach the open lot.

It's so dark that I still cannot see the bottom of the tree, but I know that's where my disobedient body is taking me.

It's the very spot I don't want to go.

Not now.

Not ever again.

As I approach, I begin to see shadows of others, standing and kneeling near the tree's base. They are but whispers of people I know, smoke that even the lightest breeze will carry away.

Another person lies on the ground, the focal point of their attention. Only she is not smoke, not a whisper, not a shadow.

I am in control of my body again, but I've come too far to run away. I drop to my knees beside her. Even the darkness can't hide the bullet hole in her chest.

I pull her into my lap and place a hand on her cheek. "Liz, don't go. Please don't—"

I wake with a start.

It's been weeks since the dream last paid me a visit. I was hoping I'd moved past it.

I'm here, Liz says. *I'm still here.*

"No, you're not," I whisper even as I feel her all around me.

I'm still here.

Hot tears run down my cheeks. "You're not."

I am.

I can't argue anymore.

I'm here for as long as you need me.

How about forever?

CHAPTER TWENTY-THREE

I decide I've wasted enough time on Adam and Linderhoff for now, and leave the hotel on Sunday evening, refocused on Marissa. I start by returning to the scene of the hit-and-run. I don't expect to discover something new. It's more symbolic than anything else. A way to remind me why I've come to Jenson.

The makeshift memorial (for that's truly what it is now) is still there, though there are fewer candles than before, and most of the stuffed animals have been removed. The only people on the sidewalk are a few houses away, a young couple walking their dog. I'd like to get out and look around again, but it's still early enough in the evening that someone might notice me. I drive past.

About a quarter mile from the neighborhood, I park at the empty end of a supermarket lot. I've brought my laptop with me tonight, and I use it to access the Jenson PD servers. I haven't checked the case file in over twenty-four hours, and even though it's Sunday, I'm hoping there's been some progress. Or, at the very least, something they may think is unimportant but I can use.

Sadly, it appears the investigation has hit a wall. From the notes, I see that the two Mikes have been working the case all weekend but have absolutely nothing new to show for it. I'm sure they're fine detectives, but they've had very little to work with, and without someone phoning in a tip, they're treading water.

I know the feeling. While I have methods open to me that they can't lawfully employ, my own pursuit of Marissa's killer hasn't fared much better.

The smoking gun is the car. Find that, and it should point directly at her murderer. There's no way the offending vehicle has been driving around town for the last week and a half unnoticed. Not with the accident on the mind of everyone in Jenson. And the Mikes have checked all the body shops, not only in Jenson, but within a twenty-mile radius of town, and nothing has the kind of damage they're interested in.

That means either the car has been stowed out of sight somewhere, or it has been taken beyond the Mikes' twenty-mile search area.

Even in a small town like this, performing a garage-to-garage check could take a week or more. I don't have that kind of time. But I can look beyond where the police have been hunting.

Well, not me. Jar.

I send her a message, asking if she can do a wider search of body shops, and include the Sacramento area. Though that would be a ton of places, she should be able to create a bot that can automatically check the computer systems of each shop. If something of interest pops up, I can call the place directly.

With that delegated, I temporarily scratch looking for the car off my list.

There are a few minor things I could probably do now, but what I really want is to talk to someone and ask the questions I need answered. If this was happening in somewhere like L.A., I could call whomever I wanted and pretend to be the police. But

Jenson's too small for that, and my ruse could easily fall apart before I ask my first question.

I ponder the problem while aimlessly scrolling through the Instagram feeds of Marissa's friends. I work through Luke's and Julia's and Noah's and finally reach Fara's. From the amount of times she and Marissa used to show up in each other's feeds, I'm guessing they are...*were* best friends. When I see the link in Fara's profile to her Twitter handle, I click on it, an idea scratching at the back of my mind. I've checked her Twitter before and noticed that basically all she does is retweet others.

As I scroll through her feed now, I see it's filled mostly with pop culture stuff from a few different sources: Buzzfeed, E! Online, Hype Scene, PopCultureNerd.com, and the like. My idea gels. Perhaps I can't pretend to be the police, but there are other professionals who can get certain people to talk.

I reconfigure my phone so that its ID reads HYPE SCENE. Hype Scene is a California-based streaming service focused on millennials and Generation Z, and the account Fara retweets most. Hype Scene gives its audience the inside scoop on all its favorite singers, performers, and social media stars. The service also covers some news and human interest stories. It wouldn't be entirely out of the realm of possibility for Hype Scene to pick up Marissa's story.

At least, that's what I hope Fara will believe.

I call her cell phone.

After the third ring, I begin to worry she's not going to answer, but then there's a click followed by a very tentative and slightly confused "Hello?"

"Yes, hi. My name is Calum McLean. I'm wondering if I could speak to Fara Nelson."

"This is Fara." Still tentative.

"Oh, fantastic. Fara, I work at Hype Scene. Have you heard of us?"

"Well, yeah. Who hasn't?" A touch of excitement now.

"Before I say anything else, I want to tell you I'm very sorry about your friend Marissa."

"Oh, um, thank you."

"I'm sure this is not an easy time for you. It sounded like she was a wonderful person."

"She was."

"That's what I thought. See, my boss and I were talking, and we believe it would be a great idea to do a story about her. You know, to honor her life."

"Really? I think that would be great."

"Then you don't mind if I ask you a few questions, do you?"

A beat. "Oh, um, I'm not supposed to."

"Not supposed to what?"

"Talk to the press."

"Who told you that?"

"The police...and my dad."

"Well, I don't want to make any problems for you. Maybe you can tell me the name of someone who might be able to talk to me."

"Are you really from Hype Scene?"

I'm not starting to feel guilty at this point; I've been feeling guilty since the moment she answered. But I'm fooling her for a good reason, and I'm sure if she knew what it was—which she never will—she'd understand.

So, it's with a clenching of my stomach that I say, "I am."

"I guess I could answer a few questions, then," she says, but quickly adds, "You can't tell anyone you got anything from me, though."

"You mean you want to be off the record."

"Yeah. That's it. Off the record."

"I promise. Our conversation will only be between us." I'm relieved to say something that's true.

"Okay. What would you like to know?"

"From the news stories I've read, I take it Marissa was a good friend of yours."

"She was my best friend."

Check. "Then this is extra hard on you. I'm so sorry."

"It's...awful."

"I'm sure it is. If any of these questions are too difficult for you to answer, just say so."

"Okay."

I ask her several questions about the type of person Marissa was, hoping it will ease her into being more comfortable with me. Her answers align with pretty much the picture I've already pieced together. Marissa was a happy, kind, well-liked teen who should still be going to school and hanging out with her friends. Fara tells me about a trip she took at the beginning of summer with Marissa and her family. They spent three days in a rental house near the ocean in Monterey, visiting the aquarium, spending some time on the beach, and generally goofing around.

"I saw this cute shirt in a shop one day," she says. "I really wanted it, but I didn't have a lot of money with me so I couldn't buy it. When we came back to Jenson and I was unpacking my things, the shirt was sitting right on top. There was no note or anything, but I knew Marissa had bought it for me. I have no idea when she could have done it, we were together all the time, but she made it happen. That was Marissa."

"She sounds like she was special."

"She was."

I spent a couple more minutes asking her general questions about Marissa and their friendship before turning to what I really want to know. "The night of the accident, Marissa was apparently walking down the street alone. Do you have any idea where she was coming from?"

"No. I wish I did."

"Did she have a job? Could she have been coming home from that?"

There's a slight hesitation before she says, "She quit her job a while ago."

"I see." I pause for a moment. "I understand that the police don't have any suspects yet. Any thoughts on who you think it might have been?"

"I have no clue. Probably some drunk driver who doesn't even know what he did."

"Or she," I say.

"What?"

"The driver could have been a woman."

"Yeah, I guess."

She doesn't believe it was a woman, which makes me think that even if she doesn't know who did it, she has her suspicions.

"I guess that's all for now. Thank you for giving me some time."

"No problem."

"If I have more questions, can I call you again?"

"Yeah, that would be okay."

"Great. Oh, there was one other thing. I was planning on calling a couple of Marissa's other friends. Julia Torres and Luke Reed. I understand he was Marissa's boyfriend."

"Luke wasn't her boyfriend."

"Really? The story I read—"

"They broke up."

"I'm sorry. I didn't realize that. Perhaps I shouldn't call him."

"Whatever he says would probably be a lie. He was pretty hurt when they split."

"That's good to know. I appreciate the info. Was Marissa dating someone else when she died?"

"No, she wasn't."

I hear a voice in the background.

"Sorry," she says. "I've got to go."

"Of course. Thank you again."

"Uh, when do you think the story will be online?"

"I'm still not sure if there will be one, but if there is, then I would think it would be up pretty soon."

"Okay. Cool. Maybe I'll talk to you later."

"I hope so. Goodbye, Fara."

"Bye."

I type some notes into my computer. The call was a lot more informative than it seemed on the surface. A) Fara thinks the driver was a man. B) Marissa had been working but she'd quit. C) Fara's slight hesitation could mean Marissa had another job. D) Marissa and Luke had definitely broken up prior to the accident.

Among the many things I'm still not sure about is whether or not Marissa was dating someone new. I couldn't tell if Fara was being truthful about that, but I didn't have time to push her on it. If she was lying, maybe it was because Marissa wanted to keep the relationship secret.

There's an obvious answer to this potential mystery boyfriend: could be Adam Nyland/John Smith. That would also explain why she didn't want anyone to know. I doubt it's much of a secret that Adam is a bad boy. If Marissa's parents had found out, I bet they would have forbidden her from seeing him. I doubt it would have mattered to them that he was going to college on the sly.

Oh, what a tangled web we weave.

I check the tracker and see the Camaro is still parked behind Adam's apartment. I'm starting to feel I need to switch my attention back to him, but only in regard to how he fits in with Marissa, not because of his work for Linderhoff. Before I do, however, I put in calls to Julia and Luke.

Julia is not quite as starstruck by my Hype Scene caller ID. She's even less interested in answering questions about her deceased friend. I get a couple of short responses from her before she tells me she doesn't want to talk anymore. Our conversation isn't long enough for me to get a sense whether or not she has any secrets that could help me.

Luke is a different story.

I don't use my Hype Scene ID with him. Instead I change it to read MCD CORP and hope he fills in the missing letters.

Either he doesn't even look at the caller ID or he does and it springs him into action, because before the first ring is even done, he answers, "Yes, hello?"

"Luke Reed?"

"Yes. I'm Luke."

"This is Richard Cruz. I'm from human resources at McDonald's Corporate."

"Oh, um, hi. What can I do for you, Mr. Cruz?"

Boy, does he sound nervous. And, yes, I am feeling guilty again.

"I've received a report about an incident at our location in Jenson, California, where you are employed. Are you familiar with what I'm talking about?"

"Yes, sir."

Not only is it Sunday but it's nearing seven p.m. here in California, which means it's almost nine p.m. in Chicago, where McDonald's Corporate headquarters are located. Why someone from the HR department would be calling a teenage restaurant worker at this exact moment should be the first question on his mind. His second should be why would corporate deal with a petty altercation involving said teenage restaurant worker in the first place. But he lacks enough real-world experience to realize either. As far as he's concerned, he probably thinks it's normal for the higher-ups to get involved in something like this.

I recount enough of the incident to let him know I am aware of what went down, then say, "I'm sure you understand that this doesn't look good. But I'm told, outside of this altercation, you've been an outstanding employee. What I need you to do is explain to me why you felt the need to attack some of our customers."

"I-I'm so sorry." His voice wavers as he tries to keep from crying. "I made a bad mistake. It's all my fault."

"I'm happy to hear you take responsibility. That shows maturity. I would still like to know why it happened."

"My, um, girlfriend was killed a week ago. Someone hit her with a car."

There's no need for me to fake sympathy. "That is horrible. I'm sorry to hear that. What a terrible tragedy."

He sniffles something that sounds like yes.

"I can't imagine what you're going through," I say. "Did these people you fought with have something to do with her death?"

A pause. "I'm not sure."

"Please, son. Help me understand."

He takes several seconds before saying, "The main guy I fought with...he...well, my girlfriend and I..." Another breath. "She broke up with me not long ago and-and started seeing him. I know it was wrong. I should have just ignored that he was there. But her funeral was yesterday morning, and when I saw him last night, I just...I just lost it."

Huh. Contrary to what Fara said, Luke seems to think Marissa and Adam were an item.

"Did he provoke you?" I ask.

"Other than just being there? .... No."

"Has he ever provoked you?"

"This is the first time I've seen him since Mar—my girl-friend left me. Well, and that morning at the funeral."

"Was he a friend of yours?"

"Not really. Just someone I'd see around sometimes."

"Sounds like you got yourself wound up and decided to take it out on someone."

Luke says nothing to this.

I let the dead air hang for another couple of seconds and then say, "It's not been a good few weeks for you, has it?"

"No, sir."

"While I can understand your desire to lash out, you can't behave like that, whether you're working for us or just walking down the street. You don't want to do something stupid that could get you into worse trouble than talking to me."

"I'm sorry. I'm really sorry. I wasn't thinking."

"No, Luke, you weren't."

"Am I...fired? Mr. Kendall sent me home to cool off and told me not to come back until next weekend."

"Mr. Kendall. Let's see, that's your manager."

"Assistant manager."

"I'll tell you what, Luke. I think this is one of those situations we'll leave up to our local management team. If he says you can come back next weekend, then you can come back next weekend."

"Thank you," Luke says, relief pouring through the phone.

"I wouldn't mention anything about talking to me unless your manager asks you specifically. Sometimes, if they think we're looking over their shoulders, they won't be as lenient. Know what I mean?"

"Yes, sir. I appreciate that."

"You take care." I hang up.

I'm a damn good judge of character, and everything I know tells me Luke had nothing to do with Marissa's death. He didn't slip out of work and secretly drive over to kill her. He didn't arrange for someone else to do it. He's just a poor, brokenhearted kid whose girlfriend dumped him, and then she went and died before he had a chance to try to win her back.

I feel like a complete asshole for questioning him like that, but at least now I can officially cross him off my suspects list.

I need a beer, but the night is still young so I settle for coffee.

From McDonald's, of all places.

CHAPTER TWENTY-FOUR

When I'm ready to hit the road again, I check to see if Adam has gone anywhere. The Camaro hasn't moved, so I decide to drive by his place.

Since it's still relatively early, lights shine in the windows of several apartments. Among these is the window to the unit I've pegged as Adam's. But an educated guess is not the same as definitive proof.

I park my car and grab a few items out of my bag before I walk over to the building. Why waste a chance to increase my surveillance on him, right?

The individual apartment entrances are off an interior hallway on each floor, reached via a small lobby. Within the lobby is a directory board listing who lives where.

On the line for apartment 209 are white capital letters spelling out NYLAND. There's no other name next to it, which I hope means Adam lives alone. I take the stairs to the second floor and pause on the landing to listen. I hear the muffled sounds of voices and TVs coming from inside apartments. The hallway itself sounds empty.

I enter and take a left toward the apartment I think is

Adam's. Thankfully the unit numbers back up this assumption, and before I reach the end of the hall, I know that the last door on the front side of the building is indeed 209. I examine the wall opposite his door, and pick out the perfect spot for one of the mini cameras I have in my pocket.

I need to make this fast. The last thing I want is to have him or one of his neighbors step out and catch me in the act.

I pull the camera out and stick it above the frame surrounding the doorway of the apartment opposite Adam's. I adjust the lens so that it's pointed correctly. The camera is designed to be used in plain sight. It resembles one of those ant traps. You know what I'm talking about—black, two-inch square, raised on one side like a dome, with openings for ants to walk into. The micro camera's lens is on the raised section and looks like part of the design. The person who dreamed it up deserves an award, if you ask me. It's a work of art.

I'm making my way back to the stairs when I hear a door open behind me, on the side of the hall Adam lives on. I hear some clinking, like bottles knocking together, and other rustling sounds that I identify as garbage in a bag.

I keep walking, not turning my head even a little, to prevent the person behind me from seeing any of my face. When I approach the stairwell, I angle my path so that I enter it without having to turn until the wall is between me and my follower.

The stairs are built with a switchback halfway down, which means if the other person is coming down the top half while I'm still on the bottom portion, I'd be seen. I double-time it so that I'm already off the stairs and entering the lobby by the time the follower starts down. I head straight outside and move off the path, into the relative darkness of the lawn in front of the building. But I go only far enough that, when I look back, I can still see into the lobby through the windows on either side of the door.

The other person has reached the last of the steps. It's Adam, all right, and he's holding a couple of trash bags.

Talk about a close one.

When he reaches the bottom, instead of heading out the front door, he turns right without looking my way and disappears down the hallway.

Though I can see the light is still on in his apartment, I'm hoping he'll head out in his car after he dumps his trash. That way I can let myself into his place, hide another bug there, and have a look around.

I hear Adam leave through a side door and, a few moments later, the squeaky sound of a lid being raised on a trash bin. Unfortunately, I also hear him return to the building. So much for the easy way.

After he disappears upstairs, I walk around to the carport. The flattop roof that shields the cars is high enough to accommodate a truck with a camper shell. The structure is L-shaped, the shorter end extended over to the building at the other side of the parking area but not actually touching it.

The apartment windows on this side are mirror images of those along the front. Pretty awful view if you ask me. Two of the apartments have lights on, but their drapes are closed. The rest of the units are dark.

Using one of the trash bins, I climb onto the carport's roof and quietly move around to where it meets the main building. There's a difference of about seven feet between the top of the carport and the top of the apartment building. I'm a tad over six feet tall, so I easily reach the lip and pull myself up onto the larger structure.

The roof is sloped though not drastically, and is covered in asphalt shingles. I ease across it to not cause any noise that might be heard below. Right before I reach the apex, I get onto my hands and knees and crawl from there. Seconds later, when

I reach the front edge of the roof just above Adam's window, I lower myself to my stomach.

I'm sure you've all heard stories about the CIA or foreign agencies being able to listen in on conversations by pointing a laser at a window that picks up sound vibrations off the glass. I don't have one of those lasers. What I do have is a specialized bug that, when attached to a window, does pretty much the same thing. It's smaller than a dime—just a microphone and a Bluetooth-type transmitter. It has a companion recorder/cellular transmitter that needs to be hidden within a hundred feet of where I place the bug.

I peek over the edge. The eave sticks out about a foot from the building, and Adam's window is another two feet below. Adam has curtains but they're open, hanging over each side of the glass about half a foot. That suits my purpose perfectly.

I check the street to see if anyone is out and about. It's nice and quiet. Still, I pull on my ski mask in case Adam chooses the wrong moment to look outside, and then I lean over the edge.

My plan is to stick the bug on the glass, near the top corner where it will be hidden by the drapes whether they're open or closed. As I'm reaching for the spot, I hear the front door of the building open. I shoot my hand out to place the bug, and though I'm successful, in my rush I connect with the glass harder than I planned, creating a small but not insignificant tap.

I jerk back up and crawl away from the edge as a young guy and girl exit the building and walk toward the street.

I'm only halfway to the top when I hear Adam's window open.

"Did you just throw something at my window?" he yells.

The couple take another step before they realize he's talking to them. As they turn, the guy says, "Wha—" but stops himself and his gaze switches from Adam's window to me. "Hey! What are you doing up there?"

Crap. (A word of warning. I overuse this word. Better get used to it.)

I scramble over the apex as I hear Adam say, "Who are you talking to?"

"There's a guy on the roof."

Crap. Crap. Crap.

I don't worry about the sound of my steps anymore as I run down the other side and jump onto the carport. To my left is the driveway that leads back around to the front of the building, where the couple are. That could be a problem.

I look to the right. A chain-link fence sits about a foot beyond the end of the carport, and after that is the parking area of the building next door. Unfortunately, it does not have a carport I can hop onto. But it'll have to do.

I pick out the best landing spot, and leap. The height is enough that someone who doesn't know what they're doing could easily break a leg, but I've trained for situations like this. I've been *in* situations like this. And besides, I have only one and a half legs to break.

Even before my toes touch the ground, I'm collapsing into a tuck, then it's a quick roll to defuse momentum and I'm back on my feet. But I'm not out of the woods yet.

I run along the back of the building, climb another chain-link fence, and drop into a third parking lot, surprising two young women walking toward a parked car.

One shouts, while the other says, "What the hell?"

Crap. (I did warn you.)

Maybe if I'm not wearing the mask I wouldn't be as scary, but then again, they would see my face and I would have to leave town. Scaring them is—with apologies—preferable.

I turn down the driveway and run past the building toward the street. As I clear the end of the structure, I glance toward Adam's building. Only the girl is still out front.

She yells, "There he is!"

Immediately her companion and Adam come rushing out from the building. They must have been standing in the doorway, talking. I turn left and sprint away.

I hear someone running in my direction behind me. With the way things are going tonight, I have to assume it's Adam.

I don't like making mistakes. While they do happen, it's not often. But I have made a doozy tonight. The only bonus is that I use the anger I feel at myself to fuel my escape.

Adam is younger than me, but even with two good legs, there's no way he's in better shape. I sprint to the end of the block and turn right. As I do, I take the opportunity to check how far back he is.

First off, it *is* Adam. And annoyingly, he's about ten yards closer than I expected. But that's only because of the burst of speed he used when he started. He won't be able to keep it up. I race down the new road, sticking to the shadows as much as possible. It's a short block, so I'm nearly at the next intersection when Adam turns behind me.

"Stop, asshole!" he yells, breathing hard.

Me, I'm in my rhythm now, my breaths measured and consistent.

I turn left at the end of the block, and almost trip on a section of the sidewalk that's been pushed up by a tree. (That's what I get for being cocky.) I am able to skip over it at the last second. To avoid a repeat, I veer into the street.

When Adam takes the corner behind me, he's not so lucky. I hear a shout and a thud as he crashes to the ground. This gives me the opening I need.

I swing around the next corner and do it again two blocks later. When I'm sure I've lost him, I take off my mask and slow my pace so that it's more of a fast walk.

About a minute after this, I hear the sound of a police siren heading into the neighborhood. I doubt Adam told anyone to call them. The young couple must have done it on their own. Or possibly it was the girls I scared.

Whatever the case, the cops are a new problem. I have to assume that at some point they will get around to writing down all the license plate numbers in the area. Though the Versa is parked around the corner a block away, it's likely to get noted. I need to get it out of there.

But it's not like I can just waltz back the way I've come. I may not be wearing the mask anymore, but I'm still in the same clothes the others saw me in.

I work my way back in a wide loop that takes me to my rental car from the other side. When I reach it, I see the reflection of police emergency lights flashing off buildings on Adam's street, but thankfully there's no one in view.

I get into the car and start the engine. It's not loud, but I still wince. When I pull out and check the rearview mirror, the road and sidewalk behind me remain empty.

CHAPTER TWENTY-FIVE

M y biggest concern now is that Adam will discover the
bug on his window. It's not that it'll lead him back to
me or anything, but it will make him realize someone is
watching him, and that in turn will make him overly cautious.
It's more of a challenge to keep tabs on someone who is always
checking his back.

If I could listen to the bug, I would know he's found it if its
feed suddenly cuts out, but at the moment, I can't. The booster
is still in my pocket. So, while the bug is doing its job, it's
sending the information to nothing.

I'll have to go back later. Not tonight, of course. Profession-
ally, we'd call that being stupid. I've had enough brushes with
stupid for one night.

I check the tracker. The Camaro is still at the apartment.
No shock there. Adam will likely be tied up with the police for
at least another hour. If he suspects I did something to his
window, I have a feeling he won't tell them that, and will wait
until they're gone before he inspects it himself. The fact that
he's so involved in Linderhoff's world has got to make him think

my visit has something to do with that. It's the most logical conclusion.

Me, I'm thinking I should head back to the hotel. It's been quite a night and sleep sounds like a good idea. But there is one thing I should check first. I switch the focus of my tracker app to the bug I put on Linderhoff's car. Since it's Sunday night, I expect him to be at home, which would mean Residence Inn, here I come.

Only he's not home.

Well, at least his car isn't.

Damn.

It.

Why can't these people cooperate with me for a little bit?

The Lexus sits at a property just north of the city limits. According to the tracker, it's been there for over two hours.

I bring up Google Maps, flip to a satellite view, and zoom in on the location. A large building sits a hundred yards from the road, with a pair of smaller buildings not too far from it. The driveway leading onto the property is mostly obscured by trees, which also cover most of the rest of the land. If the main building is a home, it's a big one. Half a city block long, and two —maybe even three—stories high.

The entire property appears to be surrounded by a wall. I switch to street view. The wall is made of stone and looks about eight feet high. Sitting across the driveway entrance is a large gate. On the wall next to the gate is a rectangular stone plaque, like the kind used to identify the name or owner of a place. When I zoom in on it, however, there's nothing to read. Not because Google has blurred the sign as it sometimes does, but because whatever was once on the plaque has been removed.

Curious, I use my bookmarked shortcut into the county tax assessor's database and look up the owner of the property.

Not a person. A company, with the innocuous name Yante/Kendall Limited Partnership.

I do a search of the name, hoping the company has a website, but no go. In fact, there are no internet entries for the company at all.

What is this—the 1980s?

Nearly everyone has a website these days. Even new companies that haven't built websites yet can't completely avoid their names appearing somewhere in cyberspace.

I recheck the assessor's information and see that Yante/Kendall has owned the property for twelve years.

Twelve.

That's a long time not to get your website up.

Whatever Yante/Kendall is, it doesn't appear to want anyone to know about its business.

I am intrigued.

I shoot Jar an email to see if she can dig up anything, and then I follow the glowing dot on my tracker north.

CHAPTER TWENTY-SIX

The first thing I note as I near the Yante/Kendall property is that there aren't a lot of other homes or buildings in the area. In fact, the last place I pass before I reach the stone wall is a good mile away.

The wall is very well made and quite aesthetically pleasing. The stones are long and flat, like fossilized wooden planks, and, in the small sampling lit up by my headlights, range in color from medium gray to dark tan. The wall has an old look, like it's been here for decades. Scaling it seems as if it should be easy, but I have a feeling, based on the owner's apparent sense of secrecy, that its appearance might be deceiving.

The gate is a work of art in itself. Thick oak boards, stained reddish brown, nestle against one another at a forty-five-degree angle, all set in a decorative metal frame. It is a single piece that I surmise rolls to the side when opened. It's so sturdy looking it wouldn't surprise me if you'd need a tank to knock it down.

A well-secured place like this almost certainly has cameras about. I drive by without slowing and don't stop until I come into view of the next home, a full two miles away.

Chateau Yante/Kendall might as well be on an island by itself.

I make a U-turn and head back. Two hundred yards shy of the wall, I ease off the road between some trees to a place where my car can't be seen by anyone passing by.

I climb out, circle to the rear, and open the hatchback. I've brought along a piece of hardware that is perfect for my current needs. It's a specialized drone, the kind you wouldn't be able to find at any retailer. Most drones make a lot of noise when in use; mine does not. That near-silent flight comes with a hefty price tag, but I don't know anyone in my business—my day-job business—who would use anything else. It's small enough to fit in my pocket and can take off from my outstretched hand.

I grab it, a pair of night vision goggles, one gun and suppressor, a variety of bugs, some rope and other tools I might need, putting all but the drone and the goggles in my backpack.

As I hike through the woods toward the stone wall, I pay very close attention to the ground in front of me. I've had plenty of experience dealing with secured locations that had trip wires or other warning devices hidden in the land leading up to them. But by the time the wall comes into view, I haven't found anything. Apparently, the good people at Yante/Kendall don't feel it's necessary. My presence here indicates they're wrong.

I stop fifty feet short of the wall, still hidden in the trees, and send my drone aloft. Using my phone as the controller, I ease the drone through the woods, five feet off the ground, until it is an arm's length from the wall. There, I direct it to rise, stop it again when it passes the top, and set it to hover. I pan its built-in camera and study the fence.

Running parallel along the top, about three inches above the stones and with another three between them, are five strands of wire. Though I can't hear a hum over the camera's microphone, from the connectors used to keep the wires aloft, I know they're electrified.

I send the drone higher so that it's lost in the night sky, and fly it toward the building at the heart of the property. I catch glimpses of the driveway through the trees. When it reaches the front of the main building, the road veers to the right, into what looks like a narrow but long parking area.

As for the main building itself, my first thought is that someone must have purchased an old English manor and transported it here, stone by stone. You know the kind I mean, right? Two stories of gray, carved rock, with a slate roof and over half a dozen chimneys. The kind of place that looks like it's survived five hundred years already and could survive five hundred more, relatively unchanged.

I bring the drone down so that it hovers over the trees in front. A wide staircase leads up to large double doors. There are numerous windows, all dark except the one near the entrance. Through the latter, I can just make out a large entryway or lobby, but the light is dim so I can't see details.

I don't detect anyone outside, but to be sure, I switch the drone's camera to thermal mode. (The multiple modes are another reason why the thing is so damn expensive.) I pan across the area between the front of the house and the trees. The only heat signatures I pick up are small and indicate the presence of electronic devices, not people. Cameras, most likely. I'll deal with that later. When I'm done with the front, I send the drone around the entire building, repeating the process. No signs of life anywhere.

Before I send it in for a closer look, I fly the drone over to the two smaller buildings. They sit next to each other at the end of the parking area and appear to be identical. From the large, closed doors along the road side, I'd say these are garages. What I can't tell is whether or not they're in use.

There are, however, nine cars in the outside parking area. Another heat scan reveals the cars are cold enough to have been sitting there for well over an hour. It also tells me no one else is in the area.

I flip back to visual mode and slowly fly by the backs of the vehicles, taking pictures of each license plate. Linderhoff's car is the one closest to the house. I don't recognize any of the others.

I bring the drone back to the house, activate thermal mode, and let it hover above the place. Most drones have a battery life of maybe fifteen minutes. This one can go almost three times that long, but I don't know if anyone will come outside before I have to recall it to put in a new battery.

The answer turns out to be yes.

With around ten minutes of power left, the heat signatures of three people exit the house. I switch to night vision, and carefully lower the drone until it's about thirty feet above the ground. More people trickle out, until there are twelve individuals standing in front of the house.

They are all men. I'm pretty sure none is younger than forty, and the oldest appears to be in his late seventies at least.

They stand in a loose group, talking. After about a minute, a thirteenth person exits the building, closes the door, and locks it.

The night vision function tends to make all the men's white faces fuzzy, but it's clear enough for me to recognize the door locker is Raymond Linderhoff.

When he reaches the others, everyone shakes hands before they head in twos and threes toward the parking area.

I take pictures of each person, hoping I can ID them later, but again, they're not the greatest shots.

Soon, the cars begin to leave, most with only a driver, but a few of the vehicles carry a passenger or two. Linderhoff is one of those alone. He waits until the last car is on its way to the gate before pulling out of his spot.

A red light in the corner of my display flashes, telling me the drone's battery is down to its last two minutes. I let the drone stay where it is for a few more seconds, to make sure Linderhoff keeps heading to the gate, before I hit the recall button. This turns the camera off and diverts all the power to the motor.

I'm sure it's not surprising that I have a few questions.

First and foremost, what the hell did I just witness? Was it an innocent gathering of friends? Or a meeting to discuss plans for more of Linderhoff's criminal activities?

(This brings up a couple of tangential questions. Other than shakedowns, what is Linderhoff into? And why is he shaking down people in the first place?)

By all appearances, the house is now deserted. But does that mean there's no one still inside?

I think it's definitely worth a check. I just have to figure out a way to get onto the property.

The electric fence troubles me. Not that I can't come up with a way to get past it, but that it's there in the first place. Other than Linderhoff and his merry band of thugs, I can't imagine Jenson is a high-crime town.

The tall wall and five electric wires make me think what takes place in that house is not exactly on the up and up. Maybe I'm wrong. I *hope* I am, but I don't think so.

You need to check, Liz whispers.

I grimace but say nothing. I already know I need to check. She didn't need to tell me that.

Which begs the question: If Liz is a part of my subconscious, "she" would have already known I'm planning on paying the house a visit and didn't need to say anything. Does the fact that she did—

I close my eyes and shake my head. Forget that tangent. That's a rabbit hole I'm not even close to being ready to go down.

The drone returns and I catch it before it reaches the ground. I replace the battery and send it back up to make sure all the cars are gone.

They are.

I leave the drone hovering, redon my backpack, and jog though the woods toward the road.

CHAPTER TWENTY-SEVEN

I can see via the drone that the county road is empty for at least a mile in either direction.

To entirely avoid dealing with the wires, I'm hoping I can either climb over or open the gate. The problem is the same one I stated earlier: the potential for cameras. I've already had one near disaster sneaking onto a property tonight. I don't need this to be another.

I start with a thermal shot looking down from fifteen feet above the gate.

There. A hint of heat. It's in one of the first trees on the property side after the gate.

I move the drone sideways down the road, to check areas previously blocked by branches.

The one signature is it.

I take the drone up and fly it past the warm spot, then bring it down through an opening between branches over the driveway. I carefully work it back until it's behind the heat signature.

Yep. A camera, all right.

I search for a Wi-Fi signal but there's none, which means

the camera must be hardwired, making it impossible to hack into from where I am.

I study the camera again. It's in a case about one foot long and four inches wide and is mounted on a metal arm that's bracketed to the tree. The support appears to be designed so that the camera can be tilted, raised, or panned.

This gives me an idea. It may not work, but it's worth a shot.

I move the drone so that it hovers directly above the camera casing, and slowly lower it until its skids touch the box, near the front end. A part of me has been hoping the weight of the drone would be enough to move the camera, but it's not. My plan, however, does not rest on that being the case.

I command the drone to "fly" downward. At first, nothing happens, but then the box begins to tilt. When it finally stops, I move the drone away and turn it so I can get a look at the camera. The angle of the box is almost forty-five degrees from where it was, and definitely no longer pointing at the gate.

I set the drone to hover and stuff my phone back in my pocket.

Along the top of the gate are several metal spikes but they aren't a deterrent, and I'm up and over without a scratch.

Once I'm safely among the trees, I head toward the house. At the same time, I guide the drone above the road, looking for more cameras. There are none until we near the main building, where the drone's lens once more picks up the electronic thermal signatures from earlier. They are identical to the one belonging to the camera near the gate.

I have the drone circle the building again, and determine there are seven cameras—three along the front, one on each end, and two at the back.

Someone is apparently very concerned about potential intruders.

This only makes me want to get a look inside even more.

Unfortunately, I can't use the same trick I did with the gate cam. All these cameras appear to be mounted to fixed arms. But even if they weren't, pushing them with the drone wouldn't be a good idea. One camera "becoming loose" and tilting from its preferred position can be explained away as a naturally occurring annoyance. Two or more having the same problem on the same night? Not so much.

While I consider alternatives, I direct the drone to the two garages and check the surrounding area. I find a single camera sitting across the road, aimed so that it covers the fronts of both buildings. There are no cameras behind the garages, but there are no doors, either.

I head back to the house, stop among the trees, and call Jar.

"I do not have anything for you yet," she says. "I have been busy."

"I'm not calling about that."

"Then what is it?"

"I've run into a little problem." I tell her about the cameras and my desire to get past them.

"The house probably has an alarm on it," she says.

"I agree, and if you can get me past the cameras, I'll be able to get close enough to check for sure."

"What kind of cameras?"

I send her a still image from the drone footage.

"SerDey Secure Tecs," she says. "How many of them are there?"

"Seven on the house. One covering the garages. And one at the main gate."

"I take it these people have money."

"I'm sure they do, but why do you say that?"

"Nine SSTs will run you around two hundred thousand dollars US list. Even with a discount, they would still cost at least one hundred and fifty. Have you been able to hack into their Wi-Fi?"

"They don't seem to have Wi-Fi."

Silence.

"Jar?"

"They are only hardwired?"

"That's what it looks like."

"Do you have wire cutters, a line tap, your laptop, and a cable to connect to it?"

"Um, well, I have my laptop. Though it's in the car."

"Then how do you expect me to take control of the cameras?"

"So you're saying it's not possible."

"No. I am saying it is possible with the right equipment."

"Which I don't have."

"Apparently."

"Okay, thanks anyway."

"You get the right components and I can help."

"I'll see what I can do. Talk to you later."

I hang up.

I was afraid she'd say something like that.

I walk over to the garages, approaching from the backside so I won't be seen by the camera out front. Unlike the house, the garages are built from wood, and are probably a story and a half high. Though there are no doors along the back of either build-ing, there are several windows. Each is about a foot and a half high by three wide, and sit in rows of four on both structures, twelve feet up the wall.

Since there's nothing around I can use to climb up to them, I move the drone so that it's hovering next to the glass of the garage to my right and point its camera inside. There's enough room for at least six cars, though there are only two present, both Lexus sedans. GS F models, just like Linderhoff's. Other than the cars, I see a few boxes but that's about it.

I fly the drone over to the other garage.

Space-wise, it's identical to the first building, but it contains four of the upscale sedans. Though night vision makes it hard to tell, I believe they are all the same dark color, maybe black. Apparently, whatever this place is, it has its own fleet.

Something about the sedan at the far end catches my attention. I scoot the drone along the windows until it's in front of the one closest to the car.

Well.

Well.

Well.

The front passenger side fender and the hood of the vehicle have been removed. The same two car sections the Sacramento crime lab said would've been damaged from the hit-and-run. I pan through the space, looking for the missing pieces, but I can't find them. Without those, I'm left with only circumstantial evidence. The car *could* have hit Marissa, but then again, it could just be coincidence that those two parts were taken off.

I know where my suspicions lie, but before I make a move to do something about it, I must be one hundred percent certain.

I need to get into the garage, but I won't be able to do that without a trip to an electronics store, which, at this late hour, will be closed.

I'll have to come back tomorrow night.

I leave the way I came and am back in Jenson at a quarter after twelve. As much as I want to hop on the interstate and go to the Residence Inn, I drive back to Adam's street. It's with relief that I find the police are gone and the street is quiet.

The tracking app tells me the Camaro is still parked in back, but the lights are out in Adam's apartment, so he's either asleep or he went out without his car. All the other front-facing apartments are dark, too.

I pause on the road and retrieve the booster from my bag. I then pull into the driveway and take it around to the carport. There, I hide the booster in a bush by the back entrance.

Back in my car, I pull up my surveillance app and tap on the line item for the bug I placed on Adam's window.

I subconsciously hold my breath until I receive a message reading CONNECTED and hear someone softly snoring.

The bug is still in place.

In my relief, I feel as if I could just lay my head back and fall asleep.

That would be a supremely bad idea.

I put the car into reverse.

CHAPTER TWENTY-EIGHT

Monday at the diner goes by quickly. We're not super busy, but there's a steady stream of customers from not long after we open until the end of my shift. That's okay. The faster the time goes, the sooner I can get back to my real work.

As soon as I'm off, I head over to my Jenson piece-of-crap motel. I change into a pair of non-diner work clothes I've brought with me. Then, as has become my habit, I mess up my bed and throw one of the towels on the bathroom floor.

After everything's set, I drive to an electronics store in Brighton, where I hunt for items from a list Jar emailed me. In that message, she also wrote she's had no success tracking down a car with the appropriate damage at any body shop in the expanded search zone. This makes me suspect the Lexus with the missing parts even more.

She has, however, found information about the stone house north of Jenson. Apparently, it was built in the late 1800s and served as the Huntington Boarding School for boys from elite San Francisco families. It was founded by a man named Willard Jenson (which answers the riddle I wasn't even trying to solve of whom the town was named after), and was in use as a school until 1951. After that, someone tried operating it as a hotel for about a decade, before it was turned into a vacation home for Langston Heller, one of the very boys who had gone to Huntington. Heller died in 1976, and the property was inherited by his daughter, who passed away in 1995, childless. The place was locked up in probate court until 2003, when the owner was declared to be Heller's nephew, who then promptly sold the place to Yante/Kendall Limited Partnership. They have held on to it ever since.

Jar ran into the same brick wall I did when trying to dig up more info on Yante/Kendall. If Jar can't find something, then likely nothing is there. Which tells both of us Yante/Kendall is a shell company for something or someone.

After I find everything I need at the electronics store, I head to the Residence Inn and collapse on the bed. It's been an exhausting couple of days, and I have a feeling it could be another long night, so I want to catch up on as much sleep as I can now.

When I lift my head off the pillow again, it's nearly 6:30 p.m. I was even more tired than I thought. Forty-five minutes and a long shower later, I make my way to my car.

I've basically been living off fast food for the last week, so I decide to grab dinner at a ramen place in Brighton. The restaurant is located in a large strip mall, anchored by one of those chain drugstores at one end, with a TGI Fridays-type restaurant in a standalone building in the middle.

My ramen's not great, but it's better than another sub sandwich or burrito. (My Yelp review: Brighton is probably not a hotbed of ramen connoisseurs.) As I walk back to my car, I feel the prickling sensation on the back of my shoulders I often get when sensing trouble. The urge to whip around and search for the cause hammers through me, but I don't even twitch.

After a few additional steps, I allow my head to swivel

slightly to the right and focus on my peripheral vision. A man is standing at a car in the next row over, looking in my direction.

No, not just in my direction.

At me.

Because I'm not looking at him straight on, it takes a few moments before I realize it's Raymond Linderhoff. He looks confused. A second later, a woman calls out and he turns away.

I reach the Versa and duck inside before he can look back. Leaving the engine off, I sit in the dark and watch as he walks over to a woman I can now see is his wife, and together they head toward the restaurant in the middle of the lot.

He looks back once before they get there and searches around, trying to figure out where I went. He has the same expression I noticed previously, and I'm pretty sure I know what's confusing him. He recognizes me but can't place from where. It's one of those seeing-someone-out-of-context situations.

I'm happy for that but am annoyed he saw me at all. This could be a problem in the future. Okay, sure, if he sees me at the diner and makes the connection, it's easy to write off that I was out getting something to eat here in Brighton. But this will cement my face in his mind more solidly. And if he sees me somewhere else, say, driving down the street in front of his house or on the road near the old boarding school, he could become more suspicious. He's into some bad stuff, after all. The instinct to watch his back will be strong.

As soon as Linderhoff and his wife enter the restaurant, I leave.

If I was into omens, I might mull over the possibility of calling off my evening plans, but I'm not, so I don't.

It's nearly 9:30 p.m. by the time I park in the same hidden spot near the Yante/Kendall property as before, and make my way back to the fence. The first thing I do is place one of my video bugs in a tree along the road, and aim it so that it can record everything coming in and out of the gate.

Next up, an overhead check of the property via the drone. This reveals eleven cars parked in the area near the stone house.

Huh. I was hoping that since Linderhoff is in Brighton, the place would be empty, but maybe it's better that it's not. I can learn a lot more if I can look inside with people there.

I fly the drone to the gate and take a look at the camera I messed with last night. As I expected, someone has adjusted it back to its normal position. It would have been surprising if no one did. That would have revealed a neglect for security, and that's not the vibe this place gives off.

I land the drone on it again and try to push it down, but the camera barely budges. Whoever fixed it has tightened the fasteners. Wonderful.

I pull the drone back a bit and study the tree branches surrounding the camera. There are a few that, if broken the right way, would fall and obscure the camera's view. But short of my hitting one of them with a lucky shot from my gun, I don't know how I can make that happen.

What I think I can do is to use the drone to temporarily bend one of the branches down to hinder the camera's view and allow me to sneak over the gate unseen.

I do a test run, landing the drone on the narrow, flexible end of the branch and pushing downward. It's a success, sort of. The branch bends far enough, but as soon as it reaches the point of covering the camera, the drone slips off the side and nearly crashes into the ground before I'm able to get it hovering again.

I know where I went wrong, and when I test it again, the branch stays in place until I let the drone rise.

I pull my ski mask over my face, get into position next to the gate, and repeat the branch procedure. As soon as the leaves cover the lens, I hurry over the top, and move along the wall to a spot where I'll be out of view when the branch returns to its normal position.

I recall the drone and move into the woods.

As I near the building, I hear music coming from inside. It's muffled, but I recognize the tune as Justin Timberlake's "Can't Stop the Feeling!" The volume must be cranked if I can hear it from where I am.

I have the drone circle over the main building and the garages. The only human-sized heat signature is mine.

For Jar to assume control of the cameras, I need to tap into a line leading to one of them. The ones on the big house won't work, because to get to any of them, I'd have to travel through their field of view first. But that's not an issue for the camera covering the gate, and the one aimed at the garages.

I choose the latter.

The tree the camera is attached to is some kind of pine. The metal arm that holds the camera is secured at the meeting point of a large branch and the trunk, about fifteen feet up. But I'm interested in the wire, not the camera, and it runs down the south side of the tree, held in place by nailed-in brackets every foot or so. When it reaches the ground, it disappears under the topsoil.

I kneel next to the trunk, remove the tools I need from my backpack, and, using my Bluetooth earbuds, I call Jar.

"You ready?" she asks.

"All set."

"Send me a picture of the wire."

I do so.

"Okay, listen carefully."

Step by step, she walks me through putting a tap on the line. Once it's in place, I attach a cable to it and insert the other end into my laptop.

Jar, who has initiated a satellite link to my computer, takes it from there.

"Interesting," she says after a few minutes.

"What?"

"There are cameras inside the main building, too."

"What do you see?"

"Nothing. All of them are currently off-line, but there is no question that they are there."

"Can you turn them on?"

"Tried that already. No go. The cameras probably need to be manually activated."

That's odd. If the cameras are for security, it would be a huge pain in the ass to go around turning each of them on.

"What about the outside cameras?" I ask.

"They are automated."

"Can you clear me a path to the house?"

"Already done."

"Cool. Which way do I go?"

"Does not matter. I have created loops on all the house feeds."

"Oh. Nice. Thanks."

"You are welcome."

Looping the feeds means she's taken a sample of what each camera has been showing, i.e. shots with no one in them, and set it up so that those snippets would play over and over instead of showing a live shot.

"What about the garage?"

"There, too. The only camera still live is the one at the front gate. When you are ready to leave, I can flip that one off, too."

"Okay. Then I'll—"

"And you can disconnect your laptop. I found another way in."

"What way?"

"The system is connected to a modem. Unless they turn it off, we should be able to get in and out whenever we want. I will email you the link."

Did I mention Jar is very good at what she does?

"Thank you. I owe you."

"Yes. You do. Quite a bit now."

"Dinner's on me next time I see you."

"That will not be enough."

She delivers the line in the same deadpan seriousness with which she says almost everything, so I'm not sure if she's joking or not. I laugh anyway.

"You are going to go inside?" she asks.

"That's the plan."

"Then maybe we should stay connected. In case you need help."

My first impulse is to say, *No, I'll be fine*, but given that I have no idea what I could be walking into, it's not a bad plan. "Yeah, okay. Let's do that."

I cross over to the garage in which I saw the partially disassembled Lexus.

Like its clone, the garage has three doors along the front, each large enough for two vehicles to pass through at the same time. There's also a regular-sized, pedestrian door at the north end. I go to that one and scan for an alarm.

Thankfully, my alarm scanning app also has the ability to hack into most systems and turn them off. Connecting via Bluetooth, I let the app work its magic. After about twenty seconds, the circle in the top part of my screen turns green, and a message pops up reading SYSTEM DISARMED.

I pick the locks—there are two—and soon I'm standing inside the building. Light from tonight's half-moon drifts in through the row of windows along the back, but it's not enough for me to see much of anything. I turn on my phone's flashlight and work my way past a counter in front of a pegboard wall filled with tools, to where the cars are parked. But instead of four, I find only three. The one with the removed parts is gone.

I look at the other vehicles, wondering if the car has been fixed and maybe one of them is it. But while the passenger-side front fenders and the hoods are in good condition, none looks new.

In case there's any doubt, I'm very annoyed.

I know it's unlikely, but I'm hoping the car has been moved only to the other garage. But as I turn to leave, something sticking out of a trash barrel in the corner catches my eye. I pull it out and set it on the counter, the hairs on my arms tingling.

It's a portion of a car's grille. And on one of the cross sections, a chip has broken free, leaving a triangular divot that, if my eyes are not deceiving me, is a perfect match to the piece I found at Marissa's accident scene.

The chip is in my hotel room, so I can't be sure. Yet.

I exit the garage and go over to its twin. After turning off its alarm and picking the locks, I take a quick look inside. The missing car is not here, either.

"Jar?"

"Yes."

"I'm pretty sure the car that hit Marissa was a black Lexus GS F."

"You found it?"

"Not exactly." I tell her about the grille and the chip, then explain the condition of the Lexus I saw last night. "They must have taken it someplace to get the new parts put on. But now that we know the make and model—"

"—I can refine the search," she finishes for me. "What about the damaged fender and hood? Are they there, too?"

"They're not in the garages. If I find them somewhere else, I'll let you know."

I lock up the second garage, reset its alarm, and return to the first. There, I grab the damaged grille section and close up the building.

After leaving the grille in the woods not far from the gate, I head for the big house.

CHAPTER TWENTY-NINE

W hoever's in charge of the music inside the house has eclectic tastes. The smooth, danceable tones of Justin Timberlake have given way to the screeches of Aerosmith's Steven Tyler belting out "Walk This Way."

I approach the building from the west side. The windows on this end are all dark, but the real reason I've chosen this approach is because there's an exterior stairwell that descends belowground. When I reach it, I see that, as I hoped, it descends to a basement door.

I perform an alarm scan. Sure enough, it's wired, but the alarm is off.

I pick the deadbolt first, then the one in the handle.

Before I open it, I pull out my gun, attach the suppressor, and take a deep breath.

Be careful, Liz says. She's been so quiet this evening that I almost jump at the sound of her voice.

"What do you think I'm doing?" I whisper.

"I do not know what you are doing," Jar says.

Oops. "Sorry. Just talking to myself."

"You are doing a lot more of that lately."

Her words catch me off guard. I thought I'd been careful when talking to Liz. Clearly, this is not my first flub.

I grunt noncommittally and push the door inward until it moves beyond the jamb.

Darkness on the other side. Excellent.

I ease the door wider and slip inside. When I close it again, it's as if I've stepped into a pitch-black void.

I pull out my phone and turn on the light.

The space is about five feet wide and maybe an additional foot long. There is nothing in the room but me. On the wall opposite the outside door is another door, but with no apparent locks.

I put my ear against it. Pipe sounds from farther in the house, and a low mechanical hum. I slowly pull the door toward me.

The room beyond is massive compared to the one I'm in, maybe a quarter the size of the whole building. To my right and left, it stretches from the front of the house to the back. Thanks to a few narrow windows, high on both walls, it's not a black box like the first I entered.

I swing my flashlight beam through the space. It looks like I've discovered the guts of the house. A large, ancient furnace takes up one corner, while elsewhere I see an industrial-sized water heater and several other pieces of machinery I can't identify. The space is dusty, and it's obvious no one has been down here in a while.

The way out is hidden behind one of the odd machines, a door that opens onto a long hallway down the center of the basement. There are other doors along the hall. Most open into storage rooms about the size of a standard bedroom, filled with boxes and trunks, all of which look to have been there for years. When I see a box with a label glued to the side reading

STUDENT RECORDS 1921, I revise that estimate to a century.

The two doors that don't open onto storage rooms prove to be entrances to stairwells. One is the door closest to the machine room and the other is the farthest.

When I was outside, the center and east side interior of the house were lit up inside, but the west was completely dark. Because of this, I decide to use the west stairwell.

The steps are dusty and I see no footprints. This reassures me that the likelihood of someone entering the stairs right now is low. But it adds another item to my to-do list. If someone comes in and my shoe prints are all over the steps, the person would know there was an intruder. I'll have to wipe the steps down before I go home. Sure, it's possible someone would wonder why the steps are clean, but it's likelier their condition won't be noticed at all.

The door at the top resists when I push it, and I worry that it's padlocked on the other side. But then, with a whine of wood, it pops open. I grab the doorknob to stop the door from moving, then freeze.

Seconds pass without any sounds of steps heading toward the door. Then a minute. Then two. I don't move until five full minutes have passed without any reaction.

Slowly, I push the door open. A low squeak escapes from the hinges, but it's nothing compared to the earlier pop. When I step out of the stairwell, I find myself in another hallway. Though it parallels the one below, it's much shorter.

I swing my flashlight around. Bare wooden subfloors and walls hung with unpainted drywall. A work in progress.

I head east as far as I can, and along the way I discover rooms that have either been stripped bare or are waiting to be. Those that fall in the second category are rundown monuments of peeling wallpaper, water-stained drapes, and warped floorboards. What's interesting is that whether or not a room appears to be in the middle of renovation, the amount of dust is consistent, suggesting it's been a while since any work has been done.

At the end of the hall, I discover a room at least three times the size of the others. It's also in the middle of a stalled restoration, but it's clear it's seen visitors more recently, as it's being used as a storage area. Stacked at one end are several newer-looking chairs and tables. There are other pieces of furniture, too, and dozens of boxes in neat stacks that have not been there long enough to collect the dust I've seen elsewhere.

There are three doors along the east wall. I study the floor in front of each, and see from the lack of dust at the center doorway that it's the only one getting any use.

I place my ear against it and hear the music again. Something old. I think it's Elton John, but I don't really know the names of his songs. It's coming from farther in the building. I don't pick up any noise that's closer, but I'm concerned if I try to open the door, I'll be walking into an occupied room.

I decide to check the other doors first. The one nearest the front of the house doesn't budge. Not even a little. There's no lock in the handle, so it's secured from the other side. Perhaps even nailed in place.

I try the one closer to the back. Though it opens, it's of no use to me. On the other side is a small closet with no outlet.

For better or worse, the center door is my only choice.

I listen at it again, straining to pick up even the slightest of sounds, but with the exception of the music, it's dead quiet.

It'll be all right, Liz says.

Easy for her to say. What would be nice is if Liz really is a ghost and could pass through the wall and check ahead for me. The smile the thought gives me lasts only for a second. What would be really nice is if Liz wasn't dead at all.

It'll be all right. Open the door.

"Jar," I whisper.

"Still here."

I give her a short version of what I've found so far, and what I'm planning on doing.

"Are you sure that is a good idea?"

"It's the only way I'm going to find out what's going on here."

It'll be all right.

"It'll be all right," I add.

Jar hesitates before saying, "If it sounds like you are getting into trouble, I will call the police."

"Only if I tell you to."

Jar doesn't reply, her silence letting me know she'll be the one who decides whether to call or not.

Open the door. Hurry.

I turn the knob and pull the door open enough to peek at the other side.

The large room before me stretches the width of the building and is probably twenty-five feet across. Wainscoting stained to near black covers the lower half of walls painted a calming tan, and warm light emanates from decorative sconces spread throughout the space.

Near the front windows sits a beautiful, black grand piano, while peppered around the rest of the room are at least two dozen overstuffed leather chairs in groups of two and four, with the occasional one sitting alone. By each chair is an identical wooden table, meant for setting a drink on or a book or an ashtray.

The floor below the tables and chairs is covered by a giant rug that could not have come cheap. But the real focus of the room is a large stone fireplace in the center of the wall across from me. It's nearly tall enough to walk into without bending down. At the moment there is no fire, but the black marks on the firebox speak of some pretty massive blazes in the past.

It's like I'm looking into an entirely different building. I almost expect a pair of men wearing tuxedos and monocles to walk in, carrying whiskey glasses and politely arguing about whether or not we should get involved in the first world war. There's no one present, however.

I slip into the room and, as I turn to quietly close the door, I raise an eyebrow. On this side, the door is located on a section of the wall that has floor-to-ceiling paneling, and when the door is shut, if you don't know it's there, you wouldn't even notice it.

I turn back to the room. When the building was a boarding school, I bet this space served as the dining hall and general meeting room. If I squint in just the right way, I can almost picture the sorting hat assigning students to the various houses.

Liz laughs, and I blink in surprise.

I haven't heard her laugh since...well, since before.

I can feel water building in the corners of my eyes, so I quickly wipe it away. My subconscious is apparently fine with inflicting a little self-torture.

There are exits along the fireplace wall. The largest is a set of double doors down near the front of the building. The main entrance, I assume. The other two are single doors, both located on the section of the wall closest to the back of the house. One is slightly wider than the other, and as I get closer, I see it's built to swing in either direction. Must be the way to the kitchen.

I go to it and inch it inward until I can see the other side. I was right—a prep table, a long professional stove top, and several big stainless steel cabinets. None of it original equipment. There are several pans on the stove, sizzling with whatever's cooking in them, and bins on the prep table where two people in chef outfits are working intently on something hidden from my view.

I let the door close again and move over to the other single door. I pull it open enough to clear the jamb but see nothing except black on the other side.

I ease it out more, thinking it might be a closet, but no. Behind the door is a narrow staircase leading up to the second floor. Another closed door sits at the top.

Hurry.

Liz's command sets me on edge. She's said similar things in the past, and she's always been right to rush me. (It's just a manifestation of my instincts, of course. Right?) What I don't know is if I should take the stairs or the double doors. I'm hoping she'll give me some clue, but she says nothing more.

I decide there's less chance of exposure on the stairs, so I step inside and close the door. As I'm enveloped in darkness, I feel Liz relax. I guess I've made the right decision. With my flashlight guiding me, I attempt to avoid causing potential creaks from the steps by placing my feet at the very edge of each tread, near the walls. This works, for the most part. One or two groan more than I would like, but if anyone hears the noise, I'm hoping it'll sound like the normal creaks of an ancient house.

At the top, I turn off my light and listen.

All is quiet.

I push the door open and step into a long hallway. Like the room below, there are sconces on the walls, only here they are farther apart and not as bright, creating a darker, intimate feel. A carpet runner, in the same expensive style as the big room's rug, travels down the center of the corridor. There are doors on both sides, set about fifteen feet apart from one another, and offset so no room looks into another.

"Are you all right?" Jar asks.

I tap the Bluetooth mic once, letting her know I'm fine but not in a position to talk.

"Copy," she says.

The music is a bit louder now and coming from down the hall, to my left. The unknown DJ has fast-forwarded a couple of decades and is playing "Wanted Dead or Alive" by Bon Jovi. I mean, throwback music is *fine*, but there are plenty of songs a little more current worth playing, aren't there? What happened to the Justin Timberlake? At least that was from this century.

I turn toward the noise and sneak down the hall. The first door I reach is on my right. I listen for any noise, then take a peek inside. All I can see is a short hallway that seems to open into a larger space.

Curious, I step inside. There's a door along the hall to a very nice bathroom, complete with a Jacuzzi tub and a shower. The hallway ends at a bedroom furnished with a king-sized bed, a dresser, a wardrobe, and a lounge, all the pieces looking like they could have come from a high-end hotel room. The bed is stripped so I'm assuming the room isn't being used.

I return to the central corridor and continue toward the music. Every so often, I check another door and find rooms similar to the first.

Is this place some kind of private hotel?

When I reach the midpoint of the building, the wall on my right disappears, and the hall becomes a balcony over the lobby atrium. A pair of wide-arcing stairs lead down to the first floor on either side, and at the front of the building in the center is the double-door main entrance that, until this point, I saw only from the outside.

I hear the low, muffled voices of two men. They seem to be coming from directly under the balcony, out of sight. It's impossible to hear what they're saying due to the music, which is even louder now and also coming up from somewhere below. As I creep across the balcony to the other end where the hallway continues, I realize the sound isn't just coming from below but also from ahead of me.

I'm about to continue onward when I hear a *bong-bong*, like someone double tapping a mid-range note on a xylophone. This is followed by steps in the lobby, headed toward the door. I peer around the corner and see a middle-aged man in a suit approach a table by the door, which has a television monitor and control pad on it. He presses a button and the screen fills with an image. Unfortunately he's in my way so I can't see anything.

He presses another button and there's a second *bong-bong*, this one higher in pitch. He turns off the monitor, walks over to the main door, and stands there. Several seconds later, headlights sweep across the windows on either side of the doorway.

This is apparently what the man has been waiting for. He opens the door and exits.

From outside, I hear a car door open, and then voices. After the vehicle's door closes again, the car moves away. The person who enters the building is not the man from before, however. It's Linderhoff.

I guess dinner with the wife is done.

A moment after he steps inside, a voice to his right calls out, "Raymond!"

He turns and smiles as a portly man enters. Due to my position, I can't see the new man's face.

The two shake hands.

"I was getting worried you weren't going to make it," the man says.

"I wouldn't dream of not being here," Linderhoff replies. He looks past his friend, and when he speaks next, his voice is lower. "Any problems?"

At least, I think that's what he says. I'm straining to hear.

Because the other man is not facing me, I can't tease out his words, but from the way Linderhoff relaxes, I'm guessing the answer is no.

"What about...?" That's all Linderhoff says. The rest is

delivered as an expectant expression, complete with a slight cock of the head.

Again, I can't make out the other man's reply.

Linderhoff claps him on the back, and the two men move in the direction from where the larger man came, leaving the lobby empty.

I pull out one of my audio/video bugs, affix it next to the balcony molding, and aim the camera so it will take in the lobby. It's not like the ant-trap one; it's smaller and easier to miss. Once that's done, I continue down the corridor.

Ahead, it looks as if the hallway dead-ends at a blank wall, but I'm still hearing music from that direction. Several steps farther on, I see it's not really a dead end, but a T intersection with a hall that goes right and left. The music is coming from both directions. I opt for the left branch.

This takes me to the back of the building, then turns and moves along the back wall, in the same direction the longer hall went. There are more doors but I ignore them. The music is so loud here, I want to find the source.

A heavy curtain covers the end of the hall. I pull it out just enough to see what's on the other side. Lo and behold, the curtain hides a doorway, beyond which is another balcony. This one is only three feet wide. It encircles a room nearly as large as the one with the big fireplace. Built into the walls are bookcases that start at the bottom of the first floor and go all the way up to the ceiling of the second. Each shelf is neatly filled with volumes that look as old as the house. To my right, I see that the hallway spur I didn't take also has a curtain-covered balcony entrance.

All this I absorb quickly, filing it away for reference. What catches my main focus—demands it, really—is the long table in the middle of the room on the first floor, with nine men and ten much younger women sitting around it. Everyone is dressed up, the men in expensive-looking suits and the women in seemingly high-priced dresses. On the table in front of them sit plates with the remains of a formal dinner.

The portly man has taken a seat, while Linderhoff is walking around, greeting the guests one by one. His attention is almost exclusively on the men, with the women each getting a smile and a word or two at most.

I'm not sure what's creeping me out more, that there's not a male in the room other than me who's within three decades of the women's ages, or that it all appears very civilized.

A railing goes around the balcony, but the posts are too far apart for me to get too close. I'm prepared, however, for situations such as this. From my backpack, I retrieve a long, gooseneck camera and attach it to my phone. Lying prone, I extend the lens until it lies in the gap between two posts.

I start working my way around the table, taking pictures of everyone, even those I can only see from behind. I'm about three-quarters of the way through when I stop, surprised.

The camera is aimed at the woman sitting next to a thin, silver-haired man. Though she's wearing considerable makeup and her hair is done in a way I've not seen it before, I know her.

It's Fara Nelson. Marissa's best friend.

I finish taking pictures, then very carefully place an audio/video bug along the edge of the balcony before retreating into the hallway. I put Jar on hold and direct the audio from the bug to my Bluetooth earbuds. There's a lot of small conversations, creating a din of voices that I'll need my computer to separate.

I bring up the pictures I've just taken and study them one by one. I recognize two more of the women. I don't know their names, but I'm positive both have come into the diner at least once. They're older than Fara but not by much. Maybe nineteen or twenty.

I also recognize one of the men. At least, I think I do. I was able to get only a partial shot of his face, but I'm ninety-five percent sure it's William Collins, the same guy Linderhoff had Adam and his companions take to the mobile home. He's smiling like the rest and seems to be having a grand old time. I guess he's worked himself back into Linderhoff's good graces.

"Who's ready for dessert?" Linderhoff says, his voice cutting through the music and chatter. "Eric, if you please?"

I switch my phone over to the monitoring screen. Linderhoff is sitting at the exact center on the side of the table facing me. Two men in identical outfits are circling the table, picking up dinner plates and utensils. After the table is cleared, the two return carrying smaller plates of some kind of brightly colored dessert. They serve the women first, all of whom refrain from digging in.

Once the men have their plates, Linderhoff raises a fork and says, "Please, enjoy!"

When they finish, I have a feeling they'll leave the library and either head back to their cars or visit other areas of the house, which will cut off my escape route. I need to leave, but it doesn't mean I can't do a little surveillance prep work on the way.

I switch my connection back to Jar and check my supply of bugs. In addition to a dozen tracking ones that have no use here in the house, I have another dozen of the audio/video variety left, and a few more than that of the strictly audio kind. I place four of the video bugs in the upstairs hallways, then choose three of the hotel-like rooms to receive one each. Next, I put one at the front and one at the back of the fireplace room, and plant audio-only bugs under several of the chairs. I'd really love to cover the library, too, but I'll have to settle for the single bug I attached to the balcony.

As I'm finishing the fireplace room, I hear voices coming

from the other side of the double doors. Dessert is apparently done.

I hurry over to the hidden door, open it, and slip into the unused half of the house, moments before the double doors open and the dinner guests spill in.

I pull two relay boosters out of my backpack and turn them on. I divvy monitoring assignments between them so that they'll have equal loads. It takes me only a few moments to find places to hide them. Now, not only will the video and audio be recorded and stored here in the house, both devices will also upload everything via satellite to a server for safekeeping and remote retrieval.

Theoretically, my work here is done for the night and I should head for the basement stairs. But I'm disturbed by this semi-sealed-off portion of the building. Maybe they're just taking restoration in stages. That's not unheard of. But while they've started some work in this half, I would be surprised if anyone has hammered a nail in any of the walls in over a year.

Money problems? Maybe, but my gut says no.

Maybe they decided they didn't need as much room. Okay, that's possible. But it all just seems...

Like it's staged, Liz says.

Yes. Exactly.

But why?

The obvious answer is so that when someone who doesn't know any better walks through here, they would believe the lie that this portion of the building is under renovation. And lies are ways to cover things up.

Sooooo, what's being covered up?

After walking around for a few minutes, I discover something odd. Along the rear side of the building, there is a walled-off portion of the first floor that doesn't seem to have a way in.

It's as if a whole room has been sealed off. I examine the walls, looking for a hidden door, but find none.

Hmmm.

A little more searching and I discover another staircase, accessed via a door with a sign on it reading DO NOT USE • UNSTABLE. The stairs do look a little rickety, but when I test the first couple of treads, I find they are solid. I decide to take a chance and head up. Not once do I feel like the steps are going to collapse from under me. In fact, they are so solid they don't even squeak.

The second floor, like the first, is in varying early stages of renovation. I make my way to the room directly above the walled-off space. The door is locked. It's the only locked door I've found inside the house.

To be safe, I run an alarm check, and am surprised to find it has its own self-contained system. I trigger the app to disarm it. The process takes considerably longer than usual, but finally I'm notified the alarm has been disengaged.

I pick the lock, but before opening the door, I check along the jamb for any tells that might have been set. Pros in the spy business often attach items like threads or hairs in a way that if a door is opened, the tell would fall away, and the pro, upon returning, would know someone has gone inside. I don't find any tells, so I open the door.

Inside, I find paint cans and rollers and tools and sawhorses and other supplies used for construction. In a way, it's a minia-ture version of Chuck Owens's shop in Brighton. I'm not buying the supply-room motif, though. It's overkill to have an alarm protecting the supplies, especially inside a house that already has a security system, surrounded by a wall topped by electric wires. Besides, if my supposition is true—that the refurbishing work is a lie—then all of the stuff in here must be part of that lie.

I slowly scan the room with my flashlight. Near the back

corner, sitting on a canvas drop cloth, is a wheeled paint spraying machine, the kind used for high-volume jobs. Even ignoring the fact that this section of the house is nowhere near ready to be painted, the size of this machine is much better suited for outside work. So why is it sitting in a second-floor room?

I roll it off the tarp and pull the cloth away from the floor. Though it's hard to see, there's a trapdoor. I find the hidden handle, lift the door, and shine my light into the dark room below. Someone has built a set of steep wooden steps leading down. I also see some boxes in the lower space, along one wall.

I climb down.

The first thing I discover is that the steps can be detached, so that a pair of motors mounted to the lower room's ceiling can lift a platform up to the opening, like an elevator. I swing my light around the room. Along the back wall, the boxes are stacked four high, three rows deep, and six across.

I sweep the light to the right and see more boxes, but when I sweep left, I freeze.

There are more stacks here, too, but instead of boxes they're packages, each about the size of a bed pillow and thoroughly wrapped in packing tape. I've seen packages like these before. Not often, but enough that I'm pretty sure I know what's inside.

I pick up one. The weight is right, and though the tape has stiffened the bundle, it's still a little flexible.

I pull up my right pant leg and pop out my knife from its hidden slot on my prosthetic. There's no way to tell if the packages have some kind of unseen labeling on them, so I need to take extra care. I remove the first three packages from a stack and set the fourth on the floor. With the tip of my knife, I cut a little opening at the corner and tease a bit of what's inside onto the blade, and am unsurprised to see it's white powder. I place a tiny portion on my upper gums.

Yep. It's cocaine, all right.

To borrow my partner's phrase, son of a bitch.

(And, no, I don't do drugs recreationally, but it's important for me to know these kinds of things.)

I work the tape so that it covers the hole and then put everything back the way I found it. There must be over two million dollars in coke sitting in front of me. I guess I now know what Linderhoff is really into.

I glance over at the boxes and wonder what's inside them. I'm tempted to take a look, but I've already spent enough time in the house. I can come back at some point when no one is here.

Before I head up the steps, I take a moment to place one of my few remaining video bugs in the upper corner of the room, from where it can see the entire space.

Back in the room above, I close the trapdoor and return the tarp and paint machine to their previous places. I then make my way out of the building.

When I'm outside but still at the bottom of the basement stairwell, I whisper, "Jar?"

The line is quiet for nearly three seconds, and I wonder if we've been disconnected, but then there's a click. "I am here. Sorry. Was dealing with something. Are you all right?"

"I'm fine. I'm out of the house now."

"Discover anything interesting?"

"You might say that. I've bugged the place, and it should be uploading to the server. Check it out when you get a chance. Right now, I need to confirm that the outside cameras are still looped."

"Hold on." A brief pause. "Yes, but..."

"But what?"

"There are four women in front of the house, smoking." She can see them because she's getting the real live feeds, but anyone checking inside the house would see loops with no one in the shot and wonder what's wrong.

"Can you switch that one back over to live?"

"I can."

"Do it." I climb to the top of the stairwell and quickly make my way to the trees. "I'm clear. Go ahead and switch all the ones at the house back. Just leave the garage looped for now."

"Copy," Jar says.

I circle through the trees until I can see the front of the house. The girls are standing near the top of the steps leading to the doors. Among them is one of the girls I've seen at the diner. The other three I don't know. I mount one of my three remaining video bugs in a tree that has a clear view of the front door, and then I meld back into the woods and hurry over to the garages.

"The garage camera's still looping, yes?" I ask.

"Yeah," Jar says, distracted.

"Are you sure?"

"What? Yes. Still looping. I am looking at some of this video from inside. It looks like a country club."

"Kind of, doesn't it?"

"Do you want me to try to identify some of these people?"

Hell, yes, I do. "That would be great."

"Okay. What is the room that is completely dark?"

She's talking about the room with the coke. "I'll tell you about that later. Right now, I have a few more bugs to place."

I have only one of the video variety left and am unsure if I should put it outside so I can have a view of the whole garage and parking area, or inside the building where the missing Lexus was. I finally decide the wide approach has the better chance of collecting useful information. I mount the bug on a tree right next to the one the security camera is on.

Next, I work my way down to the line of parked cars,

keeping them between me and the house as I place a tracking bug on each vehicle.

When I'm done, I'm left with one tracking bug and three audio bugs. There's nothing I need the former for, but it would be great to get one of the audio bugs inside Linderhoff's car.

His Lexus is parked at the end of the row, closest to the house. I scan it and confirm the alarm is set. With a tap of the button, the Lexus's alarm is deactivated. Another tap and my app runs through a series of combinations until it comes up with the one that unlocks the car, a task that takes less than five seconds.

I affix the bug under his dash and lock the Lexus back up.

As I move around the car, I see more people have come out of the house. I head that way through the trees, for a second shot at photos of the men who were facing away from me in the library.

Three men have come out and two more women, one of which is Fara. She's stopped about three quarters of the way down the steps by the silver-haired man she was sitting next to. He's holding her arm and smiling at her as he speaks. From the way he's swaying, I can tell he's drunk.

When Fara responds, she's also smiling, but in a way that's forced and a little frightened. She's also shaking her head.

A moment later, Linderhoff exits and comes down the stairs with one of the women I've seen at the diner, as well as the portly man from the lobby whose back was to me earlier.

His back isn't to me now, and—holy crap—I recognize him, too.

It's the cop who spoke at the news conference in front of the hospital. Jenson's own chief of police, Norman Sparks. He's dressed like the other men. No uniform tonight.

His presence puts a new spin on things, especially in light of what I found in the walled-off room, but I can't worry about it right now. It's Fara who demands my attention.

She tries to pull her arm away, and I realize she's a little tipsy, too. Silver Hair holds on, and seems to be pleading with her.

Linderhoff and Sparks notice, too, and quickly move over to them, all smiles and laughs. Sparks claps Silver Hair on the back, and his voice carries enough for me to hear. "Matt, come back in. You're going to miss the toast."

As he says this, Linderhoff works his way between Silver Hair and Fara, and takes control of Fara before Silver Hair knows what's happened.

"That's what I was just telling—hey!" Silver Hair realizes he's not holding on to Fara any longer.

"Now, Matt," Sparks says, turning Silver Hair back toward the house. "Why don't you let Ray talk to her? I'm sure he can work things out."

"What's there to work..." The rest of what Silver Hair says is lost to me as Sparks leads him back up the stairs.

In the meantime, Linderhoff has taken Fara to the bottom of the steps and off to the side. He's talking intently to her, and she's crying.

Crap, crap, crap.

I can only guess at what's going on, but I doubt I'm far off. Silver Hair wants her to come back in so he can paw her some more, or worse. I don't know what the deal is with this place yet, or what arrangements the girls have, but when someone says no, it means no. If Linderhoff convinces her to go back inside, I wouldn't have any other choice but to intervene.

Fara keeps shaking her head and mumbling something. Linderhoff, who was leaning down so that his face was level with hers, straightens up, exasperated. He takes a deep breath and turns to look up toward the front door.

"Eric!" he calls.

The man who opened the door when Linderhoff first arrived (the butler? Greeter?) steps outside and heads down the stairs. The two men confer, and then the butler (that's what I'm choosing to call him) hurries back into the house.

Linderhoff waves over the woman from the diner. As soon as she reaches him, he turns back to Fara.

"It's okay," he says just loudly enough for me to hear. "I'm not upset. Eric will see you home. Paige will stay with you until he brings the car over."

"Thank you, Mr. Linderhoff," Fara says, relieved. "I'm so sorry."

"It's all right." He starts to turn away, and stops. "I expect better of you next time."

She nods several times. "Yes, sir. I'll be better. I promise."

He may be hiding it behind his smile, but I can tell he's furious. When he cups a hand around the side of her head, I wonder if he's planning to shove her into the ground. I brace myself, ready to sprint out from the trees, but all he does is softly brush his fingers over her hair a few times before taking the stairs back to the house.

I'm conflicted about what I should do next. Do I go back into the house and make sure none of the other women are subjected to unwanted behavior? Or do I make sure Fara gets home safely?

Fara, Liz whispers.

Sorry, Liz, I need a little more convincing.

I open my monitoring app so I can cycle through the cameras inside and account for each of the women. But right from the start, I'm sidetracked by seeing Linderhoff in the lobby talking intensely with another guest, a distinguished-looking, white-haired man with large, black-framed glasses. I pause long enough to hear a snippet of their conversation.

"—a problem," Linderhoff is saying.

"I can't have him leave unhappy," the guest says.

"He won't. I pro—"

Nate! Liz says.

Right. Sorry. I hurry through the feeds and find all the women. Each one appears pretty cozy with the man she's paired with, and none seem to be in distress. This is not a guarantee the men's handsy-ness is welcomed by all. I'm pretty sure the women are acting, to one extent or another. But given Fara's exit, it should (could? Might?) be just as easy for any of the others to walk out. Or am I trying to talk myself into one way of thinking?

Dammit. What the hell do I do?

Fara.

"Okay," I whisper.

If I'm going to trust anyone, it's going to be Liz.

CHAPTER THIRTY

The moment Eric exits the house again, carrying a bag he didn't have before, is the moment I agree to Liz's suggestion to follow Fara. Which means I need to get a move on.

"Jar, I need the gate cam looped."

"Give me twenty seconds."

"Okay, but no more than that. And as soon as I'm over the gate and out of sight, reset it to normal. There should be a car coming out right after me."

"Copy."

I move quickly through the woods, stopping only long enough to pick up the piece of grille I took from the garage.

When I near the gate, I hear a car engine start in the distance. "How are we looking?"

"It's looped."

I sprint from the trees and scale the gate in record time. After I hit the ground on the other side, I run as fast as I can toward where my car is hidden. "I'm clear."

"Already switched over."

"Thanks. Let me know when the car leaves."

"Copy."

I stay on the road as it's faster than running through the field, but even then, reaching my car in time will be close. The vehicle Fara is in should be nearing the gate at any second, and I'm still a good fifty yards from the Versa.

I hear the gate open just as I turn into the woods. I run up to my car, pull off my backpack, toss it into the passenger seat, and climb in.

"The car is leaving," Jar announces.

"What kind is it?"

"Lexus."

That's what I expected. Probably one of the cars from the garages. "A black GS F?"

"Hold on...a GS F, yes, but gray."

Gray? Linderhoff was the only one driving a gray GS F.

"Thanks, Jar. I can handle things from here."

"Are you sure?"

"Yeah."

"Call if you need me."

"Will do."

I maneuver out of the trees and head down the road toward town. In the distance, I see the taillights of the Lexus. As soon as I'm past the boarding school gate, I press the accelerator to the floor. With one hand on the wheel, I bring up the surveillance app and select the audio bug I put inside Linderhoff's Lexus.

Immediately I hear the low hum of the engine, and some innocuous instrumental pop playing on a radio. There's another noise, too, and it takes me a few seconds to identify it as someone sniffling.

Fara.

"Ma'am, would you like a tissue?" Eric's voice.

Another sniff, then, "Yes, please."

There's movement, and a thank-you from Fara, and the sound of her blowing her nose.

Silence again for several moments. Then Eric says, "I'm not sure it's a good idea for you to go straight home quite yet."

I hear no response from Fara, but I imagine her exchanging glances with Eric in the rearview mirror.

"Until you're feeling a little better, I mean," he says. "You wouldn't want your parents to see you like this, would you?"

"No, I-I guess not."

"What time are they expecting you?"

"Um, eleven."

"Then you have plenty of time. I'll take you someplace where you can compose yourself and change back into your regular clothes. How does that sound?"

A beat. "Where?"

"Mr. Linderhoff has an apartment in town that no one is using. You'll have the place to yourself."

"What about you?"

"I can come in if you like or wait in the car. Whatever you're more comfortable with."

I wait for her to tell him to wait in the car, but all she says is, "Okay."

I grip the steering wheel tighter. A convenient apartment in town? All to herself? I've learned to always assume the worst, and this place sounds like the perfect spot for Linderhoff's employee to punish Fara for her refusal at the house.

I keep a one-hundred-yard buffer between our vehicles—close enough that he can see my headlights now and then, but far enough that he won't grow suspicious. I lose visual contact when we reach Jenson, but I still have him on the tracker.

The building he takes her to is almost in the exact center of town. A satellite image of the area shows me it's one of two dozen connected townhomes. Eric pulls into what I'm guessing is a private garage underneath Linderhoff's unit.

"Here's the key," Eric says. "And here are your clothes." I

hear the sound of something being passed around and guess it's the bag Eric had with him when he left the house. "The door is right there. You'll find a shower in the master bedroom on the top floor. You can leave the dress on the bed. Would you like me to come with you?"

"N-no. It's okay."

Good call.

I hear a car door open and close. After that, the only sound is Eric's breathing, and the same Prozac-laced music.

I drive by the back of the townhouse. The Lexus is indeed parked inside a private garage that has its door closed.

Back on the street, I find an open spot at the curb about half a block away. From here, I can see lights on in the townhouse on both the second and third floors. I send Jar a text with the place's address and ask:

Owner?

Not long after this, I hear a phone ring in the Lexus.

"Eric here," Fara's driver answers. "Yes, sir. She's in the townhouse now.... She was still upset, but more controlled.... I'm sure she will be fine.... Yes, sir. I'll tell her.... Of course. I'll make sure she understands.... Very good, sir. I should be back by eleven thirty at the latest."

There's a muted beep signaling the end of the call.

He must have been talking to Linderhoff.

It's another thirty minutes before I hear a muffled noise, followed by a car door opening again.

"Feeling better, Ms. Nelson?" Eric says.

"I am. Thank you. I-I don't know what happened. I just—"

"I don't think you should worry about any of that." There's a beat here, during which I imagine Eric giving her a reassuring smile. "Why don't we get you home."

"Yes, please."

It takes ten minutes to get from the townhouse to Fara's house. During the drive, I receive a text from Jar.

The townhouse is owned by a company in town called Regent Tax Services, which is owned by L.Y. Beech Corp, which is a shell corporation of MSM-Huntington USA Holdings, whose principal partner is Raymond Linderhoff.

The layers certainly are not surprising, nor is the ultimate owner.

"Thank you," Fara says when the Lexus stops in front of her house.

A door opens.

"Ms. Nelson?"

"Yes?"

"This is for you."

I hear something crinkly.

"But I didn't—"

"But you did. You were there. Remember Mr. Linderhoff's promise—you never have to do anything you don't want to."

"Thank you."

Their conversation all but confirms my suspicion there's some kind of monetary arrangement with the women at the house.

"One more thing," Eric says. "Mr. Linderhoff would like to meet with you as early as possible tomorrow."

"Why?"

"I'm not sure, but my guess is to discuss whether you would like to continue with us or not."

I hear the crinkling noise again. An envelope, I'm guessing, containing several nice, crisp hundred-dollar bills.

"Um, okay. But...but I have school."

"Lunchtime?"

"I guess that would be fine."

"Good. He'll be in touch. Have a good night."

Some movement followed by the door closing. From my position down the block, I see Fara take a few steps toward her house, then turn and watch the car drive away. She continues to stare down the road even after the Lexus's lights have disappeared. Finally, her head slightly bowed, she walks toward her front door.

I wait until she's safely inside before I return to my room at the Residence Inn.

The first thing I do is retrieve the triangular chip I found at Marissa's accident site and compare it to the grille. The color is exactly the same. I place it in the divot and discover the color isn't the only match.

Four things are clear to me now.

First, Linderhoff is definitely tied to Marissa's death. The vehicle responsible is from the garage at the boarding school, a property he is clearly in charge of. If he didn't drive the car himself, he knows who did.

Second, Linderhoff is running drugs out of the former school, and not in the direct-to-consumers way. With the amount of product I saw, he has to be a distributor. It would certainly explain the money for the cars and the boarding school, and even Linderhoff's own home. (What's still a mystery is what he's doing with the rest of the house. Were his guests part of his drug operation? Perhaps, but they didn't seem the type. If there actually is a type.)

Third, when it comes time to bring down the hammer, Chief Sparks's presence at the party means I can't rely on the local police to back me up. I'm sure some or even most of the Jenson police force are on the up and up, but with a boss who appears to be involved in this mess, I can't take the chance of talking to the wrong person.

And fourth, before I do bring down said hammer, I still need the answer to the original question that brought me to Jenson. Precisely who is responsible for Marissa's death?

Before I turn my attention back to Marissa, I call Jar and fill her in on the details of my adventures inside the house, including what I discovered in the secret room. Though she's not necessarily talkative, she gets unusually quiet after I tell her about the drugs.

"What I need you to do is find out everything you can about Linderhoff," I say.

"I will." Her voice is clipped, like she's holding something back.

"Are you okay?"

"I am fine. I am...I will get you everything you need. I promise."

"Thanks."

She hangs up.

There are things I don't know about Jar. She doesn't easily talk about her life. But I can tell something about the drugs has upset her. I guess she's had experience, whether directly or indirectly, in that area. But the what and why, I don't know.

I put those thoughts aside for now and turn my attention to the Marissa front.

Unfortunately, I've gone about as far as I can while operating in a (mostly) passive role. I need to talk to someone. In person.

I need to talk to Fara.

Luckily for me, there is a way I can do that while keeping my anonymity intact.

I call a friend who lives in L.A. Well, technically Santa

Monica, but to all you non-Californians, it's basically the same thing.

"Hello?"

"Hey, Anny. It's Nate."

"Well, well, well. I'm glad to hear you're still alive."

This is her usual response when she hears from me. Sometimes I go months between talking to her. She used to call and leave me messages, but after a few years of dealing with my slow responses, she grew frustrated and now waits for me to ring her.

"It was touch and go there for a while, but I'm still breathing." I have a rotating set of replies I use. This is No. 4 on the hit parade. "How are you?"

"Great, actually. We just got picked up for another season."

Anny works in Hollywood. (I mean in the metaphorical movies/television kind of way, not the actual location. Though I guess sometimes the actual location, too.) For the past couple of years, she's been on staff of a space drama on Netflix.

"That's awesome. Congratulations. When do you go back?"

"We begin prep in November, and start shooting in January."

"You working on anything right now?"

"I'm doing a couple weeks on an indie starting October first. Been pretty quiet otherwise. How have you been?"

"You know me. Keeping busy."

"Seriously, Nate. Are you doing okay?"

Anny knows about Liz. Well, she knows I had a serious relationship that came to a sudden end earlier in the year, and that I was crushed by it. Liz being dead, I never brought up.

"Yeah, I'm okay."

"You sound better."

"Thanks."

"How did that...thing I helped you with go?"

That "thing" was a previous Liz-instigated mission, though Anny doesn't know any details.

"It went great, thanks. That's, um, kind of why I'm calling you now."

I can almost hear her raise an eyebrow. "Am I sensing a job offer?"

"As a matter of fact..."

"Where and when?"

"Up near Sacramento, and tomorrow afternoon would be great."

I've known Anny since before my life took a crazy turn into the world of spies. She was dating someone I knew when I was going to UCLA. After they broke up, I ended up staying closer to her than to him.

And I know you're wondering *didn't he say that he doesn't bring people in to work these hobby cases?* I did, and I stand by that. Anny's not going to work the case. In fact, she won't have any idea what I'm doing. She's a makeup artist, trained in special-effects makeup. She'll merely be providing me with a service.

"I'll arrange for a ticket and text you the info," I say.

"Maybe you should give me a hint of what you're looking for so I bring the right stuff."

CHAPTER THIRTY-ONE

M orning at the Sunny Creek Diner starts busy but tapers off quickly after nine a.m. I spend the time between then and the beginning of the lunch rush refilling salt and pepper shakers, making sure each table has enough sugars—both real and faux—and cleaning the bathrooms. I have to say that last thing is my least favorite ever.

When lunch gets going, I sneak peeks at my phone every now and then, tracking Linderhoff's car. I want to know where he's planning on talking to Fara. If it's close enough, I might be able to feign an emergency and skip out of work for a little while. I'm sure it won't make Donna and Bree happy, but I'm not really here for them, am I?

No, you're not, Liz says.

See?

We get crowded around 11:45, and I no longer have time to check my phone. At 12:05, the door opens with the familiar *ding* of the bell and more people come in. I'm thinking I'll just have to sneak into the back to see what's up on my tracker, when I notice Linderhoff and Fara near the back of the new arrivals.

It's actually not surprising they would come here. It's

lunchtime, and we're the only restaurant that's not a fast-food place within ten minutes of Fara's school.

"I'll be right back," I say to Bree.

"Where are you going?"

"Two minutes, I promise."

I hurry past her into the kitchen before she can say anything else. A few moments later, I'm out the back door and running to my car. From my gear bag, I retrieve a couple of my audio bugs and a signal booster. I turn the booster on and leave it in the car. I'm parked close enough that it should pick up the signals no matter where in the restaurant I put the bugs.

I'm back in the dining room ninety seconds after I left.

I catch Bree's eye and say, "Did you miss me?"

She sneers. "Tables five and fourteen need clearing."

"On it."

Linderhoff and Fara are now second in line to get seated. Meaning I'm in control of which table they get. Table five is along the front windows, near the customer restrooms, while fourteen is in the back corner with no window at all. I know Linderhoff favors tables like five, but I'm betting in this circumstance he'll prefer a little privacy. And the more secure he feels, the more he might talk.

I clean table five first, and as I finish, the group at the front of the line is led over. Table fourteen isn't as messy, so it takes me only a minute to get it ready, and it would have gone even faster if I didn't spend time placing the bugs underneath both sides of the table.

I look over at Christine, who's dealing with the waiting diners, and signal that the table is ready. She points Linderhoff and Fara to it. Surprisingly, Linderhoff does not look pleased. He scans the tables near the window, but none of the diners there are close to being done. With a grimace, he nods and motions for Fara to lead the way.

Over the next forty minutes, I have to fight the continual urge to walk by their table and listen in. Instead, I settle for glances from wherever I happen to be. Each time I look, Linderhoff seems to be the only one doing any talking. Half the time, Fara isn't even looking at him, her gaze instead on the table in front of her.

Right after their food arrives, the table next to them—number thirteen—finishes up. Since we now have more free tables than waiting customers, I can take my time cleaning it off. Unfortunately, either Linderhoff is leery of talking with me nearby or he's famished, because the only thing he says the entire time I'm there is "How's your sandwich?"

To which Fara replies, "It's fine."

More and more tables empty, and I'm kept so busy clearing and cleaning that I'm taken by surprise when I look up and see Linderhoff and Fara walking toward the exit. She looks marginally less introspective than she did when she arrived. I wouldn't say she looks happy, but not as troubled, I guess. It's only by a matter of degrees, but noticeable.

By 1:45, the post-lunch lull has fully set in, and we are slow enough that Bree tells me I can go home.

Home, or at least my hotel room, is not my first destination, however. As I drive out of the lot and head toward the interstate, I play the recording from table fourteen.

"Are you hungry?" Linderhoff asks.

"I guess." Fara's voice is soft, flat, like she's saying something she's expected to say.

The sound of menus opening is followed by about two minutes when neither Linderhoff nor Fara says anything.

The next voice I hear is Donna's. "Good afternoon, Mr. Linderhoff. Are you ready to order?"

"I am. Fara, how about you?"

I don't hear Fara say anything, but she must have nodded because Donna says, "Great. What can I get you?"

"I, um, guess the grilled ham and cheese," Fara says.

"With fries?"

"Yes, please."

"You want something to drink with that?"

"A Coke. Thank you."

"You're welcome. And Mr. Linderhoff?"

"I'd like the roasted chicken and mashed potatoes. And water's fine for me."

"All right, then. I'll get this started."

Silence reigns for several seconds after Donna walks away. Then—

"I guess we should talk about last night," Linderhoff says.

Nothing from Fara.

"I want you to know, you did absolutely the right thing. Like I've told you from the beginning, you never need to do anything you feel uncomfortable with." A long pause. "It would help if you could tell me if it was something your companion did to provoke your reaction?"

No verbal response, but again, from what Linderhoff says next, I'm guessing she shook her head.

"Then something he said?"

Silence.

"If not that, then was it something else about your companion that bothered you?"

"No...I don't know." The words soft, but with more emotion that before.

"Let me ask you this. Are you having second thoughts about your job?"

"I-I-I don't know."

"If you want to stop, you know you can at any time. I can arrange it so you can get your old job back at the drugstore.

The pay will be considerably less, but I don't want you miserable."

"I...I didn't say I wanted to stop. I just...I'm not sure."

"Maybe you'd like some time off. A week or two, for you to think about things?"

"You'd allow that?"

"Of course I would. And if you decide not to come back, then you don't come back."

"A little time off would be great. Thank you, Mr. Linderhoff. I appreciate it." She pauses. "And I am sorry about last night."

"There's nothing to be sorry about."

Donna arrives with Fara's Coke a moment after this. "Your food should be coming up soon."

"Thank you, Donna," Linderhoff says.

When she leaves, I'm expecting Linderhoff and Fara to take up where they left off, but instead Linderhoff starts telling Fara about a trip he and his wife took to San Francisco a few weeks earlier. I'm tempted to scroll forward, but I don't want to miss anything important. Turns out I shouldn't have worried. By the time their food arrives and the two start eating, he's said nothing I need to know about.

Now I do scroll forward until I hear voices again. It's Linderhoff asking Fara about her sandwich. I also hear me in the background, clearing table thirteen.

Another jump ahead. When I stop, Linderhoff says, "I'm glad we did this. How about you?"

"Uh-huh. I mean, yes."

"Let's give it a full two weeks, shall we?"

"Really? Thank you."

"You won't hear from me until then, I promise. But you can always call if you've come to a decision early or want to talk to me about something."

"Okay."

I hear the squeak the booth seats make when someone is scooting across them. Then Linderhoff says, "I don't need to remind you not to say anything to anyone, do I?"

"No, sir."

"And I mean *no one*."

"I know. I won't say a word."

"Good. I would hate for a young life like yours to get ruined before it really has a chance to start." He says this in such a friendly tone that it sounds like a compliment.

I hear them get up and walk away.

I already loathed Linderhoff. Now I abhor him.

When I turn off the playback, I'm ten minutes from Sacramento International Airport.

I check the time. It's 2:25 p.m. Anny should be picking up her bags right about now.

CHAPTER THIRTY-TWO

Three forty p.m., and Anny and I are in the bathroom of my room at the Residence Inn.

Anny's makeup kit sits on the counter. It resembles a fishing tackle box on steroids. She opens it and extends the four layers of trays so she can get at whatever she needs. This is only one of the four pieces of luggage she's brought with her. On the floor next to the bathtub is one of her two carry-on suitcases. It, too, is open, and inside are many clear plastic packages, some with hair in them, some with things I can't identify. Anny's other carry-on and a suit bag are in the bedroom.

As for me, I'm sitting on a chair, facing the mirror.

Anny stands behind me. She's a slight woman, five foot four maybe, and thin as a rail, but it would be a mistake to use her size as a gauge of her character. She's fierce, opinionated, and even bossy when she needs to be. And since she deals with a lot of A-list actors, she often needs to be. She tells me they actually like it, with few exceptions. She's also sweet and kind and one of the most loyal friends anyone could ever ask for. If you need her to do something but you can't tell her why, she'd do it and never ask questions.

Her hair comes down to the middle of her shoulder blades when she wears it ironed out like she does today. I've seen her in cornrows, an afro, and even bald once in college. She describes herself as America personified, white and black and Latina all over, with a little Asian thrown in for luck. To me, she's probably the best friend I have outside the business.

She tugs strands of my hair on either side of my head while looking at my reflection. "When was the last time you got this cut?"

"I don't know. When was the last time you cut it?"

She rolls her eyes. "If I'm the only one cutting your hair, you're going to have to see me more often."

"Deal."

She frowns as she runs her fingers over my scalp. "Let's take care of this mess first."

She snips away until she's happy. I'm happy, too. Like always, she's made me look better than I deserve.

"So, we're going for middle-aged government employee, correct?" she says.

"Yeah."

"DMV or White House staffer?"

"Law enforcement."

"FBI?"

I shrug in a way that tells her that'll work, when in truth she's hit the nail on the head.

"And you need to be able to sell it up close."

"Uh-huh."

"But you don't want to look anything like *you*."

"Not even close."

"How much time do I have?"

"I'd like to be out of here by six thirty."

She looks at her watch. "Two and a half hours?" She shakes

her head and leans down to the carry-on. "Fine. I guess I'll have to make that work."

We spend the first thirty minutes doing what she calls playing. Items come and go from her bag. Some she sets on my face for a minute or two, while others she holds at arm's length in front of me, eyeing the tableau like a painter checking her canvas. She's saved time before she left L.A., by waking early and making a variety of chins and cheeks and noses and brows using molds she already has of my face.

When she finally decides on a look she likes, the real work begins. I probably fall asleep a couple of times during the process, but with all the prodding and poking I'm never under for long. Around five thirty, she takes several wigs from her suitcase and tries them on me. When she decides on a winner, it takes another fifteen minutes for her to properly affix it to my head and make sure none of my own hair is showing.

She takes a step back and gives me a long look. Unfortunately, she's blocking my view of the mirror so I can't see the finished product.

"Well?" I ask.

"Say something law enforcement-y."

"Uh, okay. You have the right to remain silent. Anything you say can and will be used against you in a court of law."

"Remember, you're fifty-plus years old. You've got to roughen up your voice."

I repeat the Miranda rights, with her suggested adjustment.

She smiles. "Okay. I think this might work."

"Might?"

"You be the judge."

She steps to the side.

If I didn't know I'm looking into a mirror, I would think someone else is sitting across from me.

Anny's changed my jawline, my nose, my cheeks, and my

brow. My new face is more oval and older. There's a hint of weariness around my eyes, suggesting someone who's seen almost everything. My new hair is light brown sprinkled with gray on top, and gray sprinkled with light brown on the sides.

I turn left and right, checking my profile. She did a fantastic job. I could be six inches from someone's face and they wouldn't know they're being deceived.

"Wait," Anny says. "One more thing."

She digs into her makeup kit and pulls out two contact lens containers. "Hazel or grayish-blue?"

I look at myself in the mirror again. "Grayish-blue?"

"Correct. That's the right answer. I was testing you."

She puts the contacts in my eyes with the skill of someone who does this on a daily basis. When I look at the mirror again, the illusion is complete.

I am not me.

After I put on the black suit she's brought for me, I am not only not me, but my whole new identity screams federal agent.

Perfect.

"You brought my camera?" I ask.

"Yeah, hold on."

She disappears into the bedroom and comes back with a Polaroid-like camera designed to take passport and other ID pictures. I stand in front of a neutral section of wall and she snaps my photo. Thirty seconds later, we're looking at a typical ID shot.

"You want to take it again?" Anny asks. "Maybe this time with less smile?"

"Hilarious." In the picture, my mouth is a horizontal line, making me look like someone who has better things to do with my time. "This will work just fine."

While Anny cleans up in the bathroom, I'm in the bedroom, cutting the picture to the needed specifications. Once it's ready,

I adhere it to a fake FBI ID card—agent name, Gordon Wallack —and study the results.

Yep. This is going to work just fine. And bonus, we're ahead of my 6:30 deadline.

I give Anny some cash and the keys to the Versa and advise her of the locations for the best places to eat in the area. I then email her the confirmation of the reservation I made for her here at the Residence Inn. How long I'll need her depends a lot on how tonight goes, and since she has nothing scheduled until next week, she's happy to hang out on my dime.

I have her drive me to the Hertz Rental Car office where I've arranged for a government employee-looking sedan. To make sure no one at the office connects us to each other, I ask her to drop me off around the block.

"I'll call you when I get back," I say, grabbing my gear bag off the backseat.

"How long do you think you'll be?"

"A couple hours? Not sure, though. Could be later."

"Maybe I'll catch a movie."

"Good idea."

"Have fun doing...whatever it is you're doing."

CHAPTER THIRTY-THREE

The sedan I'm given is a dark gray, four-door Chevrolet Impala.

The car. The badge. The suit. The makeover. Anyone I come in contact with will think I'm FBI through and through.

I drive off the lot, then stop on a deserted street a few blocks away. There I quickly replace the car's license plates with a set I appropriated off another sedan while I was on my way to the diner that morning. Doing little things like this, to cover my tracks in case I run into problems, is second nature to me.

It's nearing 7:00 p.m. by the time I reach Jenson. According to a conversation on Fara's Hulla-Chat account, she promised to attend a study group that started at 6:00 this evening and is supposed to go to 7:30.

I ping her phone and see it's at the Jenson Public Library.

Good. Fara hasn't left early.

The library is on the northern edge of the old section of town. The central portion is clearly the original building. Its art-deco style hints at Depression-era construction. Branching out from either side is a wing built in a more modern style.

The parking area is on the west side and is about three-quarters full as I enter it. Fara drives an older, light blue Prius, and it doesn't take me long to spot it. I check the license number to be sure, and then park in a spot three cars away, from where I can see everyone entering and exiting the building.

At 7:27 p.m., Fara walks out with two other girls. I hope she's not giving them a ride. That would make things...complicated.

As they enter the parking lot, one of her friends heads off to the left. The other girl continues with Fara until they reach the Prius. They stop and talk for a few moments. When they finish, they hug, and the girl walks over to the Jetta parked next to Fara's vehicle.

I was hoping to approach Fara here in the library parking lot, but if I do that now, her friend will notice and that might affect what Fara tells me. So, I remain in my car and follow her Prius out of the lot.

Based on the direction Fara's headed, I'm pretty sure she's going straight home.

Dammit.

I absolutely do *not* want to involve her family in this. I bet they know nothing about what she's been up to with Linderhoff, which means she'd be even less talkative than she would have been in front of her friend.

But less than a half mile from her house, she pulls into a strip mall, and some of the tension I've been holding on to eases.

There are only a few open spots. She takes the one in front of a karate studio and heads to the 7-Eleven that sits at the other end.

I take the empty spot in front of a dry cleaner and wait in my car until she walks out a few minutes later, carrying a fountain drink and a bag of chips.

Let me stop a moment to say, I know some of you will think what I'm about to do is despicable. I get it. Fara's lost her best friend. She's being threatened by Linderhoff. So I kind of feel the same way about my plan. But the reasons for my actions are good, and I don't just mean solving Marissa's murder and dealing with the drugs issue. I have zero doubt whatever's going on at Linderhoff's party house is very, very bad for Fara, and will only get worse if she isn't freed from it.

I exit the Impala and time my steps so that I reach her car at the same time she does. "Ms. Nelson?"

She jerks to a stop and looks at me in surprise.

"You are Fara Nelson, correct?"

"Who are you?"

I pull out my ID and show it to her. "Agent Wallack. FBI."

"FBI?"

"I'd like to ask you a few questions, if you have a moment."

"About what?"

"Raymond Linderhoff."

Blood drains from her face, and the bag of chips crinkles slightly as her hand shakes. "Why would you...I don't know any...I-I have to go." She turns for the driver's door. "My mom is expecting me."

"We know you were at his property north of town last night. We know you left early. And we also know you met with him today at lunch."

Her car key hovers near the keyhole, shaking but not moving forward.

"You're not in trouble," I say. "But the best way to make sure it stays like that is to talk to me."

"I can't. He'll-he'll—"

"You're worried about Mr. Linderhoff?"

She looks over and then away.

"I promise you, whatever you think Mr. Linderhoff might do to you is not going to happen. We won't let it. Besides, he will never know you talked to me."

She musters up enough willpower to turn back to me. "How can you be sure?"

"Because it's my job to see that nothing happens to you. And I never fail at my job."

I hear something buzz in her pocket.

She curses and pulls out her phone. "Hi, Mom.... Yeah, I'm on my way. I just-I just stopped at 7-Eleven.... Yeah, okay.... No, I'm fine.... I'm sure. I'll see you in a few minutes." She listens for another moment and hangs up. "I really have to go," she says to me. "They're waiting dinner for me."

"Can you get free after?"

"I...don't know."

"Then maybe I should come by your house and talk to you there."

"No!" Her fear meter just blew past its previous high. "I'll meet you."

"What time and where?"

She considers it for a second. "Nine o'clock. There's an Arby's on Catlin Avenue. It's being renovated so it's closed. We can meet behind it."

"Are you sure you don't want somewhere a little more public?"

Her location actually sounds perfect, but she's just met me and shouldn't be planning meetings in quiet, dark places.

Apparently, her fear of Linderhoff is greater than any concerns she might have about me, because she says, "No. The Arby's."

"Okay. But if you're not there by nine, I am coming to your house."

"I'll be there. I promise."

CHAPTER THIRTY-FOUR

She's scared, Liz tells me as Fara drives off.

"Yeah, that was hard to miss."

Save her.

"I'm trying."

CHAPTER THIRTY-FIVE

I'm all dressed up and have about an hour to play with. It would be a shame to waste Anny's good work. I decide to take the fifteen-minute drive back to Brighton and pay a visit to the Larkin Professional Center.

Most of the businesses are either still open or in the process of closing up. I pull into the gap between the middle wing and the last one on the left, and stop near the unit belonging to general contractor Chuck Owens. His newly repainted roll-up door is down, but light is spilling out from under it and the regular door beside it.

I walk over to the smaller door and try the knob. It's unlocked, so I let myself in. The puddle of paint is gone from the floor, but the concrete on which it pooled is now stained blue. The other spray-painted messages on the walls have also been removed.

I hear some noises to the left and step farther into the room. The same man I saw painting over the graffiti on the roll-up door last time I was here is moving some items out of a box and onto one of the shelves.

"Excuse me," I say.

He stops what he's doing and looks over. "I'm sorry. We're closed."

"Are you Charles Owens?"

"I am, but that doesn't change anything. Call me in the morning and make an appointment. I'll be happy to talk to you then."

I hold up my ID. "Gordon Wallack. FBI."

"FBI?" I would say over ninety percent of the time when I introduce myself as an FBI agent, people ask me that exact question.

"I promise I won't be long. I just have a few questions I'm hoping you can help me with."

"Um, sure. Okay."

I walk over.

"Do you mind if I keep working while we talk?" he asks.

"Not at all."

He digs into the box and pulls out a couple of small boxes of screws. "How can I help you?"

"We've had a report that your shop was recently vandalized."

Owens's brow furrows as he places the boxes on a shelf. "Who told you that?"

"Multiple sources. We were told someone spray-painted your door, and that it looked like there was damage inside, too."

He scoffed. "Just a few mischievous kids. They tagged the door and spilled a can of paint. Nothing to get bent out of shape over."

"You didn't report it."

"Wasn't worth my time."

"You say mischievous kids—does that mean you have an idea who did it?"

"No, but who else would it be? It was my mistake, really. The door latch was sticky. I thought the door was closed but I

was wrong. I've fixed it, so there won't be any more problems."
He gives me another look. "Since when is the FBI interested in
petty vandalism?"

"It's part of a larger probe. We've seen some cases in
Nevada, Oregon, and here in California. A place gets tossed, the
owner is extorted for some cash so that it doesn't happen again,
and the group moves on."

Owens forces a smile. "Nothing like that here."

I didn't come here expecting Owens to admit to what
happened or to flip on Linderhoff. I came for two reasons. First,
I wanted to see him up close, get a sense of him. And the sense
I'm picking up is that Owens is a man running scared. Why is
easy to answer. He's somehow involved in Linderhoff's drug
business.

And second, I want him to know the FBI is buzzing around,
so if I do decide to come back and press him, he'd be more likely
to cave. I call this the classic double visit. It's worked for me way
more times than it hasn't.

I stare at him, a hint of a smile on my face, just long enough
to make him more uncomfortable than he already is, then I say,
"I'm glad to hear it. These people can be...nasty."

If he's already troubled, meeting me might trigger him to
reach out. I've seen that happen, too. I give him a business card.
If he calls the number, it'd trigger a relay that will send him to
my phone. My screen will display both his number and a special
message indicating the call is coming in on my FBI line so I'll
know how to answer.

"If you hear of anything you think might help us, don't hesitate to call."

"Sure, sure. I'll keep an eye out."

He's sweating now. A few drops on his forehead. And
there's something in his eyes more than just worry. Hope?

Maybe. But I have little doubt his mind is twisting itself in knots.

"You have a nice evening," I say, and head for the door.

Before I reach the exit, Owens asks, "How long do you expect to be in the area?"

I glance back. "As long as it takes."

His smile slips, as he realizes I know more than I'm letting on. Good. Because I do. Just not as much as I would like.

I'm on the interstate, half a mile from the Jenson exit, when my phone buzzes. A number appears on the screen, and below it: FBI REDIRECT.

Well, that didn't take long.

I don my Bluetooth earbud and answer, "Wallack."

"Hi, um, this is, um, this is Chuck Owens. You were just here at my office?"

"Yes, Mr. Owens. What can I do for you?"

He doesn't respond.

"Mr. Owens?"

"Sorry. Well, um, I may know something that can help you."

"About the vandals?"

"About all of it."

"All of it?"

"I...don't feel comfortable talking about it over the phone. Can you come back?"

There's no way I can go back to Brighton, talk with Owens, and make it to my meeting with Fara on time. And, with apologies to Chuck, Fara is more important to me right now.

"I have something else scheduled," I tell him. "But I should be able to get back there by, say, ten o'clock. Would that work?"

"Yeah, I guess." He doesn't seem happy, but at least he's not saying forget about it. "Ten o'clock."

"Okay. I'll see you then." I hang up.

This night just became even more interesting.

I exit the freeway and pull into a gas station just long enough to text Anny.

You'll definitely want to catch a movie. I'm going to be late.

She sends me the thumbs-up emoji, which probably means she's already sitting in a theater.

On the way to my rendezvous with Fara, I stop to pick up a coffee. I want to get something to eat, too, but I'm worried that putting food anywhere near my mouth might screw up my makeup. As it is, I drink the coffee through a paper straw.

By the time I reach the temporarily shuttered Arby's, it's ten minutes until nine. I park behind the building and call Jar.

"I cannot talk to you right now," she says. "I am doing something for your boss."

"He's not my boss; he's my partner."

"Then I am doing something for your partner, and *he* actually pays me."

"Point taken. But can you at least tell me if you were able to identify the men in the pictures last night?"

"I sent you an email about that." She's annoyed and rightfully so. I haven't checked my email since not long after I woke up this morning.

"Okay, cool. Thanks. What about Linderhoff?"

She hesitates. "He is not a good man."

"Yeah, I already worked that out. I was hoping for a little bit more."

"Later," she says and hangs up.

I chuckle to myself. She obviously loves me.

She does, Liz says.

This stops the laughing. "Don't say that."

Liz remains silent.

I was joking. Jar is like a sister to me. To contemplate a

closer relationship is not something I want to do. And not just with her, with anyone.

Not now. Not tomorrow. Probably not ever again.

Sometimes my subconscious can be cruel, and "Liz's" comment threatens to take my mood on a dramatic dive into the dark. It's where I've spent much of my time since her death. It's been only in the last couple of months that I've been able to (mostly) keep my head above water. I don't want to go back to where I was.

And I don't, but not because of some drastic mental work on my part, but because headlights turn into the Arby's parking lot and moments later Fara's car parks next to mine.

I pull myself together, get out of my car, and walk over to the passenger side of her Prius. When I hear the lock release, I open the door.

"I thought you'd want to do this in your car," Fara says.

"Here is fine."

I want her to be as comfortable as possible and conducting our conversation in familiar surroundings is the best way to achieve that.

I climb in and shut the door.

"Thank you for meeting me again."

"You would have come to my house if I didn't." The fear that gripped her earlier seems to have transitioned into dread-filled resignation.

I respond with a half-smile and a shrug, meant to convey that she's right. The truth is, I wouldn't have knocked on her door. I would have parked across the street, called her cell phone, and told her to look out the window to remind her I *could*.

I'm glad it didn't come to that. I already feel bad enough.

I pull out my phone. "I need to record this. I hope that's okay."

She frowns. "Do you really have to?"

"It's only to make sure I don't misunderstand anything. I promise, it will never be made public."

"Okay. I guess."

I turn on the voice recorder app and set the phone on the dash. "Please state your name."

"Oh, uh, Fara. Fara Nelson."

"Middle name?"

"Madeline."

"And your age?"

"Eighteen."

I cock my head. "You're a senior now, aren't you?"

It's only the first month of the new school year, and for the most part, high school seniors don't start turning eighteen until around January.

She infers the real question I'm asking. "I did third grade twice. I was sick a lot the first time."

"I see. How long have you lived in Jenson?"

"All my life."

"And how long have you known Raymond Linderhoff?"

She shifts uncomfortably. "I don't know. As long as I can remember, I guess."

"You knew him as a child?"

"Probably. I mean, everyone knows who he is."

That's not quite what I asked, but I let it go for now. "Do you know his sons?"

"John and Michael? A little. John more. He graduated last year. Michael graduated when I was a freshman. They were both on the football team, so kind of hard to miss."

"Popular?"

She nods.

"Was it because of them you got to know their father better?"

"What? No. That just...kind of happened."

"Explain to me how that just kind of happened."

She presses back against the driver's door, as far from me as possible. It's the action of someone about to hide something. "I can't remember. It just did."

I watch her, waiting.

After a few moments, she says, "I think it was at the spring fair. At the food tent. He sat down next to me and we started talking."

"Were you alone?"

"Yes," she says too quickly. She wasn't.

"What did you talk about?"

"I don't remember. The fair, probably. Or the food. Or...I don't know."

"Was that when he brought up coming to work for him at the big house outside of town?"

"The Club," she says.

"That's what they call it?"

Another nod. "It's the Huntington Club, but they just call it the Club." She pauses. "Shouldn't you know that already?"

"I never said we didn't. The purpose of this interview is to find out what *you* know."

The Huntington Club. No need to figure out how Linderhoff came up with that.

"So was it at the fair that he brought up working at the Club?"

"No. That was a couple months later. When he called me."

"Called you? You gave him your number?"

"No. But it's a small town. All he had to do was ask around, I guess."

"Did it surprise you he called?"

"Sure."

"What did he say?"

"That he had a job I might be interested in."

I motion for her to continue.

"I...I told him I already had a job at the drugstore. He asked if I liked it, and I said it was okay. He said the job he was talking about was better than okay."

"Is that when he told you what he had in mind?"

"Sort of. He said he could get me a hostess job at a private club." She looks away, embarrassed. "I thought he meant I'd be greeting people. You know, like they do at restaurants."

"But it's not greeting people, is it?"

She shakes her head.

I wait, hoping she'll go on. When she doesn't, I say, "So, you took him up on the offer?"

"I told him I'd try it out. See if I liked it."

"When was this?"

"June. Two weeks after school ended."

"Did your parents know?"

She looks away. "Mr. Linderhoff told me that until I was sure I wanted to stay at the job, we should keep it between ourselves. He said I could tell my parents I was working at his distribution facility in Brighton."

"Distribution facility?"

"For one of those online retailers. I think they just put stuff in boxes. I've never been there, though. Mr. Linderhoff said he'd set it up so if my parents called, someone would confirm I worked for them."

A place like that would be a convenient way to move his drugs around.

"Didn't all this strike you as odd?" I ask.

"A little, but it was exciting, too. It made me feel grown-up, know what I mean?"

"When was your first night of work?"

"The night after he called. Mr. Linderhoff picked me up

near the hospital. Thought it would be easier that way. Then he drove me out to the Club. I had no idea a place like that was out there. It's so big. And inside it looks so...rich. I remember I couldn't stop smiling at the thought I was going to be working there." She takes a moment before going on. "There were three women inside when we arrived. Older women, in their twenties. Mr. Linderhoff said they'd 'show me the ropes.' They took me upstairs to a room filled with beautiful dresses. I spent over an hour trying on different ones. They were all so gorgeous. I felt like a—" She stops herself, embarrassed.

"A princess?" I offer.

"I know it sounds stupid, but yeah. I ended up in this purple and black cocktail dress. It was my favorite, and the other girls said I looked perfect. They took me downstairs into the library."

"The room where you had the dinner last night."

I can tell she's a little freaked out that I know this, but after a beat she says, "Yeah, where we had dinner. Only the table wasn't set up that night. There were couches and chairs. We sat down, and that's when they told me what being a hostess really meant."

She falls silent, but I say nothing. This time she continues without a prompt.

"It wasn't greeting people. Not in the way I was thinking, anyway. A club hostess, um, entertains. We're assigned a club member for the evening, and our job is to make sure that person has a good time."

I hate myself for what I'm about to ask, but I need to know the extent of the club's debauchery. "How good of a time?"

Her eyes widen. "I haven't slept with anyone, if that's what you mean. I would never do that." She looks away. "Some of the girls, I think they might. But not me. No way." She looks at me again. "I'll let them put an arm around me, hold my hand, kiss me on the cheek, but that's it. They know I won't do more. They're told that ahead of time."

"Do they ever push for more?"

A whisper. "Sometimes."

I'm the one who needs a moment now, so I can rein in my anger. "What did you think when they told you what the job really was?"

"I was shocked. But then they told me how much I would make."

"How much?"

"Five hundred dollars a night, plus any tips the members give me. I still wasn't sure, though. That's when the girls said Mr. Linderhoff's rule is that I'd never have to do anything I didn't want to do. They then convinced me to give it a try at least once. There were a few members coming in that evening. A small group. The girls would be there the whole time to make sure I was okay."

"So you tried it."

"Yes."

"And?"

"And I liked it. It was like getting paid to go to a party. The man I was assigned gave me three hundred dollars. That was on top of the five hundred Mr. Linderhoff gave me on the drive back to my car. That was more money than I made in a month at the drugstore."

"And you kept going back."

A nod.

"You've been going since the summer and everything's been fine?"

A tentative nod this time.

"Until last night," I say.

"That was my fault. It was my first night back since..." She falls silent.

"Since Marissa died."

Her brow narrows. "You know about Marissa?"

"I know she was your friend. I know she was killed by a hit-and-run driver less than two weeks ago."

"Yeah." She looks at her lap. "It hit me hard, that's all."

"Why did you go back so soon?"

"I thought I was ready. Mr. Linderhoff promised me double pay if I did."

"Did the member you were assigned get a little friendlier than you wanted?"

"He tried to...touch me." Her hand unconsciously moves to her left breast. "I should have just told him no, and it would have been fine. But..."

"But it pushed you over the edge."

"Yes."

"And now you're taking a couple weeks off."

"I don't think I can ever go back."

There's something she's not telling me, but I have a pretty good idea what it is. As painful as this might be for her, it's time to root it out. "Marissa was with you at the fair when you talked to Mr. Linderhoff, wasn't she?"

Fara, who has been looking down at her hands, rubbing a thumb across her fingertips, freezes.

"When she quit her job at McDonald's this summer, that was because you got her a job at the Club, wasn't it?"

She takes a swallow, but otherwise remains still.

"Is that why she broke up with Luke? He found out and didn't want her going there anymore?"

"He never knew," she whispers.

Another connection snaps into place in my mind, and suddenly almost everything becomes clearer.

"You said Mr. Linderhoff drove you to the Club your first night. Did you drive yourself after that?"

"No. I'm always picked up."

"By Mr. Linderhoff?"

"No. He only did it that one time."

"And the other girls? They're all picked up, too?"

A nod.

"By Adam Nyland, right? Or one of his friends?"

She nods. "Toby and Kirk."

"There's a third guy, too."

She shrugs. "Those are the only ones who drive us."

"Adam usually drove Marissa, didn't he?"

"Every time."

"Were they in a relationship?"

"Like boyfriend and girlfriend? No. Never."

A definitive answer, with no hint of cover-up.

"But Luke thought they were more, didn't he? That's why Marissa broke it off with him."

"He was getting insanely jealous."

"Because he saw her getting rides from Adam?"

"Yeah, that. But Marissa would also sometimes spend time with Adam during the day. I think Luke found out about that, and it sent him over the edge."

"Why was she hanging out with Adam outside of work?"

"She liked him, as a friend, I mean."

"She was helping him, wasn't she? That's why he's going to community college."

"You know about that, too?"

I ignore her question. "Do you think either Luke or Adam was involved in the accident that killed Marissa?"

"No way." From her tone, I can tell she's given this serious thought. "They both cared about her too much."

"You did say Luke was insanely jealous."

"Yeah, but he would never do anything to physically hurt her."

"I've seen jealousy make people do crazy things."

"I'm sure he didn't do it. Besides, he was working when it happened."

Our conversation is getting to her. I want to let her go, but I can't just yet. I open my phone and bring up a photo of the man who was her companion the night before and turn the screen toward her.

"Was this the club member you had problems with last night?"

"Oh, my god. That picture's from *inside*."

"Fara, please."

"Yes. That's him."

"What's his name?"

"Hank."

"Hank what?"

"We aren't given real names. Hank is just a nickname."

"You don't know the names of any of the members?"

"Only Mr. Linderhoff and Chief Sparks. Oh, and Mr. Collins. He's from Jenson, too, and sometimes comes in. But that's it."

"Have you seen any of the other members around town?"

"No."

"Never?"

"Never."

"Do you know what any of them do for a living?"

"They never talk about that stuff, and we're not supposed to ask."

I take a moment, acting like I'm mulling that over, then I say, "You're eighteen but Marissa wasn't. Wasn't that a problem for her working at the Club?"

"Mr. Linderhoff didn't care. He just said if anyone asked, she was to say she was eighteen. I think...I think he kind of liked her."

I'm not surprised by this, but I *am* further infuriated. To put it in Jar's terms, Linderhoff is not a good man.

I keep my feelings from showing on my face, however, and instead smile and say, "Okay. I think that's it for now."

"For now?"

"I may need to talk to you again. I assume you'll be willing to do that?"

"Do I have a choice?"

"Of course you do."

Her expression says she doesn't believe me. "Do you want my cell number?"

"I already have it."

She's not shocked by this. "Then I can go?"

"One last thing. You are not to talk to anyone about our conversation or even the fact that we have talked. I mean your friends, your teachers, your parents, and especially not Mr. Linderhoff."

"Why not?"

"We are at a critical point in our investigation. By telling anyone about our meeting, you could be putting them in grave danger."

"I won't tell anyone. I promise."

"Good. And so that we're clear, lying to the FBI is a crime. If you break your promise, you can be arrested and spend up to five years in jail."

"I swear. I won't. I don't want anyone to know."

I want to reach over and give her arm a reassuring squeeze, but I know it's not the right move. I settle for a kind smile. "You've done the right thing."

"Are you going to arrest them?"

I hold her gaze for a moment before I open the door. "Thank you again for your time."

CHAPTER THIRTY-SIX

I head back to Brighton for my meeting with Chuck Owens, feeling dirty. I'm sure Fara and my conversation hasn't left her feeling great, either, and I doubt she'll be getting much sleep until I finish my mission.

You had no choice, Liz says.

"I know. But it doesn't make me feel any better."

As I exit the interstate and head toward the Larkin Professional Center, I realize I might already have one of the missing pieces to the puzzle. Jar said she sent me an email regarding the IDs of some of the men from the Club. I'm hoping there's a connection between them that will give me an idea what the Club is all about. This may not be the crucial bit of information I need to bring everything down, but you never know how something might help. I'll take a look at Jar's email after my meeting.

It's almost ten p.m. when I pull into the business park. There are only a few units with lights still on. I pull into the lane where Owens's shop is located, and stop behind a pickup truck parked in front of his place that wasn't there before. The vehicle has that beat-up look of a truck that gets a lot of use, and I note a bumper sticker on the back that reads OWENS

CONSTRUCTION with a phone number printed beneath it. Owens either left and came back, or moved his vehicle so he could leave as soon as our meeting finishes. Though I guess one of his employees could have stopped by in the meantime.

The big roll-up door is closed, while the smaller door is propped open a few inches. I can hear music coming from inside, low, maybe jazz or swing. Before I go in, I grab a few of the bugs from my bag. Sure, Owens said he wants to talk to me, but I'm not going to count on him being truthful. Planting a bug that will allow me to eavesdrop on him later is a smart play.

I knock twice on the door and push it open. "Mr. Owens?" I step over the threshold and walk into the room. "It's Agent Wall—"

I spot him at the other end of the room, but he's not going to be telling me anything. He's not going to be telling anyone anything ever again.

Owens is slumped against the wall, his legs stretched out on the floor in front of him. His eyes are half open, staring at me but not seeing me. The cause of death is whatever created the hole in his chest, heart high. It's surrounded by a blood-soaked stain on his shirt.

Crap.

I listen for any noise that indicates I'm not alone in here. A quiet breath, the brush of cloth against cloth, anything. But there's only the music.

A scan of the room reveals no signs of other violence, no overturned furniture, no spilled paint, nothing. There's just the one body against the wall. Everything else looks exactly as it did when I was here earlier.

I don't like this.

Not one bit.

Is it a coincidence Owens was killed right before a planned meeting with me?

Right. Sure. That's it. And there are fairies flying around granting wishes, and leprechauns who will give you their pot of gold if you catch them.

No, of course it's not a coincidence.

Owens called me.

He called me because he had something he wanted to share, something others would rather he didn't. If he was being monitored, and at this point I'm inclined to believe he was, then those doing the monitoring would have known about the call. And they would have done something to keep him quiet.

And just so I'm clear, by *they* I mean Linderhoff and his friends.

If I were them, in addition to silencing Owens, I would want to see who he's meeting with. Which means someone likely watched me walk in. The question is, will he or she let me walk out again and leave? Or does the assassin have orders to terminate me, too?

Whichever the case, I need to assume the plan is not to let me leave alive.

I open my tracking app to see if Adam's Camaro or Linderhoff's Lexus or any of the other cars from the Club are in the vicinity. The Camaro is parked outside a pizza place in Jenson, and all the Lexuses (Lexi?) are at the Club. Except one—a GS F from the Club's fleet that's parked directly behind the building.

Unfortunately for me, my gun is in the bag in the Impala.

I step over to the door and flick the light switch off, plunging the unit into darkness.

If I were the shooter, I'd be set up on the roof across the way, the same roof from where I spied on this place when Adam and his friends were trashing it. If I'm not mistaken, Owens's truck is parked close enough to the building to block at least the bottom quarter of this unit's doorway from the view of anyone over there. Unless that person is standing. But doing that would expose the potential shooter, so whoever's up there is likely keeping a lower profile.

I lie down on the floor and tease the door open half an inch. I'm right about the truck, and the angle, too. Also, I don't see any silhouettes standing on the opposite roof.

I take a deep breath and push the door all the way open. As soon as it's out of my way, I crawl quickly over to the truck. Once there, I head toward the back end in a crouch, and when I reach the rear fender, I sprint across the short gap to the Impala.

The moment I'm shielded by my rental, I hear a muffled bang, followed immediately by the sound of a bullet slamming into the asphalt where I was a second before.

Apparently the answer is yes. Someone has been waiting for me.

I open the Impala's back door and pull out my gear bag. As I do, I glance toward the opposite roof and see a silhouette rising. I move away from the car's door just as a bullet slams through a window on the other side and embeds itself in the rear seat. Good thing I took the optional insurance, though I doubt it was meant to pay for this kind of damage.

I retrieve my gun but don't attach the suppressor because the shooter is far enough away that the device would affect my accuracy. Better to live with whatever problems the noise brings.

I sneak back to the car's open door. The shooter is still standing there, sweeping a gun back and forth. Though I can't see the person's face, the shape is of a man, and a vaguely familiar one at that. It's not Linderhoff. He's got more meat on him than whoever this is.

As much as I'm not a fan of people who shoot at me, I don't want to kill him. That's a promise I made Liz when we started doing these little excursions. I will not kill anyone unless it's absolutely necessary. Granted, this is right on the line of that but hasn't quite fulfilled the criteria.

I aim at the roofline, right below his feet. It'll damage the building but better that than sending an errant bullet flying into the surrounding neighborhood. When I pull the trigger, the shot booms through the interior of the Impala and sails through the previously undamaged window on the driver's side.

The shadow jerks away from the roof's edge and starts running toward the back of the building, where his car is parked.

I jump into the Impala, fire up the engine, and reverse out of the gap. As I clear the building, I glance to the side and see two people peeking out from the next gap down, undoubtedly drawn by the gunfire.

Too bad if either of them takes note of my license number and reports it; it will only lead the police to a dead end. (This is why you put in the prep work, boys and girls. It can save your ass.)

I drop the transmission into drive, race around the end of the last wing, and down the side with the Dumpsters. When I round the back corner of the complex, I'm just in time to see the gray Lexus speeding away at the other end.

Though I can track it on my phone, that won't tell me who's driving the car. And I want to know who that is.

I follow the vehicle onto the main street toward the interstate. If I had the Versa, the Lexus would be long gone already, but in the Impala I'm able to close ground a little. This clearly agitates the shooter, as he suddenly takes a turn into a quiet neighborhood about four blocks before the freeway.

I follow.

Nate, slow down.

I stay on him for a block. Then a block and a half.

Slow down.

I grip the steering wheel, ready to take whatever turn I need to.

Nate.

With a shout of frustration, I let up on the accelerator.

Liz is right. I can't chase the shooter through an area like this. Even though it's late evening, it's still early enough for people to be out and about. The last thing this area needs is another pedestrian killed by a car.

I pull to the curb, give myself a moment to calm down, and send Anny a text.

Still in a movie?

She responds right away.

Nope. Having a drink at Dave and Buster's and watching the Dodgers.

My reply.

I'll be right there.

CHAPTER THIRTY-SEVEN

I don't go inside the restaurant. The less Anny is seen with me—whether in my current guise or not—the better.

While I'm waiting for her to come out, I carefully remove what remains of the two busted windows from their doors. I break off the sections of each that were hit in the (brief) shoot-out and put these pieces in my pocket to throw away later. After that, I dig out the bullet from the back cushion, and make sure the batting looks as undamaged as possible. Then I rip the leather around the entry point so that it's larger and no longer resembles a bullet hole. It's not the way I usually like to return rental cars, but it's better than leaving a trail that might be connected to the events at the Larkin Professional Center.

Anny follows me back to Hertz, which at this hour is closed. I park the Impala on the street a block away, and under the driver's seat, I hide an envelope containing the keys and a thousand dollars from the emergency stash in my gear bag. (Sure, the insurance will take care of the damage. The cash is more of a sorry-for-the-inconvenience tip.)

When we get back to the hotel, Anny helps me take off my makeup.

"Did it work?" she asks, after the last of Agent Wallack is gone.

"Perfectly."

"Glad to hear it. I always want my customers happy."

"I'm very happy. Thank you."

She smiles and washes her hands.

"I'll get you on a noon flight and have a car pick you up at nine a.m.," I say.

"Are you sure you aren't going to need me again?"

"I've kept you here long enough already."

She snorts. "I haven't even been here a day yet. Seriously, if you need me to stay, I've got nothing going on right now."

The truth is, I don't know if I'll need her or not. I know I'm coming to the endgame, but I still haven't figured out what that looks like. "You wouldn't mind? It shouldn't be more than another couple of days at most. And I'll pay you."

"Hell, yes, you'll pay me. And no, I don't mind. I've got my Kindle and a hotel room. What more do I need?"

"Deal, then. And thank you."

After she's gone, I call Hertz and leave a message, letting them know where the car is and where to find the keys. I don't mention the money. I'll let that be a surprise.

I pull out my laptop to check that email from Jar. There's actually more than one from her. I open the oldest first.

It contains information about Yante/Kendall Limited Partnership. As expected, it's a shell company, owned by a corporation that, it turns out, is also a shell. The hopscotching goes on for a bit, but eventually Jar was able to trace bank accounts and transfers to MSM-Huntington USA Holdings, the company where Linderhoff is a principal partner. While this is not unexpected, it's nice to have confirmation.

I open the next email. Embedded in it are six pictures. Three are close-up shots I took of guests at the Club last night, each paired with a more professional shot of that same person.

Under the first set is a paragraph:

EDWARD HAILEY — 64, member of the Nevada senate. Hailey has been involved in Nevada politics for thirty-one years, starting as mayor of Carson City, and working his way up through the state assembly before being elected to the state senate, where he currently serves in a leadership position. He has indicated he plans on running for Nevada's US Senate seat in two years.

Jar has obviously copied and pasted the information from somewhere else. Wikipedia, maybe.

Under the next photo set, the paragraph is similar.

PERRY BRIAN STONE — 61, member of the California State Assembly. Stone was elected to the assembly after serving fourteen years in the US House of Representatives and losing his last reelection bid there. When asked if he plans on trying to get his old seat back in Washington, he responded, "There's plenty for me to do right here in California."

The last set's mini-biography is similar, but different.

DANIEL K. ELLIS — 72, founding partner of Ellis, Gaines & Crandell, Attorneys-at-Law, based in Washington, DC. The firm focuses mainly on lobbying lawmakers on behalf of organizations in the energy and mining industries. In his forty-eight years of practice, Ellis is said to be personally responsible for the election of five senators and thirty-three members of the House. He has argued in front of the US Supreme Court on four occasions, winning three times.

What the hell? These are some pretty high-profile club members. And on the surface, none of them should have anything to do with the drugs I found.

The first one, Hailey, is the man Fara was paired with. And Ellis is the guy I saw in serious conversation with Linderhoff, the one who said, "I can't have him leave unhappy."

Holy crap. Could that be what the Club is all about?

The location is only about forty minutes from a decent-sized airport, which also happens to serve the capital of the most populous state in the nation. If a Club member is in this half of the country, it would be relatively easy to get to.

Politicians and lobbyists and booze and girls. The Club would be a great place to entertain someone you're trying to persuade to a particular point of view. I mean, if the persuadee is into this kind of entertainment.

And Linderhoff has been involved in area politics for years. That could have given him the connections to start a place like this.

Damn.

I'm not completely clear yet how a club like this would tie in with a drug-distribution operation, but it's not hard to imagine them intertwining.

Jar's final email arrived a half hour after I last talked to her. I'm hoping it's the information about Linderhoff, but instead, she's written only three words.

You are famous.

Below this is a website link. I click on it and am presented with a page from the *Jenson Examiner*.

The headline reads:

ALLEGED ATTEMPTED ROBBERY FOILED

And below this, the sub-headline:

NIGHT MAN ESCAPES AS RESIDENTS GIVE CHASE

There's a picture of the two girls I scared when I jumped into their parking area.

Ugh.

I'd rather not read the story, but I know I'd better.

Most of the information comes from either the police or the two girls (named Amanda Hill and Kari Reese); the rest seems to be comprised of guesses on the reporter's part. Though Adam is mentioned, he isn't interviewed. I have a feeling Mr. Linderhoff frowns on having his employees gain too much notoriety.

Like the headline states, my bugging operation has been categorized as an alleged failed robbery. Residents of Jenson are warned to keep their windows and doors locked, and to be on the lookout for a man around five foot ten, a hundred eighty pounds. While the weight is close, as you already know I'm six foot, thank you very much. There's a vague description of my clothes and a mention of the mask, but that's it.

As I'm about to close the message, I realize Jar has added something at the bottom of the article.

Keep up the good work, Night Man.

Did she try to crack a joke? Humor is not her best skill, but I have to give her props for this. I'm not going to tell her that, of course. Just keeping a mental tally of her accomplishments.

I close the message. The article is annoying but it's not going to stop me.

Especially since I need to make one more visit tonight, one that I'm hoping will clear up the few remaining questions I have.

No makeup this time.
Just my mask.
And my gun.
Some rope, too.
And maybe my brass knuckles.

CHAPTER THIRTY-EIGHT

It's 12:30 a.m., and I'm sitting in the Versa at the side of Riegle Road. Half a block away, parked in front of a 7-Eleven, is Adam's Camaro. I watch him through my binoculars, as I nibble at a sandwich.

There are two others in the car with him, his two friends from the mobile home debacle. Not the big guy I sideswiped in the knee, though. I wonder if he's had his surgery yet.

The music's cranked, and they seem to be having a good time. Well, Adam seems subdued, but the other two are laughing and grooving in their seats.

At 12:33, Adam answers the phone on the dash.

Over the audio feed, I hear him say, "Okay.... We're on our way."

After he hangs up, he starts the Camaro and backs out of the space.

I let him get a two-block lead and then follow via the tracker.

He heads in the direction I expected—north, out of town, to the road the Club is located on. I don't follow him all the way to the old boarding school. Instead, I stop next to a used car dealership at the edge of town, on a side street that gives me a nice view of the main road.

Fourteen minutes after Adam and his friends enter Club property, the Camaro is on the move again. Two of the Lexus GS Fs from the garages also leave. When the Camaro passes my position, I see that Adam's two friends have been replaced by a pair of women in the backseat. Next come the Lexuses, each driven by one of the aforementioned friends. They are also chauffeuring women, three each.

This is my cue. Not to follow any of the cars but to head to Adam's neighborhood, where I park around the corner in the same spot as on the night of the foot chase. Though I have my mask, I leave it in my jacket pocket. Even though it's after midnight and the sidewalks are deserted, this is the last neighborhood I need to be seen walking around with it on.

The only light in Adam's building comes from the fixtures above the entrance and those in the lobby. All the apartments are dark. The lobby door does not have a lock, and therefore is noncompliant with the recommendation for the public to secure all dwellings.

Tsk. Tsk.

I cross the silent lobby and take the stairs to the second floor. All is quiet up here, too. Before stepping into the corridor, I don one of my earbuds, and listen in on the audio feed from the bug attached to Adam's window. I have found no evidence that he has a roommate, but one can never be too careful. The apartment is as quiet as a graveyard.

I move to his door, pick the lock, and let myself in. There's enough illumination coming in through the window that I have no trouble moving around. A check of the bedroom and bathroom confirms I'm alone.

On the tracker, the Camaro is headed back to the Club, having delivered its passengers to their homes. Based on my conversation with Fara, and the lack of additional vehicles I saw when I visited the Club, I assume Linderhoff does not like extra cars hanging around the property. To me this means Adam will wait for the other drivers to return and then take them to their homes, or wherever they left their vehicles.

Which gives me more than enough time to conduct a proper search.

First on the list is looking for listening devices. I'm sure Owens was killed because of bugs either on his phone or in his shop. If Linderhoff would stoop to electronically eavesdropping on a client (or whatever Owens was to him), then it's probable he would also bug his employees.

In my bag of tricks, I have a highly sensitive electronics detector. I take it on two circuits of the apartment. On the first pass, it discovers one bug in the living room, one in the kitchen, and two in the bedroom. On my second, another pair in the living room. I remove the batteries from each of the bugs but leave the devices in place.

Now that that's taken care of, I start going through Adam's things.

I was hoping to find something incriminating about his work for Linderhoff, but I have no luck. There's the kind of stuff you'd expect to find in a young guy's place—cupboards with few dishes but well stocked on junk food, a bathroom that needs a good cleaning, and a bedroom where dirty clothes are thrown on a pile near the door and bed-making is a lost art. In the living room, he has both the latest PlayStation and Xbox consoles, which probably means Linderhoff pays him well.

The only thing that might seem out of place (if I didn't know any better) is a desk in his bedroom, covered with text-books and notes. It seems he's been studying for an algebra test.

I know academics haven't been easy for him. Now that the

person who motivated him to go to school is dead, why hasn't he given up? Most others in his position probably would have.

The fact that he still appears determined to succeed stirs a bit of sympathy inside me.

Dammit.

I don't want to feel sympathy for him.

Marissa saw something in him, Liz says. *Give him a chance.*

I frown but say nothing, and then check the tracker.

The Camaro is heading back to town. It won't be long now.

CHAPTER THIRTY-NINE

A key slips into the lock with a metallic *chunk-chunk-chunk.*

When the door opens, light from the public corridor slices into the room. Adam shuffles inside like he's just finished a long day working in the mines. As he closes the door, he flicks the light switch. The lamp in the corner of the room that should have turned on doesn't.

He tries the switch again. When it still doesn't work, he curses under his breath, and heads across the room to the short hallway that connects to the bedroom and bathroom. The light in the latter comes on, and the sound of Adam relieving himself soon follows.

After he finishes his business, he moves to the bedroom. I'm not worried that he won't come out again. I know his type. Something's eating at him, which means he won't be able to sleep right away. He might watch some TV, maybe have one of the beers that his friends probably had to buy for him.

Sure enough, he returns a few minutes later, wearing a loose T-shirt and gym shorts. He flicks the kitchen light switch, and curses again when that doesn't work, either. If he's halfway smart, he'd think it's a fuse. It's not, but that doesn't matter.

He opens the refrigerator, takes one of the waiting beers, and carries it over to the couch.

I'm disappointed in him. He hasn't brought a glass. Beer is much better in a glass. It activates the carbonation and allows the drinker to fully experience the aroma. I guess that's something he'll have to learn with age.

He plops on the sofa, picks up the controller for the PlayStation and the remote for the TV, and pushes the power buttons. Unlike the lights, the machine boots up and the monitor flickers to life.

He chuckles with what I think is relief. He was probably worried they wouldn't work, either. He opens the beer while the PlayStation goes through its start-up process. I use this opportunity to move out from the back side of the beat-up old recliner, where I've been hiding, and sneak over to the back of the couch. I position myself directly behind him.

I hear him take a drink, after which the couch groans as he leans forward to set the can on the coffee table.

I rise slowly to my feet.

He doesn't notice me, not yet. He's focused on the menu screen that's appeared. He moves through the options until he comes to the latest incarnation of *Gods of War* and selects it.

The screen goes dark but it's TV black, so more than enough light is still coming off it for Adam to see his reflection in the screen. And to see mine.

For a whole second, he doesn't react, and then he yelps in surprise as he jumps off the couch and spins around.

"Hello, Adam."

I'm wearing my mask and holding my gun, pointed at his chest. I'm also channeling Christian Bale as Batman, my voice low and gruff.

I know he wants to yell again, but my weapon keeps him quiet.

"I think you should sit back down."

He doesn't move.

"That wasn't a suggestion."

My words finally break his paralysis, but instead of sitting, he says, "What do you want?"

I flick the barrel of the gun from him to the couch and back, and wait for him to get the idea.

After another second, he takes a seat.

"Good."

I move around the couch, my gun on him the whole time. The magazine *is* loaded, but the chamber is not. Again, my do-not-kill rule applies.

I reach down with my empty hand and grab the coffee table, but before I move it, I say, "You might want to grab that beer."

Out of reflex more than anything, he picks up the can. I pull the table out a bit and sit on it. I lock eyes with him, but my mouth remains shut.

After several seconds of this, he says, "I don't have much, but you can take whatever you want."

"Do you think this is a robbery?"

"Isn't it?"

"I don't need your things. What I want is inside your head."

His brow furrows. "What?"

"I've come about Linderhoff."

His panic obviously keeps him from hearing me correctly, because he says, "Why would Mr. Linderhoff send you to talk to me? I've done everything he asks. Everything!"

This is a misunderstanding I can use to my advantage, at least for a little while. "Are you sure about that?"

His eyes move back and forth as he thinks, trying to see if he's forgotten something.

"What about with Collins?" I ask.

"That-that wasn't my fault. We were doing exactly what we were told. Then a guy shows up with a gun. I don't know who he was! He...he must have been waiting there for us."

"So, you didn't see him? You just ran?"

"Um, well, one of us needed to get away. To warn Mr. Linderhoff, if necessary."

"And did you warn Linderhoff?"

This shuts him up again.

"What about Owens?"

He looks confused now. "What about him? Owens paid. I picked up the money myself and dropped it off."

"I'm not talking about the money. I'm asking if you were the one who shot him in the chest a few hours ago?"

He stares at me for a moment. "Mr. Owens is dead?"

Adam's shock is genuine. I had a feeling he wasn't involved in the murder, and now I'm sure.

"How's school going?"

He blinks, the change in subject catching him off guard. Then he realizes that if I work for Linderhoff, I shouldn't know about him going to school.

"I-I can explain," he says. "I was just trying to take some... some classes that might help me with my job."

"Don't lie to me."

"I-I'm not lying."

I smile sympathetically, though I'm not sure how much of it he can see under my mask. "You're going to Sacramento City College. You're taking algebra, English comp, and biology."

Adam looks stricken. He tries to speak but nothing comes out.

"You're going because Marissa Garza believed in you."

"How did you...how *could* you..."

"I need to ask you a question, Adam. And I need you to tell

me the truth. Were you the one who hit Marissa, or did you have anything to do with it?"

"No. No! I would never have done anything to hurt her! She was my friend!" He's furious. Not in the let-me-cover-up-my-guilt-with-bluster kind of way, but in the righteous indignation of someone who can't believe he would ever be asked that question.

I have a feeling if I press him on it, gun or no gun, he would launch himself at me. But there's no need to test my theory. "I believe you."

His nostrils flare as he takes several quick breaths.

After he's calmed down a little, I say, "But I have a feeling you might know who did it."

Anger leaps back into his eyes. "I said I had *nothing* to do with it."

"And I said I believe you. I don't think you were involved at all. But I do think you know something."

He looks away, subconsciously confirming that he does. When his gaze swings back to me, his eyes have hardened. "You don't work for Mr. Linderhoff, do you?"

"I never said I did."

"Who are you?"

"I'm the man pointing a gun at you. And with your help, I'm the man who will make sure Marissa's killer is brought to justice."

"My help?"

"Don't you want whoever murdered her to be punished?"

I can see that he does, but—

"It's impossible."

"Nothing's impossible."

"You don't understand."

"Then help me to."

"I-I can't."

"You're afraid something will happen to you if you say anything."

A pause, then a nod.

"Does that mean you already knew they have your place bugged?"

His eyes widen again. "What?"

Huh. Apparently that's not what it means.

"You've got two bugs in your bedroom, one in the kitchen and three in this room. That lamp there." I nod toward the lamp on the table at the other end of the couch. "Pick it up and look underneath."

Warily, he scoots down to the end of the sofa and picks up the lamp.

"It's that black thing attached right where the power cord disappears inside."

He stares at the bug for a moment before turning to me and whispering, "They can hear us?"

"I wouldn't be talking to you if they could. I removed the batteries."

He reaches for the bug.

"Don't," I say.

He stops and looks back at me.

"You get rid of the bugs and they'll know you're on to them. How do you think they'll react to that? Will they trust you're not saying something they need to know about? Or will they get suspicious and pay you a visit like they did to Owens?"

He pulls his hand back and sets the lamp down.

"Aren't they going to be suspicious if they can't hear anything now?"

"If someone is live monitoring your bugs, which I doubt, they'll just think you haven't come home yet."

He sinks against the couch. "What am I supposed to do?"

"That's up to you."

As he stares at the floor, I'm sure he's thinking he has no good options. But he's wrong. He has an excellent option. He just hasn't realized it yet.

"Tell me about Marissa."

He blinks. "What do you mean?"

"How did you meet her?"

"The first time? I don't know. That was when she was a freshman, I guess." Though he's acting annoyed with the question, I can tell he's relieved by the shift in focus. "I think I had a class with her. Art, or something like that."

"You didn't become friends then?"

"No. We didn't become friends until..."

"Until you started driving her to and from the Club."

"Yeah."

"How did it happen?"

He loses himself in a memory for a moment before saying, "One of the first few times I drove her, she told me she remembered me. I had no idea what she was talking about, but then she mentioned a few things. The class we had together, parties we were both at, people in common we knew. It got to the point where we used to talk the whole trip. I looked forward to the nights she was working."

"And at some point, she convinced you to go back to school?"

"I never specifically told her about all the other things I do for Mr. Linderhoff, but she guessed close enough, and could tell working for him didn't make me happy. I eventually confessed that I wanted to get out but didn't know how. I mean, the money's good, really good. And, well...you know."

I did know. You don't walk out on someone like Linderhoff. That's something Fara would find out in two weeks, if I'm not here to put a stop to things.

"She said that maybe I couldn't leave now, but that I could

prepare for when I finally do," Adam continues. "That's when she suggested I go to college. School's never been my thing, but she persisted, even said she'd help me study, and promised me that I'd pass. One afternoon, when neither of us was busy, she asked me to take her to Sacramento. That's when we went by the school. She convinced me to register on the spot. After classes started, she was true to her word and helped me keep up. Well, until the accident."

I ask my next question in as gentle a voice as I can. "Why didn't you drop out after she died?"

He looks at me as if the answer is obvious. "Because she wanted me to go. If I give up now, that would be betraying her."

Remember what I said about not wanting to feel sympathy for him? Let's forget I ever mentioned it.

"Were you in love with her?"

"Were?" He snorts, water gathering in the corners of his eyes. "I still am. But she just wanted to be friends. And I was okay with that, because I'd rather have had her in my life as a friend than not in my life at all."

"She was special."

"Hell, yeah, she was special. She was making me...better."

I give him a little time to work through his emotions before I ask, "Why did she take a job at the Club?"

"That was Fara's fault. She told her how much fun it was. An ongoing party with free food and drinks, and men who were smart and interesting. Fara even told her that maybe some of the men could help Marissa with recommendation letters for her college applications. It would have been against club rules, but they probably would have. Really, though, it was because of the money. Marissa has...had three brothers and a sister. Her parents do okay, but that's a lot of people to put through college. In a few weeks at the Club, Marissa could make an entire semester's tuition."

I can see it. Practical, kindhearted, helpful Marissa doing what she could to lessen the burden on her parents.

"But didn't it trouble you that she was working there?"

"Sure. I mean, not at first. I didn't think about it then. But the more that I got to know her, definitely."

"She was underage."

"I know. But she said she wasn't doing anything bad. Just talking. No sex stuff."

"Some of the girls do sex stuff, though, right?"

Another snort. "Most of them."

"Weren't you worried that she'd eventually be forced to do that, too?"

"Of course I was. I told her they were stringing her along until she was out of high school, and then they'd start pressuring her."

"How would they do that?"

"First it would be offering more money and telling her that all the girls were doing it."

"What about peer pressure from them? The girls, I mean."

"Not that much. The girls will say things when they're told to, but most of them don't like doing it. Mr. Linderhoff would rather those girls say nothing than give half-hearted encouragement."

"Okay, so if neither of those things worked, what would Mr. Linderhoff have done next?"

"Threaten to tell her parents and friends that she'd already been having sex for money. Back it up with pictures from the Club. Photos of her partying, then close-ups of other girls having sex that could be passed off as her."

The shame route. Not something a lot of eighteen-year-olds would be strong enough to fight.

"What about Fara? She's eighteen already. Is she getting pressured?"

"A little, but it's tricky. Bad PR if word gets out that one of the Club's full-service hostesses is in high school."

What Adam doesn't have to say is that if nothing changes, the full press would come soon enough, and my sense of Fara is that she wouldn't be able to fight it for long. More reason to make sure she never has to deal with that.

"What did Marissa say after you told her about the pressure?"

"I don't think she believed me at first. But the more nights she worked, the more she started to see I was right. That's why she finally told Mr. Linderhoff she wanted to quit."

"Wait. She told him she was quitting? I can't imagine he's the kind of person who would be happy about that."

"He's not. He told her to take some time off to reconsider. Marissa was tougher than people realized, and she was having none of it. She told him she didn't need to reconsider, and if he was going to give her problems, she would be happy to go to the *Jenson Examiner* and tell them all about the Club."

Oh, damn.

"Then she quit?" I ask.

A nod.

"She texted me right away to come get her and take her home."

"When was this?"

He hesitates. "Two nights before she was hit by the car."

I lean back.

I now know the means (the Lexus), the motive (to keep Marissa from talking to the wrong people), and the opportunity (Marissa walking alone on a quiet street). The only thing I don't know is who was behind the wheel.

Adam's head hangs down, his forehead cradled in his hands.

"Adam?"

For a moment he says nothing, then, "What?"

"You saw the damaged Lexus in the garage, didn't you?"

He doesn't respond, which is the same as a yes.

"Did you see who was driving it?"

He shakes his head. "I wish. There was no event that night so I wasn't working. But I was the next night. I didn't want to go in, but Mr. Linderhoff said I had to. Where I really wanted to be was at the hospital with Marissa. Her family would have never let me see her, but I didn't care. I would have sat in the lobby." He pauses. "Mr. Linderhoff had me, Toby, and Kirk come to the Club early, then he took us into the garage and showed us the car. Said we had to remove the hood and fender."

"*You* removed them?"

"I didn't have any choice."

"Did you realize then what had caused the damage?"

"I didn't want to believe it, but it was hard not to think about the accident. It was less than twenty-four hours after."

"What did Linderhoff say had happened?"

"That a Club member was using the car and hit a deer. If that were true, though, there would have been a lot more damage."

"You didn't say that to him?"

"No way. I'm not crazy. If he knew I'd made the connection and thought I might say something, he would have had me killed. For real."

"Has he had others killed?"

"I've never witnessed it, but some of the guys who've been there longer have told stories. And now I guess there's Mr. Owens."

"Tell me about Owens. What was his connection to Linderhoff?"

"That's not my business. I just do what I'm told."

"Adam, you've been doing so well. Don't blow it now. I

know about the secret room in the Club. The one with all the drugs in it. Did Owens have something to do with that?"

Adam looks nervous again. "Um, okay, yeah. I'm pretty sure he was a dealer. But I don't have anything to do with the drugs. I just deal with Club business."

I raise an eyebrow and try not to laugh. "*You* don't have anything to do with the drug business?"

He shakes his head.

"So vandalizing Owens's business and then picking up money from him had nothing to do with the drugs?"

Adam's shoulders droop, as whatever fantasy he's been holding on to fades. "I-I didn't want to work on anything to do with that side of the business, but when Mr. Linderhoff tells you to do something, you do it."

"How long has he been telling you to do stuff for that 'side of the business'?"

Adam looks like he almost wants to cry. "Too long."

I'm reminded of Al Pacino in *Godfather III*. All Adam wants is to get out, but he keeps getting pulled back in.

"I need to know all you know about the drugs. Where and who he gets them from. Who he distributes them to. How wide his network stretches. How long he's been doing this."

"I wasn't lying. I really don't know much."

Technically, he intimated he knew nothing, but I'm not going to call him on it.

"Then tell me what you do know."

For the next several minutes, Adam does just that. He has no idea how long Linderhoff has been at it. The operation was well established when Adam was hired, and he's pretty sure Linderhoff distributes to dealers over much of the northern half of the state and into Nevada. He honestly doesn't know where the drugs come from. When I ask him about the money he "deposited" at the Jenson National Bank, he tells me Linderhoff is chairman of the bank's board of directors, and that the bank president is "his man."

When I ask what the president's name is, he looks at me as though I should already know. "It's Mr. Collins."

"Then why did Mr. Linderhoff have you and the other guys take Mr. Collins out to that old mobile home?"

"I don't know for sure, but I think it had something to do with things at the bank."

Skimming, maybe? Who knows. The actual reason is not really important. But now I understand how Collins fits into the puzzle, *and* why no information needed to be on the envelope Adam dropped into the night deposit box.

"Do the members who come to the Club have anything to do with the drugs?"

"I don't think so. It's usually just a bunch of old guys, excited to party and get laid."

I'm almost at the end of my questions, but there is one other thing he can shed some light on.

"There are cameras at the Club, some on the building, one outside the garages. You know about those?"

"Sure."

"Are the feeds recorded?"

"Yeah. I think so."

Though Jar was able to gain control of the cameras and thus access the live footage, she's been unable to break through to wherever the feeds are stored.

"Where do they keep the footage?"

"There's a room upstairs, near the library balcony. All the equipment's in there."

That would be one of the rooms after the central corridor splits into two sections. The ones I wasn't able to check.

"Can you get into it?"

"It's locked. But...but I know where a key is."

I get up and push the table back into place. I have a pair of plans in my head. It's up to Adam which will be the winner.

"This is your lucky day," I say. "You get to choose your fate. Do you want to be a hero, or do you want to go down with the rest of them?"

"What do you mean?"

"I'm going to put Linderhoff and his Club out of business. It'll be a lot better for you if you help me."

"And if I don't?"

I almost respond, *You're going to have to take those college courses from a prison cell*, but Liz stops me and silently guides me to a more effective answer.

"What would Marissa want you to do?"

CHAPTER FORTY

A dam and I talk for another forty-five minutes, during which I lay out exactly what I expect of him. When we're done, I send him into the building's central corridor and then replace the batteries in Linderhoff's bugs.

After I finish, I send Adam a text.

Now

Like we discussed, he unlocks the door and opens it as if he's just coming home. Before he shuts it again, I slip out. Hopefully, Linderhoff won't be suspicious of what took Adam so long to get home. The only potential hang-up is that there's probably a bug in the Camaro, too. (You know, other than mine.) I've told Adam that if he's asked, he should say he stopped by a friend's apartment before coming home.

But I doubt Linderhoff is monitoring the feeds. My guess is he records everything, and then checks particular files if something comes up that causes him concern.

As I drive back to my hotel, Liz says, *He'll be fine. You can trust him.*

She's reading my mind again. Though I'm sure Adam was sincere when he agreed to help me, I'm concerned he'll lose his nerve, and maybe even tell Linderhoff.

"I hope you're right," I say.

I am.

Please let her be right.

CHAPTER FORTY-ONE

I sleep a total of two and a half hours, and am in my car at 4:00 a.m., heading south on the interstate. Last night, after I talked to Adam, I contacted my supplier in Sacramento with a special request. It's costing me extra because of the rush, but she assured me it would be ready for pickup by 5:00 a.m.

Since the Y doesn't open until 5:30, I have been given an alternate location. I find my package in the back of an unoccupied van, parked in an otherwise empty lot surrounding the In-N-Out Burger on East Commerce Way.

It's a cardboard box, with the Johnny Walker logo on both sides. I test the top to make sure it's glued in place, and then transfer the box to my car. It has the weight and feel of being filled with bottles, minus the clinking of glass, and with the sealed top should pass for what it's pretending to be.

I'm on the road again a few minutes after five. There are plenty of cars on the interstate, but almost all are going the other way on their morning commutes, and I'm able to get back to Jenson by 5:27 a.m. This leaves me thirty-three minutes until my shift at the diner begins.

Before I go there, I return to Adam's street and pull back

into his parking area. The building is still quiet, and no lights are on in any of the back-facing windows. As quickly as I can, I transfer the box into the trunk of the Camaro. This involves deactivating its car alarm and picking the trunk lock, but that's child's play at this point.

I arrive at the Sunny Creek Diner with ten minutes to spare, keeping my on-time record intact.

I muddle through the morning, cleaning tables on autopilot.

Linderhoff doesn't come in for breakfast, but that's what I expected. From what I now know of the Club's schedule and what I've seen here at the diner, he comes in only on days when there'll be a gathering that night. Per Adam, there is no event this evening.

Lunch is its usual tornado of near chaos, but by 1:40 the wave of diners has subsided, and by 2:00, I'm cut free for another day.

I'm anxious to get back to the Residence Inn, where I have a lot of prep work waiting for me, but in what has become my ritual, I have to do something first.

I told Adam I would meet him here at 4:00 p.m. It's a rendezvous I have no intention of keeping. If he's smart, he'll plan on coming early so he can see me arrive and find out what kind of car I drive, maybe even get a look at my face. So far, he's seen me only in my mask and that's the way I want to keep it. But there is something I need to give him.

Sure, I could have left it in his trunk with the box, but he doesn't know about the box yet. Even more than that, the meeting-that-won't-be-a-meeting will provide an opportunity to reinforce in him why he's helping me out.

And (say it with me) I don't pass up on opportunities.

I drive to the cemetery on the east side of town. Ironically, or perhaps not, it's only a few blocks from the hospital, though there are enough trees between them that you can't see one from the other.

Marissa's grave is easy to pick out. It's the one with the fresh mound of dirt on top. It's also the grave with the most flowers.

There's a pine tree at the edge of the section in which she's located. After making sure no one else is around, I wedge an envelope into the crook of one of the branches. I take a couple of steps back to scrutinize my handiwork, and am satisfied no one will see the envelope unless they go searching for it.

When I'm back at the Residence Inn, I send Adam a message, telling him I can't make four o'clock, but that I've left the items we discussed in the tree at the cemetery, and give him directions for exactly where to find the envelope. I also tell him to let me know when he has it.

Next, I pay a visit to Anny in her room. When I finish telling her what I'd like her to do, she asks, "Normally, you wouldn't pay for something like this, but I have a feeling in this case it would be better if you did."

"Okay. Does a thousand sound right?"

She laughs. "Oh, Nate, sweetie. Up here, I think a thousand might sound suspicious. Why don't I say five hundred? That's still a lot, but more believable."

"You're the expert."

"That, I am."

I mention one other thing I'd like her to do when she's out. "If you can't find them anywhere, don't worry about it."

"Okay."

I give her five hundred dollars, plus another five hundred for expenses, then arrange for a rental car to be delivered to the hotel right away. As soon as it arrives, I help her take her makeup gear out to her car.

Back in my room, I slam a couple of Red Bulls before I check my email, still expecting that message from Jar about her research into Linderhoff, but once again, it's not there. The last time we talked, she gave me the impression she had information on him she wanted to share, but that was yesterday. Between my stint as an FBI agent, finding Owens and getting shot at, my late-night chat with Adam, and the morning at the diner, I've been too busy to follow up.

It's time to give her a call.

"H-hello?"

Whoa. I think this is the first time I've ever called her and she sounds sleepy.

"Did I wake you?"

"Yes, you did."

"Sorry. Should I call back later?"

"I am awake now. What do you want?"

"I was hoping you'd tell me what you learned about Linderhoff."

"I sent you an email."

"No, you didn't."

"Yes, I did."

"No, you didn't."

"One moment."

I hear her moving around, then the sound of a keyboard clacking. This is followed by a string of words muttered in Thai. I don't know their exact meaning, but the tone is not a happy one.

"My apologies," she says. "I thought I had sent it before I went to sleep." Another clack. "There, it is on its way to you."

"Can you give me the highlights?"

"He is not a good man."

"I believe you've mentioned that before."

"Raymond Linderhoff is not his real name."

"Is that so?" I didn't expect that.

"Yes."

"What's his real name?"

"Ramon Bishop. He grew up in Florida, just outside Miami, where he got involved with the Avila drug cartel when he was still a teenager. They sent him to University of Miami and then law school at Rutgers University. That is in New Jer—"

"I know where Rutgers is. They must have been grooming him."

"Correct. My sources say that after he finished school, he took a job with the US Attorney's office in Miami, where he could feed information to his real employers. After doing that successfully for five years, he resigned, claiming he was going into private practice. And he disappeared from the Miami scene. My sources are not sure what happened after that."

"When did he disappear?"

"Twenty-six years ago."

Jar's contacts might not have known what happened to Bishop/Linderhoff, but it's not that hard to guess.

Linderhoff was probably offered the opportunity to start a "branch" office for the cartel in California. The business here took off, giving Linderhoff and his associates more money than they knew what to do with. Having already had a taste of politics from his time in the US Attorney's office, it was probably Linderhoff's idea to buy the boarding school property and turn it into a club, where the cartel could influence policy across the nation and gain valuable allies in high offices. The cartel's drugs pay for the Club, and the Club ensures there will be government officials to help the cartel when needed.

"You're right," I say. "He is not a good man."

"That is why I said that."

I smile to myself, and then go over my plan and how she will fit in.

"Are you sure you gave Adam the right things?"

"Yeah, as long as it's the same stuff from the list you gave me before."

"It should be."

"Then we're all set. I'll call you again in a few hours."

After we hang up, I start going through the hours of video and audio I've been recording from the Club and inside Linderhoff's car. I watch and listen at double speed but it's still a slog, and I've barely scratched the surface when Adam texts me back.

I have it.

I tap out a reply.

Good. Any questions?

Adam:

I don't think so. Looks easy enough.

Me:

You still okay to do this?

Adam:

Yeah.

Me:

There's one more thing I need you to do.
In the trunk of your car, you'll find a box.

Adam:

How did it get there?

Me:

Adam. Focus.

Adam:

What do you want me to do with it?

I tell him, and after a little more back and forth, he agrees.
Me:

Everything's going to be fine.
Remember, I'll be watching.

He responds:

Okay.

His lack of enthusiasm starts me worrying again. I expect
Liz to swoop in and remind me that I need to trust him, but she
remains silent. I decide to take the fact she's also not raising a
warning flag that things are still on track.

I should probably see someone about this, shouldn't I?
About Liz, I mean.

Crap.

Maybe.

I don't know.

My fear is that if I do, her voice would go away and never
come back. I don't think I'm okay with that yet.

Hours pass with me scrubbing through one feed after
another. The bugs have recorded some really juicy stuff. We're

talking career-ending conversations between politicians and lobbyists, not to mention video of the men—most of whom I'm betting are married—hanging on the women, whispering in their ears, and, in several cases, entering upstairs bedrooms with looks of excitement. I've also caught a handful of private moments between Linderhoff and the lobbyist Daniel Ellis in which they discuss the needs of certain guests, in disgusting detail.

From Linderhoff's car, I've captured several phone conversations, and while he and the people he talks to use coded language, it's not hard to figure out they're talking about moving, buying, and selling drugs. Big quantities. Which probably means Linderhoff is one of the biggest suppliers in all of Northern California.

Each one of these nuggets I copy and put in a single file I call The Good Stuff.

When my phone vibrates I look up, and for the first time realize the room around me has gone dark. The ID reads ANNY and indicates it's a video call. I put in my earbuds and hit ACCEPT.

"Hey," I say.

Anny's also wearing earbuds. "Hey, yourself. You look tired."

"Too much staring at a monitor."

"Have you been at it since I left?"

"Pretty much."

"I'll bring you up some artificial tears when I get back. You're going to need them."

I'd tell her not to bother, but I can feel the eyestrain. "Thanks. How are things going on your end?"

"I found a model."

"Excellent. Are you happy with her?"

"See for yourself."

The camera shifts from Anny to a woman sitting in a chair who looks the spitting image of Marissa.

"Please tell me she can't see me," I say.

"Nope. Just me."

"She looks exactly like her."

"I know, right?"

"Did you have to do much?"

The camera switches back to Anny, who's sneering. "I'm going to take that as a compliment of my work. Here, see for yourself."

A message appears, telling me Anny's camera is temporarily off-line. A couple of seconds later, my phone vibrates with the arrival of a text. I open it up and there's a picture of the model standing outside a shopping mall. Though she looks a lot like Marissa, she doesn't look exactly like her.

I switch back to the video call.

"Well?" Anny asks.

"You are a master craftswoman."

"That's more like it."

"Have you recorded her yet?"

"I wanted to make sure you were happy first."

"I'm happy."

"What about the dress?"

She shows me the model again.

"Wasn't Marissa wearing that same dress in one of the photos I gave you?" I ask.

The image returns to Anny. "As a matter of fact, she was. It's from Forever 21. I thought I recognized it when I first saw the picture."

"It's all perfect. Go ahead and record."

"I'll send it to you as soon as we're done. Want to make sure we're getting the right tone."

"Perfect."

Okay, so I've sort of, kind of, a little bit broken my rule about not bringing anyone in to help me. I'm not talking about the model. I mean Anny. In order to pull off what I needed her to do, I had to give her a little information about what I'm up to. Don't go thinking I laid it all out for her. I merely told her I've been hired to investigate the death of a girl, and that the video would help me root out those responsible. Anny wasn't surprised I'm involved in something like that. Apparently she's already decided I'm some kind of part-time detective. I'm not sure I like her thinking that. It's a little too close to the truth. But if I'm going to trust anyone outside the world of my day job, it's going to be Anny.

This afternoon she went into Sacramento, rented a meeting room in a hotel, and then headed over to one of the malls. There she played the part of a casting agent looking for the right teenage girl for a role in an upcoming indie film. I prepared a script for the aspiring actress to read, the video of which Anny will soon be sending to me, the "director" who couldn't make the trip north.

Anny texts me the clip ten minutes later. I watch it, and am chilled by how much it seems like Marissa. My only complaint is the voice is damn close but not exactly a match. That could be a problem. Thankfully, I know a solution.

I call Anny. "The read is great, and the look perfect. But I want you to do it one more time. On this take, make her sound a little more upset and angry."

"You want her defiant and a little emotional, but not too much."

"Exactly. You know, you should work in movies."

"Smart-ass."

She hangs up, and several minutes later, another video arrives.

After I watch it, I call Anny again. "Pay her and send her on her way."

"You like it?"

"It's better than I even hoped."

"Glad to hear it. Oh, I also found those other things you wanted. I'll drop them by later."

"If I'm not here, just slip them under the door."

"Tired of hanging around with me already?"

"Ha. No. Just busy."

"Good answer. Anything else you need from me?"

"That's it. You're done, too. I'll get you on a morning flight, and arrange for a car to take you to the airport."

"Not too early."

"Not too early."

"Drinks when you get back to town? Unless you think you'll be too busy then, too."

"For you, I'll make time."

"I'll believe it when I see it."

After I arrange Anny's transportation and email her the info, I load the video she shot into Final Cut, my video editing software. It looks pretty raw already, as I requested that Anny not use any extra lighting, but I can do a few things to enhance the unprofessional feel even more. Plus, I need to make some strategic cuts.

I insert half a second of black at the head, and then set to work editing the rest. When I'm happy with it, I send the final video to my phone, where it will stay untouched until I need it.

I check the time—8:42 p.m.

Dammit, it's even later than I thought.

My tracker indicates Adam's Camaro is already at the Club.

I bring up live feeds from my cameras, so that they appear on my screen in two rows of small, side-by-side boxes. I tap the one for the garage and it fills the screen. At the left edge I can see most of the outside parking area. There are only three cars present—the Camaro, Linderhoff's Lexus, and a pickup truck.

During the planning portion of our conversation last night, Adam told me, "Tomorrow is restock and cleanup day. After that, we're booked up through the weekend."

"What exactly does restock and cleanup day entail?"

"A company comes in and cleans the house in the afternoon. The restocking is done in the evening, usually by me, Toby, Kirk, and Connor. But Connor...um..."

"Got his knee bashed in at the mobile home?"

He looked at me, unsurprised. "That was you, too, wasn't it?"

"I'm not a fan of letting defenseless people get beat up."

"I'm not, either. I was just the driver."

"Buddy, the 'I was just following orders' excuse went out of style seventy-five years ago."

He looked away, unable to hide his guilt.

"What time do you start?" I asked.

"About eight thirty. A supply truck comes in the afternoon, too, but they leave everything by the front door."

"So it's just you and your buddies?"

"Mr. Linderhoff has to let us in."

"Does he stay there while you work?"

"He'll usually hang around for a little while, then take off and come back when I call and tell him we're done."

"And you wait until he gets there?"

"Uh-huh."

In the here and now, I switch back to the multi-camera view and enlarge the feed from my camera covering the lobby. Through the open doorway I can see some boxes stacked outside. Toby and Kirk are each carrying one in.

I don't see Adam until he enters the lobby from somewhere else on the first floor and walks outside to grab a box.

For several minutes the parade of supply redistribution continues. Then Linderhoff appears from the direction of the library. He stops Adam just inside the doorway and the two talk quietly for a few moments. When they finish, Linderhoff claps Adam on the shoulder and walks outside.

Less than a minute later, Adam steps outside and walks over to the waiting boxes. Before he can pick one up, the Lexus appears on the portion of the driveway that passes the front of the house. Adam waves at the car, then grabs a box and goes back in.

I switch views again, this time to a camera I had Adam install across from the compound's gate before the others arrived. After a few seconds, the gate rolls open. Linderhoff's Lexus pulls onto the road and drives away.

I give it a full minute, to make sure the vehicle doesn't return, before I send Adam a text containing only the thumbs-up emoji. I asked him last night for the name of someone he knows who lives out of town, and I use that as the message sender's ID. In the unlikely event Linderhoff sees Adam's phone, the emoji would be a lot easier to explain than if I send something like *He's gone*. (FYI, that's not a spy trick. That's something every kid learns when he or she gets a phone.)

I change my screen view so that I have two feeds up—the one from the lobby and the one covering the garage area. Adam returns empty-handed from wherever he took his last load. Instead of grabbing another box from the pile outside, he goes to his car and gets my Johnny Walker box out of the trunk. He carries it back into the lobby and says something to Toby, who's heading toward the front door. Toby gives him a nod and continues on his way while Adam carries my box up the stairs.

I exchange the garage feed for the one covering the central hallway upstairs, and follow Adam's progress to the T intersection. When he goes to the right, I select the hallway on that side and watch him walk up to the last door before the curtained entrance to the library balcony. He sets the box down and pulls a key out of his pocket. According to him, the spare keys are kept in a hidden cabinet in a closet beyond the downstairs lobby.

After he gets the door open, he picks up the box, steps inside, and closes the door behind him.

I'm blind now. I have no camera in the room and can't see what he's doing. I considered having him video call me once he's inside, but if something goes wrong and I'm not able to pull off what I'm planning, the call would leave a digital trail that could be used to tie Adam to my failed attempt. Same as my reasoning with sending the coded text—I don't want to put Adam at risk of receiving a death sentence from his boss because of something I do.

I call Jar.

"Are we ready?" she asks.

"Almost. He's in the room now."

"You are sure he knows what he is doing?"

"I went over it with him three times."

"That does not mean he knows."

I don't respond to this because I have the same worry. Adam seemed to understand all the steps when I talked him through connecting the bug to the Club's video server, but talking about it and doing it are two different things.

"He could be selling you out," she says.

"He won't."

"You sound pretty confident about that."

"He's not going to sell me out." Again, I don't know if I believe this or not, but Liz does.

Three minutes pass without Adam exiting the room.

"He should be done by now," Jar says. "If it was one of us, we would have finished and been out of there over a minute ago."

"Yeah, but he isn't one of us. He needs a little time."

Twenty seconds later, my phone vibrates. It's a text from Adam, the smiley-face emoji he was to send if everything went well.

"He's done," I say.

"Do you have a connection?"

"Checking."

On my laptop, I bring up the bug-monitoring program and highlight the designation number for the specialized bug Adam has just attached to the video server.

"Got it," I say, grinning. "Nice and strong. Patching it through now."

I tap a couple more buttons and link my machine to Jar's in Bangkok.

"Connected," Jar says. "This might take me a little while."

While she scours the Club's stored video, I return my attention to the feeds at the Club, just in time to see Adam exit the room and relock the door. He carries my box back to the main corridor and into one of the other rooms, where he leaves it and returns downstairs to help his colleagues.

Over the next thirty minutes, the rest of the stock is brought inside. Adam and his companions then enter the library, where they remove two leaves from the big table and four of the chairs, in preparation of tomorrow night's dinner. They take a final walk through the first floor, making sure everything has been put away. When they finish, they shake hands and Toby and Kirk leave.

Adam walks into the lobby and calls Linderhoff.

"Yeah," he says. "We're all done." A pause. "No, nothing's missing.... Uh-huh. We just did that.... Okay."

After he hangs up, his gaze swings slowly through the lobby. I have a feeling he's looking for my camera, but he doesn't find it.

He moves out to the front porch and sits on the steps. Fifteen minutes later, Linderhoff arrives.

They talk for a few moments before Linderhoff enters the house and does a quick tour of the first floor. Apparently satisfied, he exits again, locks the front door, and he and Adam walk over to their cars.

A few seconds after Adam climbs into his Camaro, I receive a text. Seven emojis this time—a waving hand, a car, and five smiley faces. It's this last group that's important. It informs me Linderhoff has told him to be back tomorrow night at five p.m.

I watch the two vehicles exit through the gate and head toward town.

The time is 10:12 p.m., and the Club is now deserted.

I stand up and stretch. As I turn to deal with my next task, I see a manila envelope on the floor next to the front door. I walk over and pick it up. Inside are the dozen red arrows Anny picked up for me. They're about a foot long and half as wide, the kind stores use for sales. I add a roll of tape to the envelope and set the package on the bed, next to where the rest of the tools of my trade for tomorrow night's mission are laid out.

This includes the drone and several extra batteries, some more bugs (though I doubt I'll be needing them), five smoke bombs and five flash-bang grenades (I'd like to avoid using these if at all possible), earplugs (in case I have no choice), industrial-strength zip ties (perfect for securing hostiles), a pair of multi-mode binoculars, an aluminum slingshot, a pair of head-mounted night vision goggles, my set of lock picks, a four-inch knife, a multitool, one of the Glocks preloaded with a full magazine (again, hoping not to use it as more than a prop), four preloaded spare mags, a fresh sound suppressor, my shoulder holster, and my two Taser guns with a half dozen spare wire cartridges.

I look over the gear and consider if anything needs to be added or removed.

No. This should do it.

I carefully load everything except the knife into my backpack, putting each item in the same spot I always put it so I won't have to think too much when I grab for something.

I place the bag by the door, and put a small duffel bag on top containing the set of clothes I will wear—black pants, black long-sleeve shirt, black gloves, black shoes, and black ski mask. My typical night mission outfit. On top of this, I place the knife that I'll insert into my prosthetic leg when I get dressed in the morning.

Speaking of morning, I don't think Donna and Bree and the others would appreciate me showing up to work in all black, so I set my diner clothes on a chair next to the bathroom.

While doing all this, I've been sneaking looks at my phone, wondering when Jar is going to call me back.

For those of you curious, the answer is fifteen seconds after I go into the bathroom to relieve myself. I try to rush things along, but by the time I'm back in the bedroom, my phone has stopped ringing.

I return her call.

"I thought you might have fallen asleep," she said.

"Not yet."

"Then where were you?"

"Do you really need to know that?"

She's quiet for a moment, then says matter-of-factly, "You were in the bathroom. Why did you not just answer?"

"Because I left the phone on the bed."

"You should have had it with you."

I want to roll my eyes, but even though she can't see me, I don't. "You're right. I should have. I'm sorry." I pause. "Did you find anything?"

"Of course."

"Was it what we hoped?"

"I emailed you a link. There is something extra at the end."

"Extra?"

"You will see."

I tuck the phone between my ear and shoulder and grab my laptop. Her link leads to a video of several clips edited together, lasting nearly three minutes.

When it finishes, Jar asks, "Well? *Is* it what you hoped?"

"No. It's beyond."

CHAPTER FORTY-TWO

I'm up, showered, and changed into my work clothes before dawn. While I was sleeping, Jar remotely took control of my laptop, and used it to copy not only the file she showed me but several others onto a blank jump drive I'd connected to my computer.

The status bar indicates the transfer was finished about an hour after I fell asleep, so I pull the drive out and put it in a protective container that already holds two other jump drives. On one is the report Jar put together on Linderhoff's illegal activities, both as the head of a regional drug-running operation and the mastermind behind the Huntington Club. There are also pictures I shot of Chuck Owens's vandalized shop, notes that make the strong case Linderhoff was behind the contractor's murder, and photos of the men who were at the Club the other night, with other pictures that identify who they are. (Jar has been able to ID everyone, and they all fall into the same categories as the ones she first identified.) On the last drive are the video and audio clips from The Good Stuff file. I place the container inside a box sitting on my dresser that already holds the car grille I found. I'd love to seal it now, but there's still one item outstanding. I interlock the box's flaps so they stay closed, and put the box in the bottom drawer of the cabinet.

With my backpack over my shoulders and my duffel in my hand, I head out.

I'm the first to arrive at the diner but since I'm still new, I don't have a key and have to wait for Evelyn, our cook, to arrive.

The morning progresses as usual, the same folks coming in at the same times and wanting the same things. At 8:20, Linderhoff arrives, further reinforcing my same-day diner visit/Club event theory.

Though the irony would be lost on him, he seems almost jovial today. He even jokes with Donna when he gives her his order.

My guess is that he's excited for tonight. If Adam's right, Linderhoff will have some particularly high-flying guests. He's probably also pleased that his Chuck Owens problem is in the past.

Oh, if he only knew.

(Is that foreshadowing? It kind of sounds like it, doesn't it? God, I hope so.)

The only (slight) hiccup in his mood comes when he spots me. I can feel him staring when I clean a table near his. When I finish and casually glance over, his eyes widen, and I know he's made the connection between me and the guy he saw in the parking lot in Brighton. But he seems to leave as happy as he arrived, which I hope means now that he's answered that lingering question about who I am, he's put me out of his mind.

My time at the diner is fast approaching an end, but it's not today. How much longer I'll be cleaning tables will depend on tonight. So I finish my shift and punch my time card and slip quietly out the back door.

I stop by a market where I pick up some water and energy bars. When I return to my car, I check the camera feeds at the Club. As I guessed, no one's there yet.

Not wanting to leave the Versa anywhere near the Club, I park at the north edge of town. Before I climb out, I don my mission clothing, and stuff my laptop and the food I bought into my backpack. I then hike through the woods until I reach the wall around the Club.

I cycle through the camera feeds again. After confirming nothing has changed, I move up to the corner near the road and call Jar. "I'm ready."

"Okay. Give me a moment." A few seconds of dead air, then, "The camera is looped. You can go now."

I look both ways down the road, and once it's clear, I swing around the corner, jog to the gate, and climb over.

As I near the clearing where the main house is, I hear a door open.

I freeze. Nobody should be here.

There are no cars in the parking area, and all the internal cameras showed empty spaces. Okay, sure, I don't have the whole building wired, but enough so that I should have picked up something.

I hear the scratch-scratch-scratch of a broom on stone.

I creep forward until I can see the house between the remaining trees. Eric the butler is sweeping the porch area at the top of the stairs to the front door, his back to me.

He must have used one of the Club's Lexuses and parked it in the garage. Good thing I didn't just walk right in the front door. That would have sucked. (And no, my plan has never been to walk in the front door.)

After Eric finishes the porch, he starts in on the steps.

I ease through the woods and circle around until I'm on the west side of the house where Eric can't see me, then I creep over to the basement stairs. Before I descend, I remove my drone from my backpack and fly it up onto the Club's roof, where I land it and put it on standby mode.

I hurry down, enter the basement, and make my way upstairs. The first thing I do is confirm no one else is in the "under renovation" portion of the house.

After that, I take the convoluted path down into the secret room. The coke isn't what interests me on this trip. I want to know what's in the boxes. I take one from the middle of the stack and open it.

Little blue pills. Not in bottles, but in bags, stuffed full. It's probably oxycodone. If not that, it's some other type of opioid.

Jesus.

I head up the stairs, close and hide the trapdoor, and return to the first floor.

In a windowless room near the back corner, I set up shop, creating a makeshift desk out of a board held aloft between two large, empty paint barrels. I place my laptop and phone on the board and don my wireless earbuds.

On the computer screen are the feeds, once more in the multi-camera view. In one of them, I see that Eric has finished with the stairs and is sweeping the sidewalk that leads toward the parking area, the sun casting his shadow on the ground. I stare at him for a moment. I've seen a similarly shaped shadow before, standing on the roof across from Chuck Owens's shop.

Well, how about that? Eric is the asshole who tried to kill me. That's a nice bit of info.

I eat one of my energy bars and call Adam.

"Hello?" he answers warily.

His response is due to the fact I've programmed my call to display the ID JENSON COMMUNITY HOSPITAL. I do this in case he's not alone.

"It's me," I say in the same hushed tone I've used with him. "Anyone with you?"

"No. Just me."

"I wanted to make sure you're ready for tonight."

"Um, yeah. I-I-I guess."

"You're not having second thoughts, are you?"

A pause. "Are you sure you can get me out of this?"

"I never said I could get you out of this. I said I could make things a lot easier for you."

"I don't want to go to jail."

You don't know how tempting it is for me to say, *Then you shouldn't have agreed to be one of Linderhoff's thugs.* I keep that opinion to myself, though, and say, "You play your cards right, and do exactly what I've told you to do, and there's a very good chance you won't. But if you try to improvise, or decide to bail on me, I guarantee you that you'll be spending a good portion of the rest of your life behind bars. And if the authorities decide to link you to Charles Owens's murder, you might never get out."

"I didn't have anything to do with that!"

"Didn't you just trash his place and pick up a wad of cash from him?"

A long silence. "I'll do like you ask."

"Good." I check my email and frown, then glance at the clock at the top corner of the screen. It's 4:05 p.m. "I don't see that email you promised me."

"I'm working on it."

"You've got to be at the Club in less than an hour. That doesn't leave you much time."

"I'll get it done. I promise."

"If I don't receive it before you arrive or I'm not happy with it, any chance of you getting off easy is gone."

"Then stop talking to me so I can finish."

"Now that's the attitude I'm looking for. Keep your chin up, Adam. This will all be over before you know it."

"If you say so."

"Talk to you soon." I hang up.

I leave my email running in the background, and at 4:33 a soft ping notifies me Adam's confession has arrived.

I read through it. He's done a surprisingly thorough job of detailing his activities for and with Linderhoff. There's some pretty juicy stuff here, stuff that could land everyone involved in very serious trouble. It's also the kind of document that will make prosecutors look favorably on its writer, if said writer agrees to testify in court. Adam knows this. We talked about it in detail. He's scared shitless about the prospect, but he seems to realize it's his only way out.

And whether he makes it through the night or not, the letter will ensure the end of Linderhoff.

Does that sound callous?

Maybe. But Adam isn't exactly an innocent in all this. I'm giving him a chance because Marissa gave him a chance. It's my posthumous gift to her, nothing more. Whether he lives or dies, goes to prison or not, will now be (mostly) up to him.

I copy his confession onto a blank jump drive and slip it into my pocket. This is the final piece I will put in the box with the car grille.

I also add the confession to an email I've prepared, which includes Jar's report and links to several of the more tantalizing photos and videos, including the montage Jar sent me last night. It does not include Anny's video, however. That's for a onetime, special use only.

Above the attached documents, I type a short message and set the email to be sent at 9:30 p.m. By then, I should be done with what I've come to do, one way or another. The email's addressees include the California Attorney General; the United

States Attorney General; the US Attorney for the Eastern District of California; several people I know at the FBI; the sheriff's department; prominent news broadcasters at CNN, ABC, CBS, MSNBC, Fox News, and, for the hell of it, BBC News; and the offices of several ranking lawmakers in DC and various state capitols whose members' names are included within the documents. Go big or go home, right?

Tomorrow should be a very interesting news day.

In theory, I could walk away now. The email should be enough to throw Linderhoff and his Club into chaos. But I don't want to chance having him or any of the others flee before the authorities move in.

The four members of the kitchen staff arrived at the Club while I was putting the email together. At five o'clock, Adam shows up with Toby and Kirk in his car. Adam goes to the house, where he spends a few minutes talking to Eric before he returns to his Camaro. While he was gone, Toby and Kirk moved two of the Lexuses out of one of the garages. The cars now sit on the road behind Adam's car, waiting.

Adam gives them a wave and gets into the Camaro, then all three vehicles head back to town.

Not much happens until the cars return thirty minutes later. Between the three of them, they have brought nine hostesses to the Club. The women are dressed casually, but have their hair and makeup done.

After the girls go into the house, Adam hands his keys over to Toby, who gets into the Camaro with Kirk and drives off until they're needed again. Adam would normally go with them, but Connor, his injured colleague who usually serves as a kind of bouncer/security person, is out of commission and Adam has, at my suggestion, volunteered to fill that role tonight.

He's walking back to the house when Linderhoff's Lexus

pulls into the parking area. Adam stops and waits for his boss, then together they head inside.

For the next two hours, preparations for the evening continue. At 7:30 p.m., Linderhoff walks slowly through the Club, performing a final inspection. Adam and Eric follow him, each taking care of things Linderhoff points out.

They finish in the lobby, where Linderhoff looks at his watch and says, "Our guests should start arriving in fifteen minutes. Gentlemen, you may go to your stations."

Eric bows his head and leaves. Adam hesitates.

Linderhoff looks at him, brow creasing. "What?"

My skin goes cold as I wonder if Adam is about to confess.

The kid opens his mouth, but nothing comes out.

"If you've got something to say, say it," Linderhoff tells him.

"I-I was wondering if you wanted me to stay here in the lobby or come outside with you."

"Didn't you talk to Connor?"

"I tried, but the drugs the doctor gave him knocked him out." This is the excuse I told him to use if he was asked something like this, though I didn't mean for him to quote me word for word.

"In here." Linderhoff points across the room. "Right over there."

"Okay. Cool. Thanks."

As Adam heads over to the spot, my attention lingers on Linderhoff. He's staring at Adam's back with a combination of confusion, concern, and caution.

I curse under my breath, worried that he suspects something's up.

It'll be all right, Liz says.

Will it?

Liz leans down so that her head is over my shoulder, her cheek a finger's width away from mine. I can feel her, like a magnet pulling my skin to hers. And I swear I can feel her breath on my ear. It's warm and feels like...home.

I want to lean to the side so that we touch, but like always I resist, knowing I would only find empty air.

I'm not going anywhere, she whispers.

I don't know if I should be happy about that or scared to death.

The truth is, I'm both.

CHAPTER FORTY-THREE

The first sedan stops in front of the Club at 8:03 p.m.

A black Mercedes-Maybach S 560 with dark tinted windows. The driver gets out and opens the back door. From the rear seat emerges a man with salt-and-pepper hair and the frame of someone who has worked out all his life. He's dressed in a dark gray suit. Linderhoff, who's been waiting outside since before the car arrived, shakes the man's hands and smiles broadly as the two exchange pleasantries.

A second man climbs out. Despite the fact his hair is all brown, he is clearly older than the first guy. His face is more wrinkled and he moves more slowly. That could be in part due to the extra weight he carries pretty much everywhere, but I'm sticking with the older theory and guessing the hair is either dyed or a wig.

Linderhoff greets him as warmly as he did the first man and leads them both into the lobby, where he turns them over to Eric. While Eric escorts the newcomers into the lounge, Linderhoff heads back outside.

Car number two arrives four minutes later. Another sedan with tinted windows, but a Jaguar this time. It also carries two backseat passengers, both men I peg to be around fifty-five. One of them gives Linderhoff a bear hug when they meet. The other is content with the standard handshake and smile.

As this is going on, a vehicle drives up with Chief of Police Norman Sparks behind the wheel, and Jenson National Bank president William Collins in the seat beside him. Linderhoff and the two from the Jag wait for Sparks and Collins to join them. From the glad-handing and smiles, it's obvious they all know one another.

The escorting process is repeated, and the four new men join the first pair in the lounge.

After the fourth car arrives—another Mercedes—with its two elderly attendees, Linderhoff escorts them all the way to the lounge himself and does not head back outside. That tracks with what I know. The eight men plus Linderhoff and the nine female companions match the number of chairs at the dining table in the library.

I stand up and roll my head over my shoulders, working out the stiffness, then rotate my torso and reach high into the air—right, left, right, left. Lunges and squats follow. Stretching can never be overrated. The last thing I want to do is pull a hammy in the middle of subduing someone. It's the kind of thing they don't show in spy movies and police dramas. Not very sexy, I suppose.

On the monitor, I watch Linderhoff raise a glass and say, "Welcome to the Huntington Club. We are honored by your presence. May the future be ever guided by those who know best."

"Those who know best," everyone repeats.

Glasses touch glasses and amber liquid flows into the men's mouths.

That was...interesting. If I have time, I'll add a clip of that to the email before it goes out. The news networks should especially love it. I can see the toast getting a lot of airplay.

Feeling sufficiently limber, I sit back down and spend a few minutes taking screenshots of the faces of each guest. Adam said tonight would be a big deal, and he's right. Four of the six guests I recognize on sight.

The man with the dyed hair is a senator from the Midwest somewhere. It takes a moment, but then I remember. Kansas. Two of the other men are congressmen who get a lot of TV face time—one, I believe, is from Pennsylvania, and the other, I think...Florida? The fourth person I recognize is not a politician (per se), but a popular cable news host. I do a down-and-dirty image search on the two I don't know and hit the jackpot on both. One is an assistant attorney general in Texas, and the other is a member of the Virginia senate.

I'm not sure how much substance is in that room, but there's a hell of a lot of flash.

"Gentlemen," Linderhoff says, "we have a lovely evening planned for you. But I understand you have some matters you would like to discuss alone. May I suggest you do so now so that we may better enjoy ourselves later?"

He motions toward a circle of six padded chairs that he directed Adam and Eric to reconfigure earlier in the evening.

As soon as everyone is seated, Linderhoff says, "When you're finished, just ring that bell." He points at a long-handled bell sitting on an end table next to the dyed-hair senator's chair, and then he, Sparks, and Collins exit the room.

The senator looks at the (Floridian?) congressman and says, "You called the meeting. What is it you wanted?"

The congressman smiles and leans forward, elbows on knees. "First, thank you, Senator, for coming tonight. We know how precious your time is and appreciate you giving us a little of it."

"I didn't come here to get smoke blown up my ass. Get to the point."

Everyone looks uncomfortable, the congressman most of all.

"It's about Senator Davidson," the congressman says.

It takes me a moment to recall that Davidson is the junior senator from Dyed Haired's state.

"What about him?"

"Frankly, sir, he's...underperforming."

The senator remains silent.

"He's up for reelection next cycle. And I think...*we* think it's a good opportunity to have someone more in tune with the party to run in his place."

"Do you now?" the senator's gaze takes in the others before returning to the congressman. "And who might that be? None of you reside in Kansas."

(Right. Kansas. That's where he's from.)

"You're right, Senator," the TV host says. "But while I don't live there now, I did grow up in Topeka. And I'm a proud KU grad."

The senator blinks. "You? Are you serious?"

"Is it really such a bad idea?"

The senator falls silent. From his expression, I can't tell what he's thinking.

Several of the others start saying why they think it's the way to go.

While I'm fascinated by this glimpse into backroom politicking, it's really no more than a sideshow to tonight's main event, and will be just another nice clip to include in the email.

I turn down the volume, don my shoulder holster, and shove my gun into it. I pull my backpack over my shoulders. My laptop I leave open and running, as it's my connection to Jar.

Speaking of Jar.

"I was beginning to wonder if you forgot about me," she answers when I connect to her.

I'm doing this via a proprietary communications app on the computer, and am using one of the comm sets from my day job. Basically, it's an earbud paired with a small microphone attached to the top of my shirt. Much more convenient in this situation than Bluetoothing through my phone.

"Got sidetracked by the conversation."

"In the lounge? I have been watching it, too."

"When they're done, can you make a clip of it and send it to me? Also of that toast earlier." That'll save me time.

"No problem. Are you ready?"

"As much as I'll ever be. Are *you* ready?"

"Why would I not be?"

I look at the monitor and see Linderhoff has reentered the lounge and a few of the men have risen from their chairs. Apparently the meeting is over, and from the smiles I take it the anti-Davidson committee has been able to win over the senator from Kansas.

I turn up the volume.

"—news. So glad to hear that," Linderhoff is saying. He smiles. "I hope everyone is hungry."

Several of the men answer in the affirmative.

"Excellent! We have quite a meal for you tonight. But first..." Linderhoff picks up the bell and rings it.

After a couple of seconds, the doors to the lobby open and the women enter. The casual clothes they were wearing earlier have been replaced by dresses that are both elegant and provocative. The men light up at the sight. Two of the women make beelines toward specific men, giving me the impression they've spent time together before. The remaining join the other men, and Linderhoff makes introductions. It doesn't take more than a minute before everyone is paired off.

"This way, gentlemen," Linderhoff says, and leads the parade out of the room.

Switching cameras, I follow them all the way to the library, where they take seats around the table. As champagne is poured, I switch to the garage cam, and see that the three chauffeurs are gathered together between the Jaguar and one of the Mercedes.

"Phase one," I say, as I pull my ski mask over my head.

"Copy," Jar replies, then, after a short pause, adds, "Exterior cameras looped."

I exit the building through the basement, circle into the trees behind the house, and make my way through the woods until I'm near the parking area.

The chauffeurs are only ten yards away, standing under a streetlamp. Two are leaning against the Mercedes, while the other stands next to the Jaguar.

I take my backpack off and lean it against the tree next to me. From inside, I retrieve my night vision goggles and mount them over my knitted cap, leaving the lens raised so I can see without them for the moment. Next out of the bag come my two Taser guns and one of the extra wire cartridges.

Facing the trio of drivers, I set the Tasers on the ground in front of me. I then extract the slingshot from the backpack, pick up a couple of marble-sized stones off the ground, and mount one in the pocket.

After pulling the rubber back, I take careful aim, and release.

I'm pretty good with slingshots, so it's not without some annoyance I watch the stone miss my target by a few inches. I prep the other stone and try again.

This time, my shot shatters the lighting element and plunges the cars into darkness. I flip down my night vision lenses, drop my slingshot, and snatch up the Tasers. As I step quickly from the trees, the three men are looking up toward the light.

"What the hell *was* that?" one of them says.

"That scared the shit out of me," the third says.

I'm halfway to them when one of the men leaning against the Mercedes starts to turn in my direction. He's probably night blind and won't see me right away, but there's no reason to take a chance that I might be wrong.

I pull both triggers.

One set of wires hits the turning man, while the other threads the space between him and the guy next to the Jaguar and hits the third chauffeur square in the chest.

The guy who hasn't been hit freaks out, but he has nowhere to go, as my initial targets have blocked off his escape routes. I pop out the cartridges and insert the spare into one of the guns before he thinks to look in my direction. When he does, I give him a dose of what his friends received.

I don't know whether these guys have been hired only for the evening or are more involved in Linderhoff's operation. Should I feel bad for my unprovoked attack?

Are you kidding me? No.

I didn't have time to question them, and I couldn't leave them out here as a potential threat, so I had to do something. Besides, it's not like I shot them with bullets. Whatever their involvement, they're getting out of this relatively unscathed. Physically speaking.

I use the same sleeper technique I employed with the Masked Raiders in L.A. Once the chauffeurs are unconscious, I zip-tie them and place each in the trunk of a car. I'm not sure I've got the right guy for each vehicle, but I don't think that's what they'd be complaining about.

Before I return to the house, I let myself into one of the garages and grab a crowbar I saw hanging on the pegboard last time I was here. I also remove my night vision goggles, as I don't need them for now, and retrieve the slingshot.

I take the driveway back to the house since there's no one to see me and the cameras are all looped. I pause right outside the lights in front.

"Chauffeurs dealt with," I say.

"Copy. Any problems?" Jar asks.

"None. Is there anyone in the lobby?"

"They are all still in the library."

"Copy."

I hurry to the stone steps and up to the Club's entrance. Each of the double doors has an ornate handle that loops out and back again, connecting to metal plates attached to the door. I slip the crowbar through the loops and secure it in place with several zip ties. No one will be using this exit anytime soon.

"Phase one complete."

"Copy."

I reenter the basement and head up to the first floor. When I reach the wall that separates the two sections, I say, "I'm at the door. Ready for phase two."

"Lounge is still clear."

"Okay. Going in."

I open the hidden door and step quietly into the lounge.

The odor of good whiskey lingers in the air. There's something else, too. I sniff again before it hits me. Old Spice cologne. For the smell to hang around like that, someone must have doused himself with a whole bottle.

That's attractive.

"What are you doing?" Jar asks.

"Uh, nothing." I hurry across to the back stairway door. "Clear to go up?"

"Clear."

With Jar watching the path ahead of me, I make my way to

the room Adam went to after he'd put the bug on the Club's video server. The door is locked, but I knew it would be. Adam said if it wasn't, it would be suspicious if discovered.

The lock is meant more for privacy than security, and it takes me little time to pick it. I slip inside and close the door. Light from a flood lamp in front of the building spills through the window, casting long shadows in the semidark room.

The prominent feature is a king-sized bed with an impressively carved headboard. Like the bedroom I checked out on my first visit, the mattress is stripped of linen and there are no pillows. Per Adam, this room is not scheduled to be used tonight.

Two doors are along the wall to my right, one on either side of the bed. The one on the far side supposedly opens onto a bathroom. It's the closer one I want. It leads to a large, walk-in closet. Along with rods to hang clothes on, there are built-in drawers for shoes and other accessories.

I open the middle drawer, bottom row. It's large and deep enough to hold several pairs of calf-high boots, side by side. It's also the perfect size for my Johnny Walker box.

I pull the box out, carry it into the bedroom, and set it on the bed. Using my knife, I work the flaps free. Inside are not the bottles of whiskey the labeling promises, but three metal canisters, each about the size of a large thermos and wrapped by a towel.

I remove the canisters one at a time and lay them on the bed. Also in the box are three valves. After making sure they are in the off position, I screw them onto the tops of the canisters. The final item is a thin but effective gas mask in a cloth bag.

"What's going on below?" I whisper.

"They have finished their salads and are being served the main meal," Jar says.

"Anything good?"

"Not in my opinion."

I smile. "What about the staff? Where are they?"

"There are two servers in the room at the moment. The other kitchen workers must still be in the kitchen. The butler is standing in the library, off to the side. Adam is also in the library, near the door to the lobby."

"Okay, I'm moving into position."

"Copy."

I put two of the canisters in my backpack, hold on to the third and the gas mask, and sneak back into the hallway. I hear music playing but unlike the other night, it's at a much more respectable volume. It's also not pop or rock, but some kind of classical piano tune.

A concerto, Liz says.

Fine, a concerto. (Look, I *do* know a lot of things, but I'm a little weak on classical music, okay? And no, I don't know how my subconscious knows it's a concerto if I don't.)

I also hear the hum of several conversations, and the occasional clink of silverware against plates. As I reach the balcony overlooking the lobby, a woman laughs. It probably sounds natural to the guy sitting next to her, who's been drinking and is in a party mood. I can tell she's acting.

I move quickly across the balcony to the shelter of the hallway on the other side, and continue down to the T intersection. This time I take the hallway to the right and stop behind the curtain covering the balcony entrance.

I set down the canister I'm carrying and remove the gas mask from its bag. The device would be ineffective if I wear it over my ski mask so I'll have to exchange one for the other, but not quite yet.

I whisper, "In position one. Am I a go?"

"The servers have returned to the kitchen," Jar says. "You are a go."

I pull out my phone and send a fist-bump emoji to Adam.

A few seconds later, Jar says, "Adam just checked his phone.... He looks nervous."

"Has Linderhoff noticed?"

"It does not look like it."

I start a new text conversation, this one going to Linderhoff's cell number. It will register as coming from a blocked number, and contain only the video Anny shot of the Marissa lookalike. Right after I press send, I switch to the monitoring app and bring up the feed of the library.

Linderhoff is laughing with the king-making senator, who is sitting next to him. I know the exact moment my message arrives by the way Linderhoff's hand suddenly moves to his pocket. While he pulls his phone out, his attention remains on the senator. Their conversation continues for a few more seconds before there's a natural pause that allows Linderhoff to look at his cell.

He stares at his screen, mildly perplexed. All he's seeing at this point is a message telling him he has a text from an unknown sender.

"Open it," I whisper.

Open it, Liz echoes behind me.

For a second, it appears he's going to ignore it and shove his phone back into his pocket. But curiosity gets the better of him, and after another glance at his device, he unlocks the screen. This is where that half second of black I put at the beginning of the clip comes in. All he can see is that he's received a video, but he has no idea what it is.

I feel Liz lean in closer, her nonexistent eyes focused on the screen. Neither of us says anything this time, but we're both thinking, *Play it.*

Linderhoff touches the screen. The moment faux-Marissa's face appears, he fumbles with his phone until the screen turns off.

The senator notices and glances over. Linderhoff smiles and says something that seems to satisfy the older man. Linderhoff then says something else and pushes back his chair.

"Here we go," I say.

As Linderhoff stands up, he gets the attention of Sparks and subtly nods toward the lobby door. After making his excuses, the police chief stands and follows Linderhoff toward the exit. It's a slight bummer. I was hoping Linderhoff would go out alone, but I always knew that would be unlikely.

I slip my phone into my pocket and say to Jar, "You're my eyes again."

"Copy."

After switching my ski mask for the gas mask, I stretch out on the floor, pull back the bottom corner of the curtain, and move the canister onto the library balcony. I make sure the valve opening is pointed toward the middle of the room, and then twist the dial.

The gas hisses as it exits but it isn't loud, and the music and voices should be more than enough to prevent anyone below from hearing it.

I back away, make sure the curtain is covering the opening, get up, and make my way around to the other hallway.

"Linderhoff is going into the lobby. The other man from the table is going with him. He has also waved for the butler to join them."

That's less of a surprise than the inclusion of the chief. "What about Adam?"

"Linderhoff said something to him as he passed, but Adam is still there."

"Copy."

I repeat the canister procedure at the left balcony entrance, but with both of the remaining cylinders.

Wouldn't it be great if I was releasing sleeping gas? The

problem is, there's no such thing. I mean, yeah, there's anesthesia that will knock out a patient undergoing surgery, but to be effective, that would entail me walking around and placing a mask over the face of each person in the library. An impractical task, to say the least.

The gas in my canisters is similar to, but not the same as, tear gas, and has the added benefit of being odorless and invisible. In a few minutes, the dinner guests will be wishing Linderhoff asked them to go with him into the lobby.

After texting Adam another emoji—a chef's hat this time—I head back to the main corridor.

"Adam is locking the door," Jar says. "Now he is walking to the kitchen entrance...okay, he has gone inside the kitchen. I cannot see him anymore."

In theory, he's blocking that door, too, so that the dinner guests have nowhere to go. I've told him to tell the cook and serving staff that a private discussion is going on, and no one is to go back into the library until Linderhoff gives the okay. It's a lie that should work until the gas takes full effect, and the diners' expressions of discomfort will be heard through the door.

As I hurry to the balcony overlooking the lobby, I make the mask exchange again, only in reverse. When I reach the end of the hall, I crouch down and sneak out far enough to see Linderhoff in the middle of the lobby, flanked by Sparks and Eric.

"Look," Linderhoff says, holding his phone so the others can see. "I'm telling you there's no number. I don't *know* who sent it."

The chief and the butler examine the screen.

Sparks says, "You might be getting worked up over nothing."

Linderhoff looks at him as if he's crazy. "It's fucking Marissa."

"Let's just play it and see."

Linderhoff takes a breath, then hits Play.

Here is what they are seeing: faux Marissa, looking straight at the camera, upset and scared.

And here's what they're hearing:

"—za. I'm seventeen, and have worked at the Huntington Club for a little over a month. The Club is a place where rich, privileged men come to be entertained by young women. There are bedrooms on the second floor where the men can have sex with the women. I haven't been taken upstairs yet, but most of the other girls have, and I know it won't be long before I'll be expected to do the same. But I have *no* intention of going up there and have decided that I can no longer work there. I'm worried, though, that the man who runs the Club, Mr.—"

Here's where I did some of my creative editing. The name Faux Marissa recorded was one I made up. If she hears the name Linderhoff on the news, she won't make the connection, at least not right away. And I'm not sending this video to anyone else. The only ones who will ever see it other than Anny and me are the three men in the lobby.

Right after Faux Marissa says *mister*, I jump cut to: "—will not let me quit. I've heard stories and know he can be very vindictive. I'm afraid he might threaten me, or-or-or—" Another jump cut to her taking a deep breath, then a jump cut to: "I'm afraid he might do more than just threaten. I know he has guys who beat up people who make him mad." She takes another breath. Halfway through it, I jump cut again. "I'm making this video in case something happens to me. If it does, I want this to go to someone who can do something about it. Not the police, though. Chief of Police—" Jump cut. "—is part of Mr.—" Jump cut. "—'s gang or organization...I don't know what to call it. I just know that if I'm hurt or...or...well, if I am, it will be Mr.—" Jump cut. "—'s fault."

The video abruptly ends.

"That little bitch," Linderhoff says.

"This problem is supposed to have been taken care of!" the chief says.

"It was. No one could have known about this."

Sparks takes a moment, and then says, "I've got a contact at AT&T. Hopefully he can find out who sent it."

Behind me, I hear the first few coughs coming from the library. It's time to send text number two.

"Call him," Linderhoff says. "He needs to do it right—"

His phone, still in his hand, buzzes again. On his screen will be the same blocked number as before. He shows the screen to the other two, then navigates to the message.

This one, too, starts off with a black screen.

Linderhoff hits Play.

The movie begins with one of the clips Jar found stored on the Club's video servers. It's from the security camera overlooking the area in front of the garages, and is stamped with the date the car hit Marissa and the time of 7:58 p.m., a little over an hour before the "accident." The door to the garage nearest the house is open, and from inside comes one of the black Lexus GS Fs.

The camera angle is perfect to see Eric behind the wheel. As he drives off, Linderhoff walks out of the garage. The video cuts to a clip from the Club's lobby. The time has jumped to 9:24 p.m. Linderhoff is pacing. After a few seconds of this, there's the sound of a phone ringing. Linderhoff stops pacing, retrieves his phone from his pocket, and holds it up to his ear.

"Well?" Linderhoff says. A few beats pass. "Are you sure?.... We *have* to be sure.... Fine. Just get back here."

He hangs up, only slightly less agitated than before.

Cut to the garage camera again. Linderhoff is standing in front of the open door as the GS F returns. Only the car is not in the same condition as when it left. There are dents in the hood and the passenger-side front fender. And, though you can't tell on the video, damage to the grille, including a tiny missing triangular chip.

The car stops next to Linderhoff and a short conversation ensues. There is no sound on the garage cam, but it's not necessary. I know what's going on, and so do the three men watching it now.

Cut to the lobby cam again. The date and time have sped forward to the next week. To Monday, 4:02 a.m., to be exact. Present are Linderhoff and Eric.

"Sparks will let you in the east door in exactly thirty minutes," Linderhoff says. "Make sure you're there."

"I will be," Eric says.

"And no screwups this time."

"There won't be any."

The next cut is not to footage from one of the Club's security cameras, but to a montage of clips from several cameras at Jenson Community Hospital. This is the something extra Jar was talking about. And, she was not wrong. The montage follows Eric as he makes his way through the quiet hospital to Marissa's room. We see him go in and come out a minute later and leave the building. There's no footage from inside the room, but again, it's not necessary. Investigators can put the remaining pieces together for the trial. But it's all the proof I need that Eric, under Linderhoff's direction and with Chief Sparks's help, killed Marissa, after failing to do so the first time.

When the video ends, I expect at least one of the men to express shock or spit out a few choice expletives. But all three are staring at the now black screen.

What finally breaks their paralysis is someone banging on the library door. They all turn toward it.

"What the hell?" Linderhoff asks.

He exchanges a glance with Eric before they both start moving toward the door.

"Stop!"

As Linderhoff and Eric halt, I cock my head, surprised. The voice came from somewhere under the balcony.

"Who said that?" Jar asks.

"You tell me," I whisper.

Before she can, Linderhoff looks back and says, "Adam, what are you doing?"

Oh, no.

My plan is to let Linderhoff and his companions panic first over the videos and again when they realize something is happening in the library but that the door is locked. After that, I would confront them with my Taser guns and give them a nice little speech about what happens to men who think they can get away with murder, before I deliver the shock. But I haven't taken the Tasers out of my bag yet, and there's no time to do it now.

I rip my Glock from my holster and run down the stairs. At the sound of my pounding footsteps, Linderhoff, Eric, and Sparks swivel their eyes toward me.

While Linderhoff and Sparks freeze, Eric jumps into action. He pushes his boss toward the front door as he pulls out a gun from under his jacket.

Having already concluded he is the one I need to worry about most, I anticipate his shot and hop over the banister a moment before he pulls the trigger.

I was more than halfway down the stairs so the lobby floor is not too far down. I'm on my feet in no time, a yard away from Sparks.

"Don't move," I tell him, my gun aimed at his chest.

At the front of the lobby, Linderhoff is trying to pull open the door, but because of the crowbar, he's not having any luck.

Eric realizes it's futile and yanks Linderhoff toward the library.

I'm about to send off a warning shot over their heads when, from the other end of the lobby, another gun roars—this one much louder than Eric's—and I feel a bullet rip through the air less than an arm's length away from me.

Linderhoff twists backward and falls to the ground, blood soaking the shoulder of his coat. Eric, realizing he can't do anything for his boss anymore, keeps running toward the library, from where the sounds of coughing and screaming continue to build.

I whip around and see Adam marching into the lobby, holding a Desert Eagle .45-caliber pistol in a two-handed grip.

"Adam, put it down!" I yell.

"No way! You heard them. They *killed* her! They killed Marissa!"

Sparks, obviously thinking this is his big chance to get away, starts to move. But I hear his first step, swing back around, and like a dirty football player, I shoot out my leg and hook one of the chief's shins with my artificial foot.

Down he goes, face-first into the floor. He tries to break his fall but it all happens too fast, and I hear the wet crunch of his nose breaking. He also appears to have done something to his leg, and I know he won't be getting up soon.

I look back. Adam is about level with me, but he's too far away for me to grab.

Stop him, Liz says.

I have only one option. I point my gun at him and say, "Put it down or I'll shoot!"

He pauses and swings his barrel over so that it's aimed at me. "Don't make me kill you, too."

You know before when I said I almost never make a threat I don't intend to follow through on? Well, I've just broken that rule again.

I don't begrudge Adam's anger one bit, and I can't shoot him for it. But Liz would not be happy if I let him kill anyone. I also don't know exactly where Eric is, but I know he hasn't gone into the library, so he must be hiding somewhere along the portion of hallway I can't see. If Adam keeps heading toward Linderhoff, he'll move right into Eric's sight. And I have no doubt the butler/bagman will be more than happy to put a bullet in the kid.

I lower my gun, and Adam moves his aim back toward Sparks, taking my action as giving him the green light. What he hasn't noticed is that I've also taken a step in his direction, which now puts him in range. The moment he starts moving forward, I lunge at him. He tries to swing his gun back toward me, but I'm already inside his arc of motion. I smack into his ribs, my arms wrapping around his torso, and push him backward.

We slam into the wall that fronts the west staircase and Adam loses his footing. As he goes down, I rip the gun from his hand before he even realizes what's happening.

"Where the hell did you get this?" I waggle the gun in front of him.

He hesitates. "It's my stepdad's."

"Son of a...you could have gotten us both killed. What were you thinking? You know what? Never mind." I poke him in the chest with the barrel. "Don't move."

He glares at me, and I'm sure he's not planning on obeying.

"Do you think Marissa would want you to spend the rest of your life in jail? Or die the second you walk into that asshole's range? Because one of those two things is exactly what's going to happen if you don't do what I say." In his eyes, I can see he's forgotten about Eric. "Stay right there. For her."

My words have gotten through to him. Whether they're enough to keep him from doing something else that's stupid, I'm not sure. But I'll have to trust he'll wise up because I can't babysit him.

I give him one final glare, then move over to the other staircase and down until I'm almost at the point where the stairs reach the lobby floor.

In a raised voice, I say, "Eric, the only way you're getting out of here still breathing is if you cooperate. I suggest you—"

The boom of his gun echoes through the lobby, the bullet smashing into the wall above the hallway to the lounge.

At least I know for sure he's there.

Over near the front door, Linderhoff groans as he tries to look toward where Eric is. In a raspy, forced voice, he says, "Goddammit, take them out!"

Eric takes another shot, the trajectory not much better than the last one.

"I'm more than happy to give you a little time to think about it," I say as I quietly slip my backpack off and unzip the top. "You're the only thing left on my agenda. So we can just sit here until you're ready to give up."

I remove a Taser and one of my smoke bombs, and study the portion of the hall to the library that I can see.

"If I were you, I'd be a little worried that whatever's causing problems in the library might leak under the door and affect you. But that's just me."

I remove the safety from the bomb, bring my arm back, and throw. Smoke begins billowing from the device the moment it hits the hallway wall. I've missed my mark by a few inches, but it's not enough to keep the cylinder from careening over to where Eric is hiding.

The cloud that quickly forms does its trick. Eric has no idea what's causing the screams in the library, so his first thoughts must be that I've tossed the same stuff at him.

He rushes out, pulling tendrils of smoke with him. As soon as he is in sight, I hit him with a pair of Taser wires.

He falls to the floor, only a few feet from Linderhoff, and dances to the electric charge. Adam—who's been good to this point—pushes to his feet and jogs toward them. I hurry over and grab his arm before he does anything stupid.

"Hey, it's over," I say.

Adam scowls. "You should have let me kill them."

"You're angry. I get it. But believe me, there are worse sentences than death."

"You don't understand. They killed Marissa. I-I—"

"Actually, I understand one hundred percent. And let me tell you from *experience*, killing them will never heal your pain."

"Putting them in jail for the rest of their lives won't heal it, either."

"No, it won't. But while they're spending every day for the rest of their lives in tiny concrete boxes, you'll be on the outside, living. And that will help the pain a little."

"The only...ones...going to jail...are you two."

Adam and I turn. Chief Sparks is trying to sit up, but his hand can't get much traction due to the pool of blood on the floor that's drained from his nose.

"Us?" I say. "I don't think so."

"Assault. Kidnapping." He glances over at Linderhoff. "Attempted murder."

"Chief Sparks, what are you talking about? The way I remember it, Adam simply tried to confront you with what he learned, but instead of talking to him, you decided to try to shoot him." I point at the three places Eric's bullets hit. "He had no choice other than to shoot back. Clear case of self-defense."

"Self-defense, my ass," Linderhoff hisses. He's been able to prop himself up on the elbow of his uninjured side. "Chief Sparks, arrest them."

I can't help but laugh. It's like a scene out of a screwball comedy. The three bad guys on the ground, making threats while they bleed. (Okay, technically, Eric's not bleeding. But he still has the electric shakes.)

I saunter over to Linderhoff. "You know where you made your mistake?"

He looks at me, eyes narrow, but doesn't say anything.

"At the fair last spring."

Now he's confused.

"You should have never talked to Marissa and Fara." I wave my arm around. "All this is for them."

I shove my foot into his wounded shoulder and push him back to the ground.

CHAPTER FORTY-FOUR

With Adam's help, we zip-tie and gag the three men, though I have to cuff Linderhoff's hands in front of him instead of behind. I'll have to do something about his wound, but first things first.

"Watch them," I tell Adam.

"Can I have the gun back?"

"Adam, look at me."

He does so, reluctantly.

"No gun. And this is important—you *do not* do anything to them. Understand me?"

He is not happy with this, but after a moment, he nods.

"I mean it," I say.

"I won't do anything. I promise."

If he's lying, he'll be the one who has to explain that to the authorities.

I hurry through the lounge and into the kitchen. One of the cooks looks over from behind a prep table, where he and the rest of the kitchen staff are hiding. He ducks back down when he sees me.

Coughing is still coming from the library door at the other

end of the kitchen, but no one is pounding on it anymore. I take this to mean the gas is working as it should. The initial stage of coughing fits and panic has progressed to eyes swollen nearly shut and loss of energy. The only people I feel any sympathy for are the women. But their condition is only temporary, and in a couple of hours, much to their surprise, they will be back to normal.

"Everyone on your feet," I say, my gun pointed in the direction of the staff, but not actually at any of them.

"Please don't shoot us," one of them says.

"You do what I say and I promise you won't be harmed."

One of the chefs is the first to rise. When he isn't riddled with bullets, the others follow suit.

"This side of the table," I say.

They come around it.

Adam has told me that any outside workers, such as kitchen staff, are relieved of their phones when they arrive and are not given them back until right before they go home. But, as we all know, being thorough is in my nature.

"Did anyone call nine-one-one?" I ask.

They glance at one another, but no one speaks.

"I'm not going to be happy if I find out later one of you did, so better tell me now."

All four of them shake their heads, then the chef who stood first says, "We don't have our phones."

Confirmation is always nice. "All right. I need you all to turn around and put your hands behind your backs."

"We-we didn't do anything!" one of the servers says.

"You're right. You didn't. But I'm afraid I can't just let you walk around free at the moment. Now, please, turn around."

I zip-tie their hands and have them sit on the floor, with their backs to the table. I use more ties to connect the secured wrists to one of the table's crossbars so that they have to stay where they are. Each gets a last tie around his ankles. I'm kind, though, and don't pull the plastic strips as tight as I did on Linderhoff and his friends.

When I stand up, I say, "I'm sorry I have to do this to you, but you won't have to stay like this for long. The authorities will be here soon."

On my way out, I grab a stack of linen napkins.

When I return to the lobby, I'm happy to see Adam hasn't killed anyone. I use some of the napkins to create bandages for Linderhoff and Sparks, and then Adam and I haul all three men into the lounge, where we zip-tie them to the legs of the grand piano. We then use the remaining napkins as blindfolds and gags on the men.

I leave Adam to watch them again and enter the hidden side of the house.

Back at my computer, I say, "Jar, you still with me?"

"Yes, of course."

"Can I assume you've been watching?"

"It has been very entertaining."

"I'm glad you enjoyed it."

"If you would like, I can make you a highlights reel."

Jar's becoming a regular comedian. "Thanks, I'll pass. Time for phase three." I pull out my phone, open the remote control app, and send my drone—which has been patiently waiting on the roof—straight up thirty feet, from where it has a clear view of the county road all the way back to Jenson.

"Camera's aloft," I say.

"Receiving video. I will keep an eye on it."

"Thanks. Hey, were you able to get me video from the lounge?"

"Of course. I sent you links."

I kneel in front of my computer, and check the time. It's only 9:12.

How about that? I'm way ahead of my goal. Nice.

I copy Jar's links from her email and add them to the group email. I'd love to hit SEND now, but I still have some cleanup to take care of so I leave it to go at 9:30.

I grab the manila envelope and make my way up to the second-floor room above the drugs. I move the equipment and tarp out of the way and open the trapdoor.

I tape one of the red arrows from the envelope on the hatch, pointing down at the hole in the floor. As I work my way back to the first floor, I place more arrows along the way so that there's no chance anyone will get lost.

When I'm done, I leave the hidden door open and return to the lounge.

"Everything all right here?" I ask Adam.

"Fine."

"Okay. Hold tight. I'm almost done."

I head back up to the second floor and retrieve my cameras from the bedrooms, hallway, and balcony overlooking the lobby. Before I get the one from the library balcony, I put my gas mask back on.

The sound of coughing greets me long before I reach the curtain. When I do, I pull it away only far enough for me to step through, and then let it drop back into place. Most of the gas should have dissipated by now, but I'd rather not chance some of it sneaking into the rest of the house.

I grab the empty gas canister and put it in my backpack. Below, I see that most of Linderhoff's guests and their companions have made their way back to their chairs, but three people are stretched out on the floor. Using my camera, I zoom in and watch each for a moment, to make sure they're breathing. When I'm satisfied no one's checked out for good, I walk down the balcony to the left-side door, making no attempt to hide. Even if the people below aren't exhausted from coughing, with their hampered vision it will be impossible for any of them to see me as anything more than a fuzzy blob.

I pick up the other two canisters and the camera and slip into the hallway. After I remove the gas mask, I check my phone. It's 9:21. Almost time to jet.

I head back to the lounge.

Adam has moved one of the stuffy chairs right next to the piano and is sitting on it, staring at our three captives.

"Adam," I say. "I need you to go in the kitchen and check that the staff is okay."

"Did you do something to them?"

"No. Well, I mean, I tied them up, but—you know what? Just go check, all right?"

"Okay."

"And give them water if they need any."

The second he leaves the room, I make my way through the lounge, snagging the two cameras and all the audio bugs I left under seats.

By the time Adam returns, it's 9:25 and I'm standing by the piano.

"They're fine," he says, and hesitates before adding, "They asked me to untie them."

"What did you say?"

"I said you wouldn't let me."

I nod, and motion to the chair he was in before. Once he sits, I say, "It's time for me to leave, which means you're going to be here alone for a while. I know you're going to be tempted to take out your anger on your friends here." I glance down at Linderhoff, who's closest.

"They're not my friends."

I snort. "Next time you go to your writing class, ask your teacher for the definition of sarcasm."

"I know what sar—"

"Look, what I'm telling you is, don't give in to any urge to retaliate. Remember, I have cameras everywhere, and if I see that you've done something I told you not to do, I'll make sure the police have evidence making it look like you were much more involved in Linderhoff's business than you already are."

He grimaces. "I won't do anything. I swear."

"You might also be tempted to leave before anyone gets here. That's a very bad idea. Your only way out of this is to be perceived as one of those responsible for stopping this asshole." I give Linderhoff a nudge with my foot.

"What do I tell them?"

"The truth."

"I mean, what do I tell them about *you*?"

"What *can* you tell them about me?"

He thinks for a moment, and frowns. "Not much, I guess."

"So tell them that."

He nods. "Okay."

"One last thing." I point at the open door to the unfinished half of the house. "Don't go back there, and don't go into the library. You know what, just don't wander around at all."

"Um, sure."

"And I'm going to open the front door. Leave it that way, got it?"

"I got it."

"There *is* one thing you can do. Five minutes after I leave, you can untie the kitchen staff."

"Didn't you tell me not to wander around?"

"Adam!"

"They're going to want to leave."

"Tell them they can if they want." I look at my phone. It's 9:29. "When the cops get here, just tell the truth and you'll be fine."

I turn to leave.

"Hey," he says.

I look back.

He's standing, his hand held out to me. "Thank you."

I shake it. "Marissa gave you a chance to make a better life for yourself. Don't let her down."

"I won't."

CHAPTER FORTY-FIVE

H*e's a good kid,* Liz says after I step into the unfinished
section of the house.

"Maybe. He wasn't always, though, that's for sure."

He never had a chance before. He does now.

That's Liz, always seeing the best in people.

I retrieve my computer ten seconds after the email was sent,
and put it in my bag before heading out through my usual basement route.

Jar still has all the Club's outside cameras looped, so I run
around the house to the front entrance, where I remove the
crowbar and push the double doors all the way open. This will
make things easier when law enforcement arrives.

On my way to the gate, I make side trips to pick up the
cameras in front of the house and outside the garages. I don't
worry about the bugs in the cars. If they're found, they will be
easily explained as being put there by someone who has a gripe
with Linderhoff, whereas the cameras and the bugs in the house
would draw greater scrutiny. No matter what, there's no way to
trace them back to either me or my supplier.

Instead of hopping over, I use the crowbar to pop the chain

that moves the gate, and push the gate open. After I grab my final camera from across the street, I pull out my phone.

The man who answers says, "Colusa County Sheriff's Department. How can I—"

"This is Deputy Chief Meyers of the Jenson PD," I whisper urgently. Meyers is the real deputy chief. "We have a potential hostage situation with shots fired. We are spread thin and requesting your immediate assistance." I give the address of the Club, and answer a few questions before saying, "I need to reposition. Send backup now!"

I hang up.

"Very impressive," Jar says.

"You should have seen my FBI act."

A few minutes later, when I'm in the woods about two hundred yards away from the wall, Jar says, "Here they come."

I bring up the drone cam on my phone. Racing up the road from Jenson are three vehicles with emergency lights blazing. I fly the drone toward the road and stop it when it's above the trees just inside the gate. There is the possibility that the sheriff's office contacted Jenson PD after my call and these cars could be from the police. That would be less than ideal.

The cars slow as they approach the property and stop on the road in front of the gate.

I smile. All three are sheriff's vehicles.

Men from the trailing two cars leave their vehicles and run up to the lead car. There's a discussion at the driver's window, then the men hurry back, and all three vehicles turn onto the property.

I hit the drone recall button.

For all intents and purposes, my mission is over.

CHAPTER FORTY-SIX

Only it's not quite.

The next morning, on my way to my job at the diner, I drop the package containing the damaged grille and the jump drives into a curbside mailbox on a quiet street. The addressee is the US Attorney for the Eastern District of California.

Some of the digital evidence are copies of what I sent in the email, but there are plenty of new items that will aid in the coming investigation.

You're probably wondering why in God's name I would be going back to the diner. That's simple. If I disappear the day after the biggest law enforcement activity in the county's history, someone might take note of that, and who knows how that might cause me problems later. I always have to think ten steps ahead.

News of what happened doesn't reach the diner until around seven a.m., when the national news channels start airing some of the footage I sent them. From that point on, things go crazy, and the diner buzzes with conversations full of shock and rumors and wild speculation. It gets to the point where we're basically hosting one giant discussion that goes on and on even as people come and leave.

After work, I am finally able to make the call I've been looking forward to.

"Fara, this is Agent Wallack."

"Oh, hi. I was, um, wondering if you were going to call me."

"I take it you've heard that the Club has been shut down."

"It's all anyone's talking about."

"We've also taken Linderhoff into custody. You don't need to worry about him any longer."

"I...I can't believe it."

"I told you, you are never going to have to worry about him."

She sniffs, and I'm pretty sure she's holding back tears. "Thank you."

There's a chance her ordeal might not be completely over yet. If investigators connect her to the Club, they'll likely want to interview her. But I don't tell her this. She deserves a bit of time to enjoy the feeling of being free.

I work at the diner for two more days. At the end of my shift on the last day, I tell Bree I need to deal with some personal issues out of town and won't be coming back. She's not happy, but I've done a good job so she can't be too mad. Before I go, I slip a note next to the cash register, saying someone named Adam called, looking for work, and I include his number.

Will Adam take a busboy job? Who knows. At least he'll realize he has options.

It isn't until I'm sitting on the plane, flying back to L.A., that I sense Liz's presence again. She's been noticeably absent since I finished the mission.

Now it feels like she's sitting in the empty seat next to me, her head tilted to the side, hovering just above my shoulder.

I knew you could do it. Thank you.

"You never have to thank me." Aware that I can be overheard by other passengers, the sound of my words barely escapes my lips. "But let's not take anything else on for a little while, okay? I'm sure I'll have some jobs coming up."

She says nothing.

"Liz?"

She's there, but she's silent.

"Liz, I'm serious.... Liz?"

She laughs, playfully, and then she's gone.

THANK YOU FOR READING NIGHT MAN

If you enjoyed it, please consider leaving a review at your point of purchase. And if you know someone who might enjoy this, consider telling her or him about Night Man. Reviews & word-of-mouth are the two most important ways people find out about novels.

If you haven't read Brett's Jonathan Quinn series, check out the Quinn original novel, Becoming Quinn.

And if you have, check out The Excoms, a Quinn spinoff series, starting with book 1, The Excoms.

Would you like a free book? Receive updates on new releases and information on what Brett is working on by signing up for his newsletter at his website: brettbattles.com. You'll also receive a FREE copy of one of his stories.

ABOUT THE AUTHOR

Brett Battles is a *USA Today* bestselling and Barry Award-winning author of over thirty-five novels, including those in the Jonathan Quinn series, the Excoms series, and the time-hopping Rewinder series. He's also the coauthor, with Robert Gregory Browne, of the Alexandra Poe series.

Keep updated on new releases and other book news, and get exclusive content by subscribing to Brett's newsletter at his website: brettbattles.com.

And around the internet:

facebook.com/Author-Brett-Battles-152032908205471

twitter.com/BrettBattles

instagram.com/authorbrettbattles